To Rosemary —

Best wishes and
en joy!

D.M. Johnston

# EXTERNALITIES

*A NOVEL*

D. McCall Johnston

◆ FriesenPress

One Printers Way
Altona, MB R0G 0B0
Canada

www.friesenpress.com

ISBN
978-1-03-834086-3 (Hardcover)
978-1-03-834085-6 (Paperback)
978-1-03-834087-0 (eBook)

1. FICTION, LEGAL

Distributed to the trade by The Ingram Book Company

# DEDICATION

In memory of my In-Laws, Paul and Anna Thurmer whose experiences
helped inspire me to write this book.

# AUTHOR'S NOTES

I WOULD LIKE TO acknowledge the assistance and support I received from friends and family while undertaking this project. Specifically my sons Scott, Michael, Andrew and my wonderful spouse and partner, Eldy. Also thanks to Al Marsh for his guidance during my early days of developing the plot.

# EXTERNALITIES:

Benefits received by a third party, wherein the third party does not have control over the generation of the benefits.

I T WAS A gorgeous spring morning, and fortunately, the sunroom where they spent any free mornings faced east, capturing the warmth and light from the morning sun. The trees were beginning to fill out as their buds developed into leaves. Mike had gone out to the kitchen for his second cup of coffee and decided to check and see if the mail had been delivered. It had.

One letter in particular caught his attention, and he opened it on the spot. "Holy crap," he gasped as the reality of the situation hit him. He had known it was coming, but he didn't realize the size of the bill until he opened the envelope and it was staring him in the face. "Holy crap," he uttered again, not sure what else to say. The envelope was from their lawyer, and the amount due "For Professional Services" was $242,799.00. "Damned lawyers," he muttered. "Damn Grasser."

"Rose!" he called.

"What!" The response came back rather sharpish from the sunroom, where Rose had spent her morning going over her mail, messages, news, and God knows what else on her iPad.

"Grasser's bill is here," he responded.

"Great," came the reply, "just what we need."

"Yeah," he muttered as he walked toward her voice, holding the rest of the morning mail and that day's local newspaper.

He handed her the invoice and the envelope and then plunked himself down in his chair, waiting for her reaction.

"Great, just great!" she exclaimed. "We can thank your sister for that." She laid the bill down. "Did you have any idea it was going to be that much?" she asked.

"No," he replied, "not that much."

Mike picked up the bill again and studied it. There were pages of itemized charges, all starting with the word "To," followed by the appropriate details, including date, place, and hours being charged. One that caught his eye was "To attending discovery." *Yeah,* he thought, *a hell of a lot of good that did.*

Glancing around the small room off the kitchen of the old house they were renting in Fergus, Mike thought, *we sure don't have a lot to show after our twenty-eight years of marriage.* He then glanced over at Rose, who had gone back to studying the news story she had been reading. He wondered how she really felt about their life together and if she had regrets about what they had done and not done in their time together. It had looked so promising when they started out, with Mike working in real estate and Rose as a veterinarian's assistant. Grasser's bill was a wake-up call, giving him food for thought and reflection.

It had all started so nicely. Because of his outgoing personality, he had been drawn to sales. After spending time in the life insurance industry learning sales techniques, he had gone into real estate.

Rose had a love for large animals and had started visiting the local veterinarian and doing odd jobs for him while she was in high school.

Over the course of time, they had been drawn to Collingwood, a town on the south shores of Georgian Bay, which had transformed into a leading recreational area after its main industry, a shipyard, ceased operation in the 1950s. Mike had heard of Collingwood well before he'd considered moving there. His colleagues and associates started talking about it and thought it could become a prime destination for retirees and others looking to sell and leave the Toronto rat race for a more laid-back lifestyle. Mike had thought it would be great if he could get in on the ground floor, so they had moved. Rose had had no difficulty finding a position because of her past experience and the amazing recommendation she had received from her former employer.

Mike remembered their first visit to the Collingwood/Thornbury area and how impressed he had been with what was available less than a couple hours away from Toronto. Rose had come with him and agreed that it certainly had an attraction for potential newcomers.

His family had bought a cottage in Sauble Beach on the shore of Lake Huron when he was a boy. It was about an hour and a half west of Collingwood. Sauble was an amazing summer destination, but it died in the off-season. Collingwood was a four-season destination offering cheaper housing, affordable waterfront living, and a ton of year-round recreational opportunities.

And now this!

He decided he'd better go and relieve himself before he settled back into his chair in the sunroom. He knew as he got older that he would drip when he thought he was finished. *This, of course, is one of the joys of aging,* he thought sarcastically. Then he remembered the poems he had read on the inside door of a public toilet he had used when he and his buddies were playing football as teenagers. Smiling to himself, he headed to the washroom.

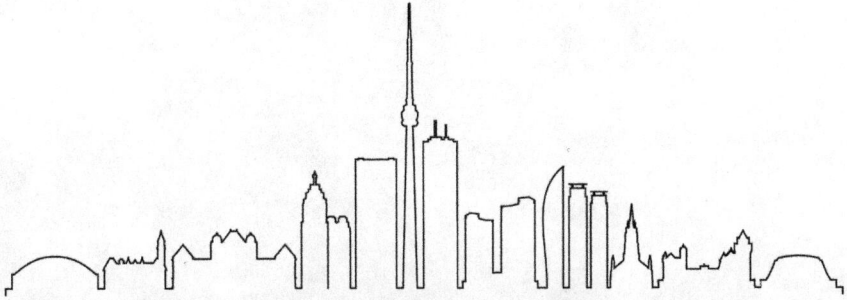

# PART ONE
## A NEW BEGINNING

CHAPTER **ONE**

I T WAS A beautiful, sunny, warm spring morning in Tuscany, and Yolanda was planning to return home from Bucine after running an errand for her father. Yolanda, the oldest daughter, had picked up her father's knives from the local knife sharpener. She had walked the twenty minutes to the town, enjoying the walk along the shoulder of the road surrounded by vineyards and olive groves. Off in the distance, the hills looked especially magnificent and peaceful this time of day. There was a slight haze near their bases, and the olive orchards and towering cypress trees that grew up the sides of the hills looked especially elegant. At the top of the largest hills, there were relics of old stone castles. Some were in a state of ruin, but many had been rejuvenated as homes and apartments.

"*Buongiorno*," the knife sharpener had greeted Yolanda as he handed her a cloth bag in which each sharpened knife was individually wrapped. She knew that they would have some weight. Her father was a butcher, and these were the tools of his trade. The sharpener was a short, stocky man with a very intense look about him. He always seemed to Yolanda to be a very serious, no-nonsense person, so upon leaving, Yolanda thanked him very seriously, with no hint of a smile.

As she was walking on the cobbled street past the next shop, the lady who owned it beckoned her to come in. It was a small shop selling seasonal fresh produce. Yolanda walked past the bins of fresh green onions, lettuce, early carrots, and other spring produce on the porch and entered the shop. It was full of pleasant, earthy smells. The lady handed Yolanda a large sack. "These are for your mother," she said. "I promised to get them, and they arrived this morning. Can you manage it?"

"I think so," Yolanda replied, taking the bag.

While neither bag was particularly heavy, the produce bag was bulky. Wrapping her arms around it, she juggled it until she had a good hold of it while balancing the package of knives. "Thank you," she said as she turned to go. "My mother will be thrilled."

Leaving the shop, she started for home. She had walked a few steps and was still trying to adjust the bags so she could carry them comfortably when a voice behind her said, "*Qui lascia che ti aiuti con quelli.*"[1]

Turning, she saw a young fellow about her age coming up behind her and reaching to take the bulky produce sack from her. She was uncertain what she should do and was feeling very ill at ease when he said, "Hi, I'm Clemente. Those look pretty awkward to juggle. Let me take this one."

His outburst had been a knee-jerk reaction. When he saw the beautiful young woman in need of assistance, he couldn't help himself. He reached to take the bulky sack. As his smile was reassuring and there was no hint of aggression, she let him take it.

"I'm Yolanda, thanks. I didn't realize I would have this much to bring home. I was only expecting my father's knives. He's a butcher just down the road," she said as she motioned in the direction she was heading, "and it is a bit of a walk. I don't want to inconvenience you."

"No problem," Clemente replied as he tried not to stare at this beautiful girl in disbelief.

She was around his age, he guessed. Slim and tall with long, black hair, beautiful hazel eyes, lovely cheekbones, and an amazing smile. He caught himself in a moment and stopped staring.

"I have the day off and really don't have any plans. I was just going to drop in on an old friend, but he's not expecting me, so I'm all yours," he said laughingly. He then thought to himself, *I'll leave the truck over where it is parked so I can walk this beautiful girl home.*

And so they headed down the road while Yolanda talked about her father's shop and his garden, her sister, her mother's cooking, her love of music, and her thoughts about her future. He was so engrossed in the

---

1    "Here, let me help you with those."

conversation, he didn't realize they had left Bucine and were walking down a country road, past fields of grapevines on both sides of the road.

Yolanda saw in her travelling companion a well-built young man who was of average height with short black hair. He had a square face and intense, dark eyes. He had a small scar on his left cheek and a warm smile.

As they walked along, he told her about his father, who was a barber, and his older brother, Luigi, who worked with his father in the barbershop. "Luigi is not a certified barber yet. He's an apprentice. This means he can do certain things around the shop, but he can't cut a customer's hair, so he practises on our father and me."

He then went on to tell her that his family had a small farm on which they grew grapes and vegetables and raised a few chickens. "As the older brother, Luigi will inherit our father's business and land. So, I became a carpenter. I'm working for a local builder and quite love the work."

He was just starting to tell her that he had an aunt and uncle who had moved to Canada when Yolanda interrupted him, saying, "We are here."

Looking up, he saw a small old two-storey stone house. There was a separate stone building beside it with the word "Macelleria"[2] painted in the window.

At that moment, the door of the house opened, and a woman and a young girl emerged. Turning, Yolanda said, "Oh, hi Moma. This is Clemente. He helped me carry these home." And she pointed to the sack and then the cloth bag. Pointing back to the bag, she said, "This one is for you from Mrs. Ricci at the produce market."

Yolanda's mother looked Clemente up and down for a second before taking the sack from him and saying, "Thank you for helping my daughter. Would you like to come in for something to drink? You must be parched after that walk." Without waiting for a reply, she took his arm and brought him into her house. "I'm Loretta, by the way, and this is Yolanda's sister, Sofia."

Looking at Yolanda's mother, he was taken aback. She was an older version of Yolanda. She had short dark hair with a hint of grey sneaking into it and the same eyes, cheekbones, and smile. He held out his hand,

---

2    "Butcher Shop."

saying, *"Ciao, piacere di conoscerti. Sono Clemente Gallorini."*[3] He felt completely at ease as he entered the house.

Loretta motioned him to the kitchen table. "Sit here," she said. "Would you like sparkling water or a glass of Yolanda's father's wine?"

"I'm quite thirsty after that walk, and I think the *acqua frizzante* would be perfect, although the wine is always good." He was always interested to taste homemade wine. In Tuscany, where the grapes were known and respected throughout the world, the locals were known to produce some amazing wines.

"Tell me about yourself and your family. Where do you live?"

"We live on the other side of town on a small farm. My mother is Amara, and my father, Tommaso, is a barber. He loves his garden and his grapes. I have an older brother, Luigi, who works with my father. We have fifteen acres, most in grapevines, and a large garden. I am a carpenter by trade and"—he pointed to the small scar on his left cheek—"this war wound is from my first argument with a saw," he said laughingly.

Clemente was just about to continue when the door burst open and a short, stocky fellow with a round face and very short hair entered the room, looked directly at Clemente, and said, *"Come va?"*[4]

*"Bene, grazie,"*[5] Clemente responded, guardedly.

"I'm Leonardo Canesdri, the best butcher in Italy and Yolanda's father," he continued in a very jovial tone, his eyes twinkling. Clemente guessed he was in his mid- to late fifties. Obviously, Sofia had gone to tell her father about their visitor. "Call me Leon," he added.

In a flash, Loretta produced a large glass of sparkling soda, a bottle of red wine, and a platter of salami, cheese, and bread. "Eat!" she announced to the room, and she motioned everyone to the table.

Yolanda sat in the chair next to her guest, smiling at him. Almost immediately, everyone started talking, telling stories, and sharing thoughts. Clemente loved the friendliness and spontaneity of the family. As he looked

---

3    "A pleasure to meet you. I'm Clemente Gallorini."

4    "How are you?"

5    "Fine, thank you."

across the table, he noticed Sofia watching him, smiling and listening to his every word. Her eyes were sparkling, and she reminded him of a young pup, waiting in anticipation for what was going to happen next.

It was well into the afternoon when Clemente glanced down at his watch. He didn't want to overstay his welcome, so he said, "I really should get going. My family will be wondering what's become of me." Standing up, he added, "This has been wonderful. Thank you for your hospitality. Leon, your wine is excellent, and thank you for sharing it with me." Once he had finished the soda, Leon had been making sure his wine glass was never empty.

"My pleasure. Just a moment and I'll get you one to take home to your family." Disappearing into an adjoining room for a minute, Leon reappeared holding a bottle of red wine, which he gave to Clemente, adding, "And thank you for helping my daughter carry our parcels home."

"It was entirely my pleasure," Clemente said as he headed to the front door. Yolanda joined him, and they walked out together. "What a wonderful family," Clemente told the now-blushing daughter. "Can I see you again? I have to work tomorrow, but we could go out on Saturday."

"That would be wonderful," she replied, trying to hide her excitement.

"Great, I'll bring my truck and pick you up at seven. We can grab a bit of supper." He took her hand in his and gave it a gentle squeeze. "It was a real pleasure to meet you." With that, he turned and headed back down the road to Bucine, walking with his head in the clouds as he went over the events of the day.

# CHAPTER TWO

TIME PASSED QUICKLY, and before Yolanda knew it, on a beautiful warm spring evening, Clemente returned. He was about to knock on the door when it was flung open, and Sofia stood there, beaming. "Hi, come on in. She'll be right here."

"That's great," he replied. "And how are you?"

Before she could answer, he caught the motion of Yolanda arriving out of the corner of his eye. Turning and holding his hand out to her, he exclaimed, "Oh, hi! You look wonderful."

Taking his offered hand, she came toward him.

"Have fun," said her parents, who had arrived and stood smiling just behind them.

Clemente and Yolanda turned and walked down the steps toward his truck.

"Have fun," Yolanda's parents called after them once more.

"Thanks," Clemente responded, taking his attention off his beautiful date for a moment.

Walking ahead as they approached the truck, he held the door open for Yolanda. As she stepped up, he lent her support, and she slid onto the bench seat of the spotless interior.

"I hope you don't mind," he said as he entered the driver's side, "but my mother insisted that I bring you home for dinner."

"No, I don't mind at all," Yolanda replied, smiling. "That will be nice." She knew her mother would have done exactly the same thing.

"Great. They are looking forward to meeting you. It is not far, just on the other side of town," he added, putting the truck in gear and heading down the road.

They were telling each other about their previous day—he on the current construction project and she working in her father's butcher shop. He finally said, "Here we are," as they pulled up to an old stone house, not dissimilar to the one they had just come from. Yolanda was thinking about how quickly they had arrived when the door was flung open, and Clemente's mother, Amara, and father, Tommaso, appeared with huge, welcoming smiles on their faces.

"*Ciao, benvenuto,*"[6] Tommaso called out as they exited the truck.

He was a tall, thin man with thinning black hair and glasses. Yolanda could see a slight facial resemblance to Clemente.

"*Questa e la madre di Clemente, Amara,*"[7] Tommaso added as his wife stepped forward and took Yolanda's hand.

"*Benvenuta,*" Amara said with a warm, personal smile. Her short hair had a slight curl, which suited her round and friendly face. Her eyes were identical to Clemente's, and her face was slightly rounder, but Yolanda could see that she was definitely his mother.

"*Grazie,*" Yolanda responded, smiling.

Yolanda was impressed with the friendly welcome she was receiving. She was taken to the dining room, and she sat as Clemente held her chair for her. The room was smaller than her mother's but was nicely appointed with dark green drapes on either side of the south-facing window that overlooked the garden. There was a beautiful old painting on the wall that showed a small lake surrounded by a thin forest and a large mountain in the background.

"I hope you like this," Amara said as she brought out a roasted pork dish with a tomato-based sauce served over homemade noodle pasta. It smelled wonderful. As she laid the dishes on the table, she added, "Clemente's brother Luigi is sorry that he can't be here, but he sends his regards."

---

6     "Hello, welcome."

7     "This is Clemente's mother, Amara."

While Luigi was not present, he was certainly talked about. After all, he was the oldest boy. Yolanda was feeling very pleased and comfortable with the evening. She thought that, while her father's wine was slightly better than Tommaso's, Tommaso's was still very good. She learned the family background of both sides of Clemente's family, and Tommaso extended an offer of a free haircut for her father.

At the end of the evening, Clemente and Yolanda pulled into Yolanda's driveway. It was a beautiful, star-filled night. After looking up at the night sky, she said, "That was a wonderful evening. Thank you. Your family is very nice and made me feel right at home."

Smiling, Clemente turned off the engine and moved over closer, giving her a kiss and saying, "You were wonderful, and I can see my parents think you are amazing."

Yolanda was thrilled and kissed him back.

All of a sudden, out of the blue, Clemente said, to her surprise, "I was starting to tell you about my uncle in Canada the other day." After pausing momentarily, he went on. "He has suggested that I should consider joining him there. He told me I could work with him in construction. Apparently, the city is quite nice and modern. He also said there is a very large Italian population. I think the city is called 'Toront' or something. I'm thinking about it. I thought it was important for you to know. I really don't see much of a future here, since Luigi will get my father's business and family land."

". . . Oh. I've never considered anything like that, although I've heard that many people have gone to America. I'll have to give that some serious thought," Yolanda replied, caught off guard and not sure how to respond.

They exited the truck and walked hand in hand to the house. At the front door, they engaged in one more passionate kiss.

"Thank you again," Yolanda said as she entered the house.

*Good,* Clemente thought, *she didn't say no.* And he jumped into his old, clean truck and headed home.

After giving her parents a rundown of the evening and ensuring her father knew that he had a free haircut, Yolanda headed to bed to let her mind wander before she fell asleep. *Why would he tell me that?* she wondered. She knew she liked Clemente, and his family seemed very nice. She also knew her parents liked him and probably would love to have him as a son-in-law. So, she lay there, mulling it over in her mind. *Is he planning to ask me to marry him? We've only just met. There would be no reason not to become his wife and venture off to a new country.* But she couldn't be sure in her mind that they would be compatible. She decided they should spend more time together to make sure they were meant for each other. She then drifted off.

$ $ $

THE KNOCK ON the door the following evening was unexpected. When Sofia opened the door, she was met with, "Oh, hi, Sofia. Is Yolanda home?"

"Yolanda, it's Clemente," Sofia called over her shoulder without taking her eyes off the handsome young man before her.

"Just a minute," was the reply from inside the house. As Sofia was inviting him to step in, Yolanda appeared and motioned for Sofia to leave. She then invited Clemente to enter.

"I just wondered if you wanted to go for a drive," he asked as he stepped through the door.

"Sure. Any place in particular?"

"Well, I thought I would show you the house we are working on, and then we can go for a cappuccino, if you like."

"Okay, let me get a wrap and an umbrella. It feels like we might get some rain." She opened the nearby closet and then called out, "Moma, Clemente and I are going out." Then, to Clemente she said, "Let's go," turning to follow him out the door.

Sitting in the truck, turning and looking at her beautiful face, he told her, "I didn't want to come across or appear too forward last night. I wasn't trying to put you on the spot, either. I just wondered if you were open to the idea of leaving your home and family and heading to a new country to start a new life, if it seems right. As you can tell, I tend to be very spontaneous sometimes."

"Well, I was surprised," she answered, "and have given it some thought. I think we should give it a few months to see if we think it will work. If it looks good and we decide to proceed, I would have no problem with starting a new life with you, anywhere."

Leaning over and kissing her warmly, he started the truck and headed down the road.

"You should know, first of all, I'm not a very religious person," he blurted out.

That started an evening of conversation about likes, dislikes, hopes, wishes, desires, and deep feelings. They talked, discussed, and argued over a broad range of things for several hours, forgetting about everything else, including the time. As predicted, the rain started falling very softly.

In the end, they had decided that if they were to leave Italy for good, they would need to save all the money they could so they could start a proper new life.

# CHAPTER THREE

YOLANDA AND CLEMENTE soon became a couple. When they felt the time was right, they went together, first to her parents and then to his, telling them of their feelings for each other and what they were considering. It was not a surprise to either set of parents, as they could see how things were progressing. Her folks were a little apprehensive about their daughter possibly moving away but remained supportive. Of course, his family was completely in tune, knowing Tommaso's brother Favio had extended the invitation to Clemente to move and join him and his wife, Ana, for a life in Canada. They were very supportive, knowing that Favio was well established and would take his nephew and his bride under his wing. His father told them he would contact his brother immediately.

With both families feeling comfortable, things moved along.

One evening a few months later, Yolanda asked Clemente, "I know you are not into music, but there is an opera in Florence next month that is one of my favourites, *La bohème*. Would you like to go and check it out?"

"What's it about?" he asked.

"It is a story that takes place in Paris in the 1840s. It tells about the lives of a young couple living in the Latin Quarter. Their names are Rodolfo and Mimi, and the story is told through music and singing. It is really touching and tragic."

"Sure, I would love to go. Where do we get tickets? How much are they?"

"I can get them through a local contact my family has known for a long time. And, if you really don't like it, it is not a problem. My father has no interest in opera or musicals, so you won't be alone. He has never gone to a production, so if you come, you will be one up on him."

Clemente could not fathom what he was experiencing a few weeks later, sitting in Florence. The train trip was just over an hour long, and they took a taxi to the opera house. Settling in, he looked around and was amazed by the surroundings: the beautiful interior of the theatre, the artwork, the drapes, the colours, and the gold-accented interior. Soon, the lights dimmed, and the live orchestra, hidden from view below the front of the stage, began to play. He had never seen or heard anything like it in his life.

He was able to follow the storyline, but everything about it was new and foreign to him. After about fifteen minutes, no matter how hard he tried, he lost his focus and started fidgeting. Rather than spoil the evening for his fiancée, he shifted his mind to the house addition he and his boss were building and the money that he was putting away. Yolanda could tell that she had lost him but was impressed that he stayed for the whole performance. It was never really talked about, although Clemente never understood why people would be so enthralled with a story about singing deadbeats.

$ $ $

THE DATE FOR their wedding was set for May the following year, and Yolanda was thrilled with her wedding. The day was perfect. It was a mix of sun and cloud and not too hot. A lovely breeze kept things perfect. It was a great celebration and an amazing party with everyone happy and having a good time. Dancing, singing, and eating were the order of the day. It had been important for Yolanda and her family that the wedding be held in the church and overseen by the priest who had been an important part of her life. She had enjoyed her upbringing in the Catholic Church and was a believer.

Clemente, on the other hand, had told her that, while he had also been brought up in the Catholic Church, he couldn't get his head around what they were trying to teach him. So while he tolerated the religious beliefs that all Catholic children were taught, he was by no means sold on them. He and Yolanda had discussed it long and hard. He had told her that he could not understand or reconcile why the church had huge, ornate, extremely expensive edifices for worship that the average person was expected to support with hard-earned money. He also felt very strongly that the church should not be involved in everyone's daily lives or extend influence on how they lived. They had agreed to disagree and let it go.

Yolanda and Clemente had decided to sail from Venice to Canada. But, to their surprise, Clemente's aunt and uncle had sent them, as a wedding present, airplane tickets for the flight from Rome to Toronto. Two weeks after the wedding, on a cloudy but nice day, with their packed suitcases—and, most importantly, the money they had been given in lieu of gifts—Luigi drove them to the airport in Rome.

After saying their goodbyes, they boarded their direct flight for Toronto, Canada. It was late May 1950. Yolanda was nineteen and Clemente was twenty-one.

# CHAPTER FOUR

N EITHER CLEMENTE NOR his bride had seen, let alone been in, an airplane before. They didn't know what to expect. Yolanda was particularly nervous and tense. She did relax somewhat when her husband took her hand and guided her into her window seat. He then bent over and whispered in her ear, "Think of this like being in a big bus and going on a trip to a new city." He took the seat beside her, still holding her hand.

As they were settling into their seats, a young, friendly stewardess came and asked, "Is this your first time flying?"

"Yes," they both responded, nodding.

The stewardess smiled, telling them, "That's great, I'm sure you will enjoy it." She then went on to explain about the seat belts and the oxygen masks and noted that the flight was twelve hours long and that Toronto was in a different time zone. They learned that the time difference between Toronto and Rome was six hours. They were leaving Rome on a morning flight, flying all day, and getting to their destination in the late afternoon, Canadian time. She told them that a meal would be served as soon as the plane had reached its flying altitude and that there would be hot and cold beverages for their choosing. Then, out of the blue, she asked, "Are you, by chance, newlyweds?"

"Yes," Clemente responded, "our wedding was two weeks ago."

Upon hearing this, the stewardess turned and announced to the whole plane, "Ladies and gentlemen, we have the pleasure of travelling with this lovely couple who were married recently. Please join me in congratulating them." Everyone on board clapped, and many offered their personal best wishes.

Yolanda smiled happily and relaxed.

Once the plane left the runway and started to gain altitude, Yolanda, who was sitting in the seat next to the window, looked out and saw Rome sprawling out below. She said to Clemente excitedly, "Look." As he did, he just caught a glimpse of the city below before the plane travelled through the clouds and the view of the ground was lost.

The flight proved uneventful as Clemente and Yolanda drifted in and out of sleep and ate as the stewardess brought snacks, drinks, breakfast, and later, lunch. They chatted about where they were going, what they would be doing, where they would live, and what their jobs would be. The clouds had cleared, and Yolanda and Clemente looked at the ocean from time to time; they couldn't believe how massive it was. Nothing but blue water for hours on end.

They drifted off. When they woke up, they saw they were over land again. They asked the stewardess where they were, and she responded, "Over what they call the Maritime provinces of Canada. It is their east coast."

They were quite excited and then surprised at how much longer they kept flying. They took time to freshen up in the tiny washroom before they were instructed to prepare for landing at Toronto's Malton Airport.

$ $ $

IT WAS LATE afternoon, and once they collected their luggage, they proceeded to Canadian immigration. They stood while an immigration officer questioned them about their intention of staying in Canada. Did they have family? What were they planning for work? After they told him of Clemente's uncle and the arrangements he had made, he took down their details. He then stood up and shook their hands, saying, "Welcome to Canada."

Taking their luggage again, they followed the signs to exit the airport. Clemente had assured his new wife that his Uncle Favio and Aunt Ana would be waiting for them and reassured her again as they proceeded to the exit. As they went through the last door, a young-looking, very well-dressed man approached them with a huge smile and open arms.

"*Benvenuto,*" he said to them both, and then to Clemente, "Was the flight good?" Before his nephew could respond, he looked at Yolanda and said, "Wow, you must be Yolanda. You are beautiful!" Yolanda blushed and was about to respond when he continued, "I'm your husband's uncle, Favio Gallorini, and this beautiful lady is my wife, Ana. Welcome to Canada."

As Yolanda extended her hand toward Ana, she was immediately pulled into an enormous bear hug. "My pleasure," Ana said. Releasing Yolanda, she turned and repeated the hug with Clemente, adding, "Wonderful to see you again and meet your lovely new bride. She is beautiful. Welcome to Canada and to Toronto. We are so pleased that you took us up on our suggestion, and we are sure you won't be disappointed."

Yolanda finally got a minute to step back and get a good look at Clemente's aunt and uncle. Favio was a short, slightly built fellow with combed-back black hair and a small thin moustache. He was very good-looking and immaculately dressed, including his highly polished shoes. Ana was similar in height to her husband but sturdier, with medium-length black hair and high cheekbones. She was well-dressed and gave the air of a no-nonsense person.

"This way," Favio said as he took part of the luggage. Clemente took the remaining bags, following as his uncle headed for their car. Favio turned and said, "We're sure you will settle into Toronto nicely. There are people here from all over the world, and there are many from all parts of Italy, right, Ana?" And then, carrying on before she could respond, he said, "As I told your father, and I'm sure he told you, I work for a fellow, Pasquali Bertollini. He has a small construction company, and he builds houses. He is from Abruzzi and is a pretty decent fellow. He is fair and honest. When I told him that you were a carpenter and would be available for work immediately, he said he wanted to meet you."

Leaving the terminal building, they went outside to find it was a beautiful, warm evening. Everything was calm, and there was no breeze to speak of. They walked through the parking lot, which was busy with travellers coming and going.

"Okay, here's the car. If you ladies care to get in the back, we'll get the luggage in the trunk and be on our way," Uncle Favio said. The girls slid in through the door he opened for them. When the men entered and Favio started driving, Ana turned to her new niece, saying, "We have rented a furnished apartment, and it's waiting for you. That's our welcoming gift to you. You must be exhausted, so we thought we would go and have a quick bite of supper, and then we will take you to the apartment, and you can settle in and get some sleep. I put some food in the refrigerator, so you won't have to worry about shopping for a few days. We'll leave you tomorrow to rest and catch up on your sleep. We'll come and get you the day after and show you around. I think you will be very comfortable in the neighbourhood. It is known as Little Italy because mainly Italians live there. There are good supermarkets and stores. I can hardly wait to show you. We live a few blocks away."

Yolanda recalled being told that Ana was from Pero in Veneto.

Leaving the airport, they saw they were driving past miles of flat farmland. No hills, stone buildings, or magnificent cypress trees. There were well-spaced rows of trees, which appeared to mark the edge of a field. It was nothing like Tuscany in any way. Then, a few buildings appeared, and this proved to be the start of the city.

As they headed down the highway, Favio turned and asked, "Did you tell Yolanda the plan?"

"Of course," was Ana's reply.

Favio turned back to Clemente, saying, "We thought you would be tired and hungry after that long flight, so we will go to a little restaurant. The owner is a friend of mine and serves good food. Then we will take you to your new apartment so you can settle in and get a good sleep. Tomorrow we'll leave you on your own and will get you the next morning around eight. Oh, you'd better set your watches to your new time." Looking down at his wrist, he said, "It is exactly seven forty-four. Ana will take your wife and show her around. I'll take you to the company to meet the boss, and then we'll see. Does that sound like it will work?"

The newlyweds nodded in unison, and Clemente said, "We want to thank you very much for the amazing wedding gift. Being able to fly and arrive within the same day is wonderful. We really appreciate it."

"It was our pleasure," Favio responded, turning to look at his wife, who nodded in agreement.

For the remainder of the drive, they sat looking at the city that was unfolding before them. Favio and Ana provided a running commentary on what they were seeing. They were quite surprised to see how modern everything looked compared to Italy and how many new houses there were. While the sun was just setting, they could still see everything, and they were very impressed.

Turning a corner, they parked in front of a small building, and Yolanda saw a sign that read, "Antonio's Ristorante." As she nudged her husband to show him, the front passenger door was opened from the outside. A small man with a huge smile greeted them and proceeded to open the rear passenger door. "Welcome to the finest Italian restaurant in Canada." He laughed. "I'm Antonio. We've been expecting you. My wife, Julie, and I have prepared a special meal just for you. As it will be your first meal in your new country, we want it to be memorable. Welcome." Clemente stepped out of the car as Antonio was helping the girls out of the back seat. "Your table is right this way," their host said as he led them into the interior of the restaurant.

It was quite dark, and their eyes took a minute to adjust to the dim light. They saw a small room decorated with pictures of different regions of their old country. There were eight tables with checkered red and white tablecloths. There was a wicker-enclosed Chianti bottle holding a candle in the centre of each table. Theirs was lit and felt welcoming. Two of the other tables were occupied.

Antonio pulled out a chair and motioned for Yolanda to sit. Once she was settled, he quickly pulled out another chair and, with a sweeping motion, invited Ana to her chair. "I'll get the wine," Antonio stated as he headed to the bar and came back in a minute with a bottle of white wine, which he started to pour. "Pinot grigio," he announced.

As he poured, a curvy, middle-aged woman approached them and placed a tureen in the middle of the table. Smiling, she said, "*Buongiorno*. I'm Julie. Welcome to our restaurant." She removed the lid with a great gesture and announced, "*Zuppa.*"

The remainder of the meal proceeded in much the same fashion, and it was amazing. All the courses were topped off with a chicken dish that was better than anything the young couple had ever experienced.

Clemente remembered that his uncle had immigrated to Canada, arriving from the old country a couple of years previously just as the war was winding down. What he didn't know was what his uncle told them while they were eating at the restaurant.

"I didn't have a job when we arrived," he told them once they had settled into their meal. "We had some money that we brought with us, so we went to a rooming house for a few days until we could find an apartment. As we were looking for an apartment in the Italian neighbourhood, I was asking around about work. We ate at Antonio's on our first evening. As we chatted, I told him we had just arrived, and I was looking for work. He didn't say anything then but told a contractor he knew about me. The next day, I was contacted by Pasquali Bertollini, and after a brief conversation, I joined his company as the office administrator."

He paused and, addressing Yolanda, explained, "You see, I had worked in a bank in Milan, and when the war came, I was lucky to be transferred to Switzerland because I had a decent working knowledge of English, and they needed me at the branch in Zurich. This turned out to be very valuable to Pasquali Bertollini. He was a carpenter by trade from a small town in Abruzzi, and he had a knack for dealing with numbers and estimating. He had started small by building houses and hiring other tradesmen as he needed them. While that worked for a while, it became obvious that the competition for skilled trades was becoming intense.

"You see, Toronto was growing quickly as more people were immigrating after the war. So, to ensure that he wasn't caught short, he hired a carpenter and a labourer to work for him. He didn't want other contractors to come along and hire them away from him, so he offered a higher rate of pay than the going rate and secured their word that they would tell him if any other contractor tried to hire them away from him. He sweetened the pot by guaranteeing them two weeks of paid holidays a year."

"But you weren't a carpenter," Clemente stated.

"Absolutely," was the answer. Favio continued. "Pasquali had developed a good reputation in the community for his work, and as more work came his way, he added additional qualified tradesmen, apprentices, and helpers. He had a good working relationship with his workers because he treated them with respect. As the business grew, he formed the company, but it was becoming obvious that he needed help with the business side of things. His knowledge of English was very limited, and this was starting to cause problems. His wife was his bookkeeper. She was finding that there was too much required to allow her to do things in a proper and timely manner. Her English was better than his but still limited.

"So, when Pasquali started asking around in the Italian community, Antonio mentioned to one of his customers about a young banker who had just arrived from Zurich and was looking for work. The customer knew Pasquali and passed the information on to him. He called me and invited Ana and me to have lunch with him and his wife.

"The rest," he added, "is history. Now I am the office manager, I have a staff of two people, and Mrs. Bertollini stays at home enjoying her garden. The company is running smoothly and is very successful. I told Pasquali about you"—Favio nodded toward his nephew—"and he is looking forward to meeting you. But understand that, while I have recommended you, you will be working for him and under his watchful eye."

"I know I can prove myself," was Clemente's response.

"So do we," his aunt stated as they finished their wonderful dinner, chatting about the differences in lifestyles between Canada and Italy.

"Many thanks for making our first meal in Canada so memorable, Antonio," Clemente said as they were leaving. "And please tell your wife that I have never had a better meal!"

"For sure," Yolanda added.

"It was our pleasure," the smiling host replied. "Please consider this your home. You are welcome any time."

After driving for what seemed to be a few minutes, Favio announced, "Here we are." They pulled up to a large, three-storey brick house. By now it was dark, and the street lights were on. Clemente and Yolanda hadn't seen much on the drive from the restaurant. They were exhausted. The ladies entered the door bearing the number 2 and went inside. Clemente and Favio brought in the suitcases, and after a brief look around, he and Ana said good night and left.

The young couple barely got their clothes off before they collapsed under the blankets of their bed and immediately fell asleep.

$ $ $

THEY AWOKE WITH the spring sun filling the bedroom. They looked at each other, and Clemente said, "Well, we are here."

After a good morning kiss, Clemente followed his wife out into the living room of their new accommodation. Their apartment was on the first floor of the brick house they had entered last night. The living room was their main room. There was one bedroom, a small kitchen, and a bathroom.

Opening the refrigerator, they saw that, true to her word, Ana had filled it with food. As Yolanda looked in the cupboard next, she discovered dishes, cutlery, glasses, cups, and an assortment of pots and pans. Turning, she said, "This looks great. We really must thank Ana and Favio. They couldn't have done more. What about breakfast? I'm starving, and you must be too."

After a delicious breakfast of scrambled eggs, toast, orange juice, and blueberry jam, Clemente suggested, "Let's unpack, put our things away, and then go for a walk around and see the neighbourhood."

Giving him a devious smile, she responded, "I've got a better idea." Taking his hand, she led him back to the bed.

It was amazing sex, after which they both drifted back to sleep. When they finally opened the front door several hours later, they saw they were living on a quiet, tree-lined street. "I wonder what kind of trees those are," Clemente said, and they stood on the porch taking in their surroundings. The trees were very large and full. The trunks were black with rough bark, and further up, when they branched out, they were grey. The leaves were large and distinctive, and the trees looked majestic. Large brick houses were set back from the sidewalk, and the street was lined with beautiful large green trees and large grass lawns.

"Come on," Yolanda said, taking Clemente's hand, and they headed out to explore the neighbourhood. It was a totally new experience, nothing like anything they had ever seen in Italy. Returning to their house, they crossed over the road, which was covered with a black, tar-like substance, and noticed a small narrow sign on a metal pole. It read, "Palmerston Boulevard."

$ $ $

WHEN YOLANDA AND Clemente woke up the next time, it was night. They went to see what the cupboards and refrigerator contained. In the latter, they found the casserole Ana had left for them.

They cleaned up after their meal, and as they were returning to bed, Clemente asked, "How many children should we have?"

"Three or four would be nice," his wife responded.

"Good. I hope we get a boy first." Kissing each other, they closed their eyes and enjoyed the feel of each other's exploring hands, fingers, lips, and tongues before falling into a deep and peaceful sleep.

CHAPTER **FIVE**

THE FOLLOWING MORNING, there was a knock on the apartment door, and Yolanda opened it to see Ana's and Favio's smiling faces. "Come in," Yolanda said, standing aside for them to enter. "Clemente is just finishing up in the bathroom. Would you like coffee?"

"No, thanks," they replied in unison.

"Are you finding the apartment okay?" Ana asked.

"Yes, it is perfect," Yolanda replied, and she went on to tell them about their walk through the neighbourhood yesterday and how different it was from anything they had ever experienced at home.

"Good morning," came the voice from the bathroom. "I'll be with you in a minute. Are we leaving now?"

"Yes, Bertollini is expecting us. Ana is going to introduce your wife to her friends," his uncle replied.

"Okay, I'm ready. I'll just get a jacket."

"You won't need it. It is beautiful outside. Warm and sunny."

"Let's go then. See you later, girls," Clemente added, planting a kiss on Yolanda's cheek.

Turning discreetly, Yolanda whispered in his ear, "I'll need money for food and shopping."

"Of course," Clemente replied, and he handed her his wallet. "Take what you need."

She removed all the paper money, saying, "I'll take it, and if I can, I'll convert it into Canadian money." With that, she handed him back his empty wallet.

Settling into the passenger seat in Favio's car, Clemente was starting to feel a little uneasy about what he was feeling as it hit him that this was a make-or-break meeting with Pasquali Bertollini. As he sat thinking about it, Favio sensed his apprehension and said, "He's quite a man, our Mr. Bertollini. I've been with him for two years now and probably know him better than anyone in the company, excluding, of course, his wife. He had a bad experience when he first started the business with a carpenter from Sicily. He hired the fellow without references, and while his work was okay, he fell for and absconded with the boss's niece, who was working in the office for his wife. She was a nice, good-looking, girl, and this guy swept her off her feet. They eloped. Pasquali was furious. He had people search, but they were never found. They probably left the country and disappeared into the States. Ever since then, he has been extremely cautious about who he hires. He checks everyone's references and makes them start at the bottom until he sees their work ethic and character.

"While I've told him about you and your training, you will still start as a labourer. You will remain there until he develops a sense of your work, skills, and personality. If he feels good about you, you will move up. If not, he will leave you as a labourer until you get fed up and leave. This way, he avoids firing people. But don't worry. You'll be fine." While the story was enlightening, Clemente still felt apprehensive.

Shortly thereafter, they arrived at an old brick building on a busy street, which turned out to be College Street. Parking the car in the adjoining lot, Favio escorted his nephew to the second floor and through a door with a glass window on which was printed, in black letters, "Bertollini Construction." Clemente followed him to an office in the far corner of the large room. His uncle paused at the door, and after glancing in, turned and motioned him to enter.

Clemente saw it was a medium-sized office with a desk in the middle of the room, which was covered in plans, paper, and booklets. Sitting behind the desk was a short, stocky man in his mid- to late thirties or early forties. He had a square jaw and short black hair. He was a serious-looking man. He nodded and motioned for Clemente to sit across from him.

"So, what do you think of Canada so far?" he asked. Clemente was taken aback. He realized that his uncle had left the two of them alone.

Gathering his rapport, he replied, "It looks very promising, but we really haven't seen too much of it yet."

Pasquali studied him for a minute and then said, "You'll start this morning at a new house we are building a couple of miles away. I'll have you driven over. The foreman is expecting you and will show you what to do." With that, Pasquali stood up, went to the door, opened it, and called out, "Hey, Francesco, take young Mr. Gallorini here over to the job just off Jarvis and introduce him to Dino. He is expecting him." Turning back, he motioned for Clemente to leave.

As Clemente exited the office, a young man with wavy black hair and a large pair of glasses approached him, saying, "Hi, I'm Francesco. Let's go."

They walked by another office where Favio was waiting in the doorway for him. Favio winked and gave him a brown paper bag, saying, "Your aunt made these sandwiches for your lunch. I'll see you later."

They got into an old blue Ford pickup, and Francesco drove off, giving a running commentary about himself, the city, the weather, the roads, and the company until they pulled up at a new house being constructed in what appeared to be a new subdivision. While Clemente had half-listened to his driver, he was looking at the roads, avenues, buildings, people, and everything else that caught his eye on their drive to the construction site. Getting out of the truck, he saw a new house that was just being framed.

A short fellow approached, nodded to Francesco, and then, looking at Clemente, said, "You're the new guy, right? I need you to move those two-by-fours in there," he said, nodding toward the house. He had motioned toward a pile of lumber, which had been unloaded and was sitting on the ground. "I'm Dino. Let me know if you have any questions or need anything. Oh, put your lunch over there," he added, nodding toward a pile of coats as he walked toward the entrance to the new house.

Setting his lunch on the ground where Dino had indicated, Clemente rolled up his sleeves. He then walked to the wood pile and picked up six of the eight-foot-long boards, hoisting them on his shoulder. They weren't overly heavy, and he carried them up the temporary ramp to the main floor of the new house. He set them down in the middle of the floor. Then, turning to Dino, who was standing a little way away and watching him,

Clemente said, "This okay?" The foreman nodded and returned to his conversation with one of the other workers.

And so, within an hour of meeting Pasquali Bertollini, Clemente commenced working as a labourer for Bertollini Construction. It was a beautiful late spring morning, and he felt exhilarated. He thought that it would take him about an hour to move the two-by-fours. It took twenty-five minutes.

As Clemente was finishing, Dino, who had obviously been keeping an eye on him, came over and said, "Bring in those sheets of plywood out there and stack them near the two-by-fours." He indicated toward the yard area on the other side of the building shell, then walked away.

Clemente stepped outside and saw the plywood and, without hesitating, moved it all. It took him just under half an hour. Again, as he was finishing, Dino came over. "You know a bit of woodworking?" he asked.

Nodding, Clemente answered, "Yep."

"Wait here," Dino told him, and he went over to his truck and came back with a carpenter's apron. He held it out to Clemente. "Put this on and come with me. Your uncle said to give this to you if I thought you were any good," he said, looking directly at Clemente and, for the first time, smiling at him.

Clemente tried to hide his surprise as he took it. Holding it around his waist, he adjusted the strap and then attached the two interlocking ends behind his back. There were two leather pouches side by side. He fastened the apron at his back and followed the foreman into the house.

Dino took him to a makeshift table and unrolled a set of plans that were lying on it.

Clemente automatically took hold of one side of the plans as the foreman, holding onto the other side, said, "We are going to frame walls here, here, and here." He went from the drawings with his finger to the plywood floor, where the location of the future walls had been marked in pencil. "There's the sawhorse, and there's the Skilsaw and the handsaws. Anything else you need, let me know. We are going to break for lunch in a few minutes, so you can study these and let me know if you are okay with them." With that, he walked away.

Clemente proceeded to spread the plans out on the table, anchoring the corners with pieces of scrap wood that were lying around. He studied the plans and the measurements and then took his new tape measure, which was included with the apron, and checked the plan measurements against what had been drawn on the floor. Once he satisfied himself that the floor markings exactly matched what the plans indicated, he went to Dino, saying, "Okay, I've checked them. They look good, so I'll start constructing the frames and installing them right after lunch."

Dino smiled for the second time since he and Clemente had first interacted, and said, "Great. Let's eat. You'll need a hand when you are ready to start. Kelly, here"—he indicated a young man who looked as if he were still a teenager, with blonde hair and a great smile—"will help you. His mother is Italian, and he speaks it pretty good."

Kelly said in English, "Hi."

Clemente responded, "Hi, I'm Clemente."

So, after lunch, Clemente and Kelly started to construct the frames. Once they were done, they nailed them to the floor and wall. As Clemente worked, he started to feel at home and comfortable doing what he was trained to do.

It felt good.

# CHAPTER SIX

A  s soon as Favio and Clemente left the apartment, Ana turned to Yolanda, saying, "I thought we would go around the neighbourhood, and I'll introduce you to the people you should know."

"That would be wonderful," Yolanda replied.

She was going to grab a light jacket but then remembered what Favio had told her husband: it was a lovely, warm day. Following her new aunt out, Yolanda paused to lock the apartment door and slipped the key into her purse. Outside, she found it to be a bright and sunny late spring morning. It was not too hot, and there was a lovely breeze. Walking beside Ana, she took everything in. The street looked majestic, with all the trees Clemente had commented on the other evening lining either side. She asked Ana what they were. Maples, she was told.

Continuing on, Ana said, "I doubt that you have any Canadian money yet, so we'll start with Scozzafava. He's a moneylender, and he will trade your lira for Canadian dollars at a good price." Yolanda nodded in agreement and was glad she had brought all the money from her husband's wallet.

And so the morning went, with Ana introducing Yolanda around the neighbourhood. Yolanda could understand why it was referred to as Little Italy. Almost everyone they met was Italian. Over the course of the morning, she met or was told about the gossips, the clairvoyants, the bargain hunters, the medical advisers, the shops, and the merchants she could trust, as well as those to avoid. She learned the ins and outs of life in her new neighbourhood.

When they finally stopped for a bite to eat, they entered a small café where a group of ladies was waiting for them. Yolanda was quite taken aback as she was introduced to each of the five women, who were all from different areas of Italy. "Do all of you know English?" she asked. It turned out that they had varying levels of understanding of the language. It seemed that those with children in school had learned the most from their children.

One of the girls told her, "I go to English classes at night school. It's just around the corner. The teacher is good, and he always gives us a new special word to learn every evening. The words are usually not ones that are used in everyday conversation. Anyway, two weeks ago, the word was 'spiffy.' It means 'a very stylish and smartly dressed person.' It is what they call slang or a made-up word. As soon as he told us, I thought of Ana's Favio. Have you ever seen anyone more stylish or fashionable?" Everyone at the table broke out in gales of laughter, and Ana broke into a very large smile.

After lunch was over and each of the ladies had gone their own way, Ana said to Yolanda, "Let's go shopping so you can see how the shops and stores work here." Yolanda readily agreed, and off they went. It was an eye-opener for Yolanda to see the large selection that the stores were offering here compared to those back home.

Finally, as they were getting ready to go home, Yolanda said she would like to pick up some groceries. "I need eggs, flour, tomatoes, garlic, onion, and olive oil. I saw you left us salt and pepper, so that should get us started making meals."

Ana nodded, and they shopped.

$ $ $

"HI," CAME THE cheerful voice of Clemente as Yolanda was putting the last of her groceries away.

"Oh, hi. Ana took me shopping before bringing me home, and I am just finishing putting things away," she said as she moved to the door and shared a kiss with him. "We had quite a day. How did things go for you?"

Putting his arm around her as they headed toward the couch, he said, "Well, it was certainly not what I was expecting." He paused and made himself more comfortable before continuing. "I assumed from what Favio told me that Bertollini would have me working as a labourer for a few weeks until he got to know me a little bit and see what I could do. I went to a job site where they were building a new house. I moved piles of lumber and plywood into the house, and the next thing I knew, they showed me a set of plans, and I started building a wall. Favio had bought me my own carpenter's apron and hand tools. I spent the rest of the day reading the plans and framing the walls. And I had a helper."

He paused and then went on, "Bertollini must have told the foreman—his name is Dino—what Favio had said about me. It seemed that Bertollini had Dino test me. When he saw that I knew what I was doing and wasn't afraid to work, I started the carpenter's job right away. The very first day!

"How about you? How was your day?"

"Well, Ana showed me around and introduced me to everybody we met. We had lunch with a group of her friends in a nice little café, and I learned two very interesting things." She paused and then continued. "Your uncle has an English *soprannome*. In English, it's called a 'nickname,' and his is Spiffy."

"What?"

"It is a made-up name to describe someone based on their character and the way they present themselves. How they comb their hair and dress. They have named him, in English, 'Spiffy.' The girl that did it said 'spiffy' means 'a very stylish and fashionable person,' and apparently, they all thought it suited him perfectly. Even your aunt thought it was funny and appropriate."

"Wow. Did you say 'siffy'?"

"No," she replied, "it is 'spiffy' with a 'P.'"

"Oh," was the reply. "He certainly is a smart dresser, and he looks pretty dashing. 'Spiffy' it is," and they both broke into laughter. Then Clemente inquired, "What was the other thing?"

"Well, one of the girls—her name is Lucia—told me that one of the best hotels downtown was looking for girls to work in their laundry room, and she wondered if I was interested. She said she would take me down and introduce me to the lady who was hiring—if I was interested. I told her that I would talk to you but that it sounded good to me. What do you think?"

"I didn't think you would start working right away. I thought you would take some time to get your bearings and get comfortable. How far is it, and how would you get there?"

"It is about a fifteen-minute ride on a streetcar, so it's not that far, and I would learn much more about things here working with other people."

"Do you want to try it?"

"Of course, and the money would come in handy. I could learn different things about the city and the country, and it will help us find a place of our own much sooner."

"Yeah, for sure. Okay, you try it and see if you like it and if it's worth your while."

"I'll go and tell Ana after dinner so she can get a hold of Lucia and tell her. They both have telephones."

"Oh, by the way, how did you make out with our money?"

"Well, I got it all converted into Canadian dollars." As Yolanda talked, she removed it from her apron pocket and gave it to him. "The money changer was a fellow named Scozzafava. Ana said he was fair and trustworthy. He seemed nice. I used some of it to buy a few groceries we needed. Oh, I should probably keep some on hand if I am going to be starting a new job."

"All right, that's great."

"Okay," his wife added. "Ana told me about the banks here and suggested that we open an account with one of them so we can deposit our cheques in one place together. She said there are five main banks here, and they are all good. She and your uncle use the Royal Bank and said they were quite happy with it. I think we should check it out and get an account set up. She said that the staff in this area mostly speak our language, so we shouldn't have any trouble."

Clemente agreed, and then Yolanda said, "There is something we should discuss and agree upon before we go too far."

"What's that?"

"Well, I don't know about your family, but in mine, my mother looked after the banking, bill paying, and anything else that had to do with finances. She and my father both had access to the account, but in reality, he left everything up to her. They took time every week to go over the accounts, so he always knew what was going on, but he left the day-to-day details to her. We don't know what we are going to be doing, but now we should start depositing your paycheques. When I find a job, my pay will go in too. We will each be able to take money out, and I suggest that once a month, probably at the end, just after dinner, we sit down and review things. What do you think?"

He thought about it for a moment and then said, "I think my parents had a similar arrangement, but of course, it was never discussed with us. As long as we can both take money out when we need it, I think that would be a good way to do it." Within a few days, they had their new bank account established.

There was one thing Yolanda's mother did that Yolanda didn't share with Clemente. She told her daughters that she always kept a separate account and added money into it without anyone knowing. She had told the girls that things happen and emergencies occur, and she always wanted a pot of money available so she could deal with such things. Yolanda had decided that she would do the same thing.

CHAPTER **SEVEN**

T
HE FOLLOWING MORNING, Lucia called for Yolanda just after Clemente left. As she got ready to leave, Lucia asked, "Do you have an umbrella? It's cloudy and looks like it could rain." Yolanda nodded and took the umbrella from the closet, thinking how smart she was to have packed it along with their other belongings. They stepped outside into a cloudy, gusty morning and walked to the end of the street, where they took the streetcar toward downtown.

As they settled into their seats, Lucia, who was about Yolanda's age, said, "I hope you won't mind working here. I've been there for close to two years, and the work is pretty routine. The pay is not bad, and there are some nice girls working with me. They are all fairly new to the city, and they come from all over the world."

"I'm really looking forward to it and hope it works out," Yolanda replied. "It would be nice to start working so quickly. I really want to start getting some exposure to English, and it would be great to start making money so soon. I was thinking that it could take me months to find something I could do without knowing the language."

Soon, they got off the streetcar. They walked a block and came to a large building with large gold letters above the main entrance that read, "King Edward Hotel." There was a doorman at the front door showing people in and out. There were quite a few people coming and going. Yolanda followed Lucia past the entrance and down the adjoining alley to the side door, where they entered.

"This way," Lucia said, proceeding down a long, dimly lit hall with a distinct smell of soap and disinfectant in the air. Turning right, they entered a huge room. As Yolanda looked about, she saw it was a large, unfinished concrete room. There were several young women dressed in blue frocks busily working. There were piles of white linen in what looked like large containers on wheels, a row of medium green washing machines, another row of dryers, and overhead, lines holding various linens, mainly sheets. Yolanda was immediately aware of the presence of noise: a constant humming and clicking from the machines and the loud chatter as the girls talked above the din of the machines. It was quite a scene to take in, and Yolanda felt as if she had arrived in a different world. She was overwhelmed.

Within a minute of their arrival, a rather portly woman in a white frock approached them and, looking critically at Yolanda, demanded in a short manner, "Who is this?" in broken English.

"This is Yolanda Gallorini. She and her husband just arrived from Tuscany. He has a job in construction, and she is looking for work. I thought that she would fit in here," Lucia answered.

"Does she speak English?" was the next question from the large lady. Yolanda noticed that she had very curly, sandy-coloured hair, a wide face, prominent cheekbones, and a bad complexion. "No, she doesn't speak any English. She's Italian."

Wanting her own interpreter, the large lady turned toward the room and bellowed, "Paola." Almost immediately, a tall dark-haired girl in her early thirties came over. "Paola, ask this girl why she wants to work here," the large lady commanded. Paola looked at Yolanda with no expression on her face and asked the question in Italian.

Smiling, Yolanda answered, "My husband and I arrived two days ago from Bucine, in Tuscany. When Lucia told me about her job, I thought it sounded good and came with her this morning to see if you needed anyone else. I worked for my father, who is a butcher, and I enjoy working."

Paola translated, and the boss lady grunted and said, "We'll see." Turning to Paola, she continued, "Take her over, get her changed, and show her what to do." She then looked at Lucia, nodded, and walked off.

Lucia went to change into her work clothes, and Yolanda followed Paola into a locker room, where Paola directed her new charge to an empty locker and opened it. "Put your clothes here and then put these on." She pointed toward a rack of blue skirts and white blouses. "Get a hairnet there." She pointed to a box on a table. "You'll be working in the best and most elegant hotel in the city," she continued, "and they only hire the best workers. I come from Milano and have been here for three years. The work is good, and the people are nice to work with. They are from all over. We have several Italian girls here, so you can get a lot of help learning English. The boss is Olga, and she is from Ukraine. She comes across as a hard-ass, but she is pretty nice once she gets to know you. Oh, if you last the first day, you'll be on probation until they think you're okay. But don't worry. Do what I tell you, and you'll be fine."

As soon as she had changed, Yolanda followed as they walked out to the main room. "You'll work with me, sorting dirty bedding. I'll show you." Paola turned her attention to a pile of sheets, saying, "You'll be looking for spots and stains that need special attention before they are washed. Don't be surprised by what you see; people can be pretty disgusting. Once you've sorted a load and found sheets that need extra attention, you take that high-powered solution"—she pointed to a large plastic bottle with a spraying spout and a trigger—"to the spots and work it into the fabric. Let it sit over here for half an hour"—she indicated another small pile—"and then add them to this pile for washing."

Paola then picked up a dirty sheet from the small pile that had been treated and held it up so they could examine it. "It's okay," she said and deposited it in a large pile beside the washing machines. She then motioned for Yolanda to continue, so Yolanda picked up another sheet, examined it, and deposited it onto the same large pile. She picked up a third sheet and noticed what looked like food stains on it. Quite a few stains. She held it up so Paola could see it. Her mentor nodded, and Yolanda deposited it in the smaller pile to her left.

Paola nodded again, saying, "Good. The next thing is to take the washed sheets out and throw them in the dryer." She pointed to the other row of machines with round glass doors. "You are responsible for these five washers and those five dryers. When the maids bring the sheets down, they will add them to the smallest pile. Finally," she concluded, "you remove the sheets and check to ensure they are clean and ready to go and then fold and then pile them on that table where they will be pressed and placed in the clean bedding area and sorted. The pillowcases, towels, and bed covers are all kept there. Any questions?"

"No, I don't think so," Yolanda replied, shaking her head.

"Good. Start now and let me know if you have any questions or need help."

"Gracious."

"You say 'Thank you' in English." And so, Yolanda had learned her first English word. She smiled and turned her attention to the pile of dirty sheets.

Lucia came over a little later, asking, "How is it going? Are you okay?"

"Yeah, I'm getting the hang of it."

"Well, it's lunchtime, and you are in for a surprise. The hotel gives us lunch, so let's eat," her friend said, taking her to the end of the room where round tables and chairs were placed and plates of sandwiches, fruit, and prepared vegetables were waiting for them, along with glass jugs of water and pots of what proved to be tea. They were joined by Paola and the three Italian girls. They chatted away, getting to know each other and enjoying their lunch. As she glanced around, she noticed Olga looking at them.

Yolanda learned that there were girls from almost every European country, including Hungary, Romania, and Russia. After lunch, they returned to their various jobs, and she realized how noisy the workplace was as the workers resumed talking above the machines in different languages. Yolanda was kept very busy but enjoyed it, as the day passed very quickly. Olga seemed satisfied with her work, but of course, she would never say anything to "her" girls.

As they walked back to the front of the hotel, Yolanda saw the street sign saying they were on King Street. Heading for the streetcar stop, which was on the corner of Yonge Street, she saw from the puddles and dampness on the sidewalk and road that it had rained. Now, the sky was a mix of fluffy white clouds racing across the blue.

She arrived home a little tired from being on her feet all day but happy that she now had a job and was meeting some very interesting people. When her husband arrived, she gave him a complete rundown of what had happened and what she had done. He was pleased that things had worked out for her so quickly.

The following morning, Yolanda and Lucia met at the streetcar stop they'd agreed on yesterday and proceeded to work together. The day went well, as she was comfortable doing her job and knew what was expected of her.

Arriving home that late afternoon, she stopped and looked at the state of the apartment.

When he arrived home, Clemente sensed something was wrong. His wife was very quiet and was not welcoming when he came into the apartment. "What's happening?" he asked. "Did something go wrong with the job?"

"No," Yolanda answered. "No, the job was fine."

"What is it, then?" he inquired.

"Well, my mother always told us that she was not our maid. It was our home, and we all had a responsibility to keep it neat and tidy. We were taught to keep our rooms neat and our clothes hung up, or if they were dirty, put into the hamper. We were expected to make our beds when we got up and not leave anything lying around the house. We were expected to leave the bathroom clean and tidy. I am thinking that your house, maybe because there were three men involved, was not run the same way."

"I am feeling pretty down because I now have a job, and when I come home from work, I find the apartment an untidy mess. Nothing has been put away, and everything is scattered all over. I've cleaned it up every day so far, but to be honest, I'm feeling that this is not going to work." Yolanda paused, waiting to see if there was any reaction. There was none, so she went on. "I think that since we will both be working, we need to decide how we are going to do things because I am not prepared to keep the apartment clean and tidy by myself." With that, she stopped, folded her arms, and waited for a reaction.

As Clemente sat and listened to Yolanda, the message was received loud and clear. He knew this was serious. He hesitated for a moment and then said, "You are absolutely right. You're not my maid. Sorry, I wasn't thinking. What do you want me to do?"

"Well, let's start with you putting your clothes away or in the laundry hamper if they need washing. You can leave the bathroom neat and tidy and start putting the toilet seat down for me when you are done. Can you imagine what it would have been like if I got up in the night to use the toilet without realizing the seat was still up? It would not be a good scene, I can assure you. Don't leave things lying around once you have finished with them, and help me make the bed as soon as we get up."

"Okay," was his response.

When dinner was over and they had moved the dishes and cutlery to the sink area, she said to her husband, "Do you want to wash or dry?"

"Okay, I'll dry."

$ $ $

WHEN CLEMENTE RECEIVED his first cheque from Bertollini Construction at the end of his second week, he immediately checked the amount to ensure it was what he had been promised. It didn't add up! Not wanting to offend his new employer, he approached his uncle. "I'm not understanding this," he said. "My cheque is for less than I was told I would be paid."

Laughing, Favio replied, "The prime minister of Canada has taken his cut."

"What! Who is this prime minister?" Clemente asked.

Chuckling, his uncle went on. "He's the head of the government, like our president back home, and his name is King. He lives in a place called Outaw, or something like that, and he takes a cut from everyone's pay."

"Is he the King?" Clemente inquired.

"No," responded Favio, "that is just his last name. His first name is McKenzie."

"Is it like protection?" asked Clemente.

"Not exactly," Favio went on to explain. "It is called income tax, and the government takes it from everyone who works. The more you make, the more they take. They use it to pay for the army and things like that. I have a fellow who looks after that kind of stuff for me, and I'll take you to meet him. He will explain everything and show you how to deal with it. His name is Georgio Cagnoni, and I think you'll like him."

A few nights later, Favio took Clemente to meet Georgio, who lived in an apartment a few blocks away. Clemente was introduced to a young, studious-looking fellow with a small moustache that gave his face a look of maturity and authority. Clemente guessed he was in his early thirties, although with his moustache, he was trying to make himself look older and more professional. Clemente immediately had a good feeling about him.

"I was a bookkeeper back home," Georgio said after they were introduced and shook hands. "When we arrived here, I started working from my apartment, helping the newcomers from the old country, and I became their accountant." He went on to explain that over time he had built himself a nice business and had a good reputation in the community. "I enjoy helping everyone and looking after their taxes for them."

"Who is this King, and why does he take part of my earnings every two weeks?" Clemente inquired.

"Well, it is no longer Mr. King. He retired, and now we have a new prime minister, Uncle Louie. Like his predecessor, he takes it from everyone who works," Georgio explained. "It's called income tax, and at the end of the year, you have to show the government how much you made. Your employer will give you the amount on a special slip of paper called a T4 slip. The prime minister is the boss. The people that work for him will look at how much income tax you paid based on your earnings and decide if it is enough."

"Enough for what?" Clemente asked.

"The cost of running the country. It was supposed to be temporary to help pay for the First World War many years ago. But I guess they became used to having the money, so it is still with us," he explained. "They set the rates for everyone based on how much you earn. At the end of the year, if you paid too much, they give you money back. It's called a refund. If they don't think you paid enough, you have to pay them more. There are certain things that you can use called 'deductions,' and they will lower the amount of tax you owe."

"Sounds like protection to me," was Clemente's reply.

"Not really," Georgio exclaimed, laughing. "When the time comes, I will help you, and it will be fine. None of my clients pay more at the end of the year. We always manage to get money back for them."

"See, I told you he would look after you," Favio added, as their host produced a bottle of red wine and filled three glasses. The conversation shifted to the old country.

As Favio had predicted, Clemente proved himself to be a good and careful worker. He was very quickly promoted to lead carpenter. His wages increased accordingly, and with Yolanda working, they soon saved enough for a down payment on their first house.

When they shared their thinking with their uncle, he agreed that buying instead of renting was a smart move. "Ana and I don't have children and are unable to have any," he confided in them. "Let me talk it over with her, and we'll see what we can do to help you."

Favio came back the next day, advising them, "We will be happy to help, but it must be a business transaction. We'll have a proper mortgage agreement drawn up, and you will pay the money back with regular payments—monthly or annually—with interest. The choice will be yours."

# CHAPTER EIGHT

GOING THROUGH THEIR first year in Canada was quite an experience, one Yolanda and Clemente would never forget. They were noticing more things now that they had settled into a routine. The change in the weather was very gradual but noticeable. By mid-September, the temperature was still nice but not as hot. The nights were cooler, and the days were noticeably shorter. The leaves on the beautiful, large maple trees on their street seemed to be losing their strong, dark green colour. As September ended, the leaves were verging on a very light yellow, and the days continued to shorten.

Then, one morning while getting into his truck, Clemente saw the first hint of red appearing on some of the leaves. He mentioned it to Yolanda, and she agreed, saying that she had been subconsciously aware of it but had not given it much thought.

That weekend, they went shopping and bought light jackets, as there was a coolness in the air. There were more rainy days, and some of the leaves had started to fall to the ground. By mid-October, the trees were covered in beautiful red, yellow, and brown leaves, which were dropping to the ground. Within two more weeks, the lawns were covered with the fallen leaves, and on the weekend, homeowners were raking the leaves, piling them on the edge of the road, and burning them. They filled the air with a very distinctive smell, which was not particularly unpleasant but very noticeable.

The sky became a deep, dark grey in November, and the first snow fell toward the end of the month. It was damp and melted within a few hours. The snow kept falling and melting into December, and then things changed. The days were considerably shorter now. Everyone was wearing warmer clothing, hats, and gloves. Then the first storm of the season flew in off Lake Ontario, the large freshwater body of water on which the city sat. They were told that this lake was one in a group that made up the Great Lakes.

It was windy and cold, and the snow blew in. Lots of snow flew around and drifted against anything that was in its path. The young couple had never seen anything like it as they looked out of their windows in awe. When it was over, it was like the whole world had changed. Everything was blanketed in snow. It was over a foot deep, and some of the drifts were close to two feet. As they watched, snowplows appeared and pushed the snow to the sides of the pavement and up onto the road edge. Everyone bundled up and shovelled their sidewalks and driveways. This was their first taste of winter in their new home.

Within days, it seemed, coloured lights appeared inside homes, where they were visible through windows. Outside, they were strung on porches, around doors, and on trees and hedges at the sides of the front doors. Beautifully shaped spruce trees, which were six to eight feet in height, were on sale as "Christmas trees." They were taken home and decorated with coloured lights and ornaments. The shop windows were decorated to encourage customers looking for gifts to give to friends, family, and loved ones. Many stores had outside speakers that played Christmas music.

While Clemente and Yolanda were very used to celebrating Christmas at home, this was nothing like what the young couple had ever experienced. They were fully immersed when their aunt and uncle took them Christmas shopping and then to Anthony and Julia's for dinner. They purchased a small four-foot tree at Ana and Spiffy's suggestion. On it, they hung a string of coloured lights, wrapping them on the outer branches, and added a few ornaments that caught their eye.

On Christmas Eve, at Yolanda's suggestion, they attended a midnight Mass at a nearby church, and the following day, after surprising each other with gifts, they went to their relatives' for a traditional Canadian Christmas dinner. It consisted of roast turkey with stuffing, mashed potatoes with gravy, and Brussels sprouts, along with steamed carrots in a brown sugar sauce.

It was an amazing time of the year.

$ \$ \quad \$ \quad \$ $

ONE FINE MORNING the following spring, just before the construction season fully started, Bertollini called Clemente into his office. "Have a look over these," he said, pointing to a new house plan laid out on his table, "and see what we will need to do for this job. Don't worry about going to the job today. I've sent word that you won't be there."

Picking up the plans and tucking them under his arm, Clemente headed out of the boss's office. To his surprise, his uncle was waiting for him. Favio ushered Clemente into a small office across the floor. There was a small desk, an old rickety chair, one window, a telephone, and a pad of paper and a pencil on the desk. "Work here," his uncle told him, and, giving him a wink, he left.

Puzzled over Bertollini's request and not coming to any conclusion, Clemente turned his attention to studying the plans. They were for a fourplex consisting of two units on the main level and two on the upper level, with a common set of stairs to the upper units in the middle of the front of the building. He had seen a few of these buildings, which were being constructed on lots where old, derelict houses had been bought and torn down.

As Clemente studied the plans, he realized the potential for the builder to demolish an older house and replace it with four new living units. *Bastardo intelligente,* he thought, and he grabbed the pad and pencil and began to figure things out.

When Clemente finished working on the calculations, he realized that it was almost the end of the day, and he hadn't stopped for coffee, lunch, or any kind of a break. He had been totally immersed in the project, and it was like everyone had forgotten that he was there. Getting up and stretching, he picked up the plans and his calculations and headed for Bertollini's office. The rest of the offices were empty, as everyone else had gone home. Bertollini was sitting at the table, obviously waiting for him. Clemente spread the plans out, saying, "This is what I've come up with. And this is what I think we would be looking at for costs." He handed Bertollini his sheet of neatly printed calculations for materials.

To the boss's pleasant surprise, Clemente had calculated the actual cost of the lumber, the drywall, and the related supplies, not just the amount of each that would be needed. "That's great," was his reaction. "However, being a carpenter, you missed a few things, like cement for the foundation, plumbing, heating, and electrical supplies, windows and doors, roofing materials, and a few other things like hardware, sinks, cupboards, et cetera."

Clemente was feeling devastated at what he thought was his boss's criticism, but not missing a beat, Bertollini went on, "What you have done is perfect, so now we'll show you how to do the rest, who to call for quotes, and most importantly, how to negotiate for the best price. We'll deal with all that tomorrow, but now give yourself a pat on the back, and let's go and get some dinner. Call your wife, and we'll go and pick her up. I've called my wife, and she is holding a table for us at Antonio's."

And so it started. Pasquali Bertollini shared his years in the industry, building his business, and learning the ropes. His understudy was a fast learner, and since all the suppliers they used were from the old country, he had no difficulty with the language. He and Yolanda, however, realized the importance of learning English, and they both used every opportunity to learn words and phrases and practise on each other.

Before long, Clemente was taking plans and doing all the estimating. His work was always carefully reviewed by his boss, and when he gave his approving nod, Clemente was happy. They travelled to meet with a plumbing and heating salesman a few weeks later, and to Clemente's surprise, he had been introduced as the company estimator.

When they left the meeting, where Clemente had done most of the talking and negotiating, Bertollini said, almost in passing, "Oh, by the way, now that you have a new title, you will need a raise to go along with it. And here, these are your new business cards." He handed Clemente a small cardboard box the size of his hand. Clemente didn't know what to say. He opened the box and removed the first card, which read, in black, official-looking printing:

**Bertollini Construction**
**350 College Street East**
**Toronto, Ontario**
**Clemente Gallorini**
**Estimator**

He couldn't believe his eyes. His own business card and a raise! He could hardly wait to share the news with his wife. When he did, she was absolutely thrilled, and so they started making plans.

$ $ $

"DO YOU KNOW a real estate agent that could help us look for a new place?" Yolanda asked Ana the next time they were together.

"Well, let me ask around. There is a fellow that I have heard the girls talk about, so let me check."

It didn't take Ana a day to get back to her. That evening, when Yolanda arrived at the apartment, Ana arrived shortly after and told her, "His name is Angelo Leonardelli, and they say he is very good and knowledgeable. Here is his number if you want to call him. Or do you want me to set up a meeting for you?"

"As we don't have a telephone yet, it would be great if you could call him for us," was the answer.

"Okay, anything else?" Ana asked. As Yolanda shook her head, Ana turned and headed back to her place.

Within twenty minutes, Ana came back and said, "I've set up a meeting for tomorrow evening here. I hope that works for you. He should be here by seven-thirty. I thought that would give you time to eat and clean up after supper."

"Wow, that's great. I'll make sure we're ready for him. Thank you."

The following evening at seven-thirty, there was a knock on their door. Yolanda and Clemente opened it to a smiling, smartly dressed fellow around their own age. He introduced himself, and they invited him in. After introductions, they all sat around the table, as Angelo had a rather large and bulky book he produced from his briefcase. He was a husky fellow with light brown hair that was starting to show signs of thinning. He was clean-shaven, and his eyes were brown and intense. He sat back and asked, "What do you have in mind? What are you looking for?"

And so, after a little under twelve months of hard work, they bought their first house in May 1951. As previously arranged, their aunt and uncle held the mortgage. It was a small two-bedroom brick bungalow with a basement, located about a mile northwest of their apartment. It was still in the College and Spadina area and had a small yard, some flower gardens, and an area in the back where the previous owners had had a tiny garden. Clemente and Yolanda thought they would plant a garden the following spring. They lived frugally and ate mainly pasta, which Yolanda made, with homemade tomato sauces.

Life was treating them well, and they never looked back.

# CHAPTER NINE

I T WAS A normal summer day. The sky was blue with fluffy white clouds leisurely floating by, and while there was some humidity in the air, a nice breeze was keeping the temperature comfortable. Clemente had arrived at work just before 8 a.m. It was early July, it was turning hot outside, and construction season was in full swing.

Just as Clemente was settling in, the boss called him. Entering Pasquali's office, he was told, "We just heard from Ronaldo, and apparently some material has gone missing at the fourplex project. Go and see what's going on." Returning to his office, Clemente grabbed his project file, which contained the calculations of the material they had ordered for the job. He then proceeded out to the parking lot, jumped in a company truck, and headed to the job site.

The city was growing, and so was the demand for new, affordable homes. This project was one of the first where the company bought an older home and then applied to the municipal authorities to change the zoning. Their objective was to have the area remain residential but to allow multi-family accommodation to be built. Under this plan, contractors bought the older homes and replaced them with fourplexes.

Arriving at the job site, Clemente entered the partially completed building, looking for Ronaldo, the foreman. Seeing him on the upper level, he proceeded toward him, calling out, "What's going on, man?"

"When we arrived this morning, all our two-by-fours and plywood were missing. Looks like we've been ripped off," was the response.

"All of it?"

"Yep. Every stick of wood."

Thinking for a minute, Clemente asked, "Did you see anybody around sniffing around the site yesterday?"

"Yeah, now that you mention it, three young guys had stopped by and said they were looking for the one guy's grandfather. They said he was supposed to be working here as an electrician. When we told them there were no electricians on the job yet, they left."

"Do you remember what they looked like?"

"They were in their late teens or early twenties. All spoke Italian and wore jeans and T-shirts. One blue, two reddish, as I recall. I didn't really pay that much attention to them."

"Okay, I'll be in touch," Clemente said, turning to go to his truck.

Arriving back at the office, he headed to the boss's office and stuck his head in, saying, "Looks like we were ripped off last night. Ronaldo said three young guys dropped by yesterday on the pretense of looking for one of their grandfathers. Claimed he was an electrician. They were all speaking Italian. Who do we call, the police?"

"*Diavolo*, no," was the answer. "I'll call Tony and let him deal with it." Pasquali picked up the phone. After a very short cryptic conversation, he hung up. "He'll be here shortly," he said, waving Clemente off.

In about twenty minutes, a stranger arrived and proceeded to walk directly into the boss's office. They chatted in very low voices for a few minutes and then called Clemente in.

"This is Tony. Tell him what you know," Pasquali instructed Clemente. Before him stood an intense-looking man who stood about five feet six and was stocky with a chiselled face. He was dressed all in black, and it was obvious from the way he looked at Clemente that he was a person not to be trifled with. After relaying the details he had gleaned from Ronaldo, including the description of the three young fellows who had appeared at the job site, Clemente waited. Tony turned to the boss, giving him a curt nod, and walked out.

When he had left the office, Clemente asked, "Who is Tony, and what does he do?"

"He's a fixer," was the answer as the boss turned, returning to his desk. Clemente, seeing that he was no longer needed, went back to his office.

The following morning, Clemente returned to the job site, intending to recalculate the additional lumber he would have to order to replace what was stolen. He didn't want things to grind to a halt because there was no more material. To his surprise, there was lumber stacked neatly inside the bottom unit. "Where did this come from?" he asked.

"It was here this morning," Ronaldo replied. "I thought you had ordered it."

"Wow! Great! See you later," he said, heading to his truck. "And let me know if you have any other problems." Jumping into the truck, he returned to the office.

As the boss was not around, he went into Spiffy's office and started to relay the details of the events of the last two days. His uncle held up his hand and stopped him. "The old man told me about what went on," he explained, "and Tony sorted it out."

"How?" Clemente asked.

"Well, the first thing you need to know is that Tony Pagotto has eyes and ears on the streets. He knows pretty well everything that is going on and who is doing what. He is from Calabria and still remains in touch with his associates there. He's a no-nonsense guy and one you don't want to mess with. Apparently, he found out within an hour of leaving us yesterday who the punks were and paid them a visit. It seems they hadn't moved the lumber yet, and Tony suggested to them that it was in their best interests to return it. Apparently, there was a brief discussion, after which a mouthy guy, who was the ringleader, ended up in the hospital with multiple injuries. The other two couldn't get the material back to the site fast enough."

"But who is this Tony?" asked Clemente.

"*Risolutore di problemi,*"[8] was the answer from behind him. Pasquali had returned. "He is paid by business owners to fix problems when they arise."

Clemente nodded and, returning to his office, turned his attention to the plans for a new house that he was going to start working on.

The following morning when Clemente arrived at the office, Bertollini was waiting for him. Motioning him into his office, he said, "Nice work on that little problem we had." He handed Clemente a small box and a set of

8    "Problem solver."

keys. "You're going to need these for your new job." And with a wave of his hand, he dismissed him.

Clemente returned to his office and opened the small box, removing a business card. It was identical to his current ones, except "Project Supervisor" was now directly under his name, and the business address was different.

*Wow,* he thought. Then he studied the keys he had been given and saw that they were new and had "Ford" embedded on them. Not totally understanding what was happening, he returned to the boss's office and again was shown to the chair. Seeing that he was puzzled, the boss smiled, saying, "I like what you do. You are smart, and you know how to deal with the men. I can trust you, and you know when to keep your mouth shut. I'm giving you a raise, and you'll need the truck to visit the job sites regularly to ensure everything is good and we are not getting ripped off. The quality of the work has to remain high, or we'll lose our reputation. We can't have our guys or the subcontractors cutting corners. I don't want anyone to ever say that Bertollini cuts corners."

"What about the estimating?" asked Clemente.

"Oh, that'll still be under you, but we'll get you some help."

The following morning, Pasquali called a staff meeting and announced that they were relocating to get more office space. Everyone was told to pack up their things. A pile of boxes was sitting in the corner. Shortly after, a crew of men arrived and loaded everything into a truck, which was taken a few miles to a new four-storey building. They proceeded to the second floor and set up the furniture and equipment they brought from the old office.

As soon as they settled into their new office, which was owned by a cousin of Bertollini's wife, a young man with thick glasses and a boyish face arrived in Clemente's new office and introduced himself as his new assistant, Georgio.

Clemente sat and listened while his new assistant explained that he had just graduated from Ryerson Polytechnic studying project management and was looking forward to putting his knowledge to work in the real world.

"Welcome, Georgio. I am happy to have you on the team. I only ask that you do your best and ask if you have questions. And always put the company's reputation first," Clemente answered.

CHAPTER TEN

CLEMENTE AND YOLANDA had arrived in Canada in late spring 1950, and it was now September 1951. Toronto was growing. The company was thriving, and Clemente was doing very well. The company was looking at taking on larger projects, like three-storey apartment buildings and upmarket houses. Yolanda continued to work at the hotel laundry. She was enjoying what she was doing and the fact that the other girls were helping her to speak English. Clemente had picked up limited English, as most of his work was done in Italian. He was quite happy with his progress in Bertollini's company.

The boss turned out to be a very fair and caring man under his rough exterior manners. He valued his employees and did not hesitate to give pay raises to accompany each well-earned promotion. However, Clemente felt that something was missing. It was a deep feeling, so he decided to take Yolanda out for dinner on the weekend and discuss it with her. He was thrilled to have such a wonderful wife and partner who had such common sense. He knew he was a lucky man.

Arriving at Antonio and Julie's restaurant shortly after eight, they were warmly welcomed. After being seated and settling in, he ordered the house wine. Surprisingly, Yolanda passed on the wine and ordered sparkling water. "I'll try your chicken parmesan and leave it at that for now," she told the server when he came to take their order.

Clemente laughed and said, "I'd like to try your linguine bolognese, although it will have to be pretty amazing to beat my mother-in-law's."

Sipping on his wine and turning to his partner, Clemente thought to himself, *She really is beautiful and smart.* He then informed her, "Your mother is an amazing cook. Better than my mother." He paused for a moment before continuing. "It seems to me that we've been here longer than we have. I've been thinking about where we are and what we have achieved since arriving in Canada. We are doing much better financially than I could have imagined when we started out, thanks to you and your level-headed approach. Oh, by the way, I forgot to tell you that I received a call this morning after you left from Marco Morett."

"Really? From Italy?" Yolanda said, remembering him from their wedding party. He had stood up with her husband.

"No, he's here and was just passing through Toronto. He wanted to know how we were getting on and was excited to hear that we had bought our own house. He sends you a big kiss. He and a couple of friends are on their way to a place in the north called Uranium City, I think he said. Apparently, there is a need for hard rock miners, so they are going to check it out. He was leaving very quickly but promised to stay in touch and to get together as soon as it was practical."

"That sounds exciting. I'll be interested to hear how things work out for them. I hope they are as lucky as we were."

"So, as I was saying, I've been giving some thought to several things and think we should talk about them." He looked over and saw Julie approaching with their meals.

"Enjoy," she said as she set their food in front of them. She could see that they were in the middle of a serious conversation, so she left, heading directly back to the kitchen.

As they started to eat, Clemente continued, "I am wondering if this would be an opportune time to visit our parents. I've just had that nice pay raise. Also, I wonder if we should be looking at starting our own company. On the other hand, I really love what I am doing, and the boss is a good guy and certainly is treating me well." At that point, he paused and looked for his wife's reaction.

Putting her fork down, Yolanda replied, "I know what you are saying, but I think there is something I should share with you first." She paused, took a sip of her water, and then continued, "I wanted to wait until I was sure, but I've missed my period, and I think I'm pregnant." She paused, watching his face as his mouth hung open for a moment before a huge grin appeared.

"What?" He was dumbfounded, and his loudness resulted in everyone stopping to look at them. He couldn't contain himself. Their life was about to take a major turn, and he was thrilled. "That is amazing." Pausing, he then blurted out, "Talk about timing. That answers the questions I've been toying with."

"What questions?"

At that point, he realized, having been caught up in the moment, that as a result of his reaction, the other patrons had stopped eating and were staring at him. Looking around, he smiled and nodded to let those around them know that everything was under control. "Well," he then went on in a much quieter voice, "I've been wondering if I should be looking at leaving Bertollini and starting our own company. But that is not going to happen now, obviously."

"It's a good thought, but starting on your own would probably take you quite a while to earn as much as you do now. Can't we do everything we want while you are working with Bertollini?"

"Of course, and we will. The other thing I have been thinking about," he continued, "is if we should build a small apartment building and rent out apartments. You could be the manager. I've been working on plans for the company, so I know exactly what we have to do to make it happen."

Yolanda was quiet as she thought and then said, "Why not? We've been saving my pay for a while now, and I think with your raise we just might be in a position to repay Ana and Spiffy what we owe them on the house mortgage. I certainly won't go back to work once we have our baby, but if we had a small apartment building, I could manage it and take the baby when I need to go and attend to something. It wouldn't be a problem, and actually, I think I would look forward to it."

"Wow, that's great!" Pausing, he thought about how glad he was that they had decided that she should look after the family's bank accounts. "How soon do you think you'll be stopping work?"

"About a month before the baby is due. I'm thinking it will arrive in the early summer, probably June."

"And what about visiting our families before the baby comes?"

"As much as I would love to, and I know our parents would be thrilled," she paused and took another sip of her sparkling water, "in reality, if we are going to undertake the apartment building, I think we should focus on that. By the way, is Pasquali going to have a problem with us doing this?"

"Hell, no! He'll build it for us. It will be just another project for him. I'm sure he'll be okay with it." Putting down his fork and getting up, he went around the table and gave her a kiss on her lips. "God, I'm the luckiest guy in the world to have you for a partner, even though you get after me for walking on your nice clean floors with my dirty boots on. Are you up for dessert?"

CHAPTER ELEVEN

OVER THE NEXT few weeks, Clemente did his calculations on their project. Each evening after dinner, he and Yolanda sat down and reviewed his thinking. One evening, Yolanda said, "I've had a thought. What if we buy the property from one of our neighbours? We could knock down their house and ours and build the apartment on the two lots. Would that work? It would give us room for a nice parking area for the tenants."

"Sure. We would have to find a new home. Maybe Ana and Spiffy could help us, but I don't think we should tell them what we are planning just yet. Let's put out a few feelers and see. I'm thinking about the guy to that side," he said, pointing to his left. "His house is a lot older and really needs work. He may just jump at the chance to sell and move into an apartment or even leave the city for a new place."

And so they continued talking and planning. Within a few weeks, they had settled on a six-unit, three-storey building with a mix of one- and two-bedroom units and a single three-bedroom apartment on the top floor. Costing it out, they were surprised that it was not that much more than a fourplex, and having the two extra units would make a significant difference in the monthly revenue.

Before briefing Ana and Spiffy and getting their blessing, Clemente was a little nervous but knew it was time to bring Bertollini into the picture and get his blessing first. Before heading to a job site the next morning, he poked his head through the boss's office door. "Have you got a minute?"

The boss looked up and nodded. Clemente said, "I wonder if we could sit down this evening. I have been working on something and want to run it past you."

"Of course," was the answer.

Returning after work with his plans and calculations, he joined the boss at the work table in his office. He had given it a lot of thought, so he proceeded to spell out what they were thinking. When he finished, Pasquali's first question was, "Does your uncle know about this?"

Clemente answered, "No."

"That will be quite an undertaking for a young couple who have only been in the country for what, two years? Well, I think it is great to see you planning to get ahead, and I'm sure we can work something out. What would you think if the company built it for you and my wife and I carried the mortgage? You said you're thinking it can be paid off in ten years, and I think you are bang on. If that works for you, and once you have the land and the approvals, we'll get started. Okay? But let me tell your uncle. I want to see the look on his face. Oh, by the way, when is your baby due?"

"Toward the end of June or early July."

"And your wife is doing okay?"

"For sure."

"Great. I know where there is a nice house for sale that you can check out. I'm looking forward to telling your uncle. I need to get ahead of him sometimes just so he doesn't think I'm not in tune with things that are going on around here."

On that note, Clemente left the boss's office and headed home feeling very pleased. He could hardly wait to share what had transpired with his wife.

"You won't believe what happened," he said, and without waiting for a reply, he blurted out, "Bertollini is going to build and finance the apartment building. His money. We will pay him back with interest over ten years."

"Are you absolutely sure we can do it in ten years?"

"I did the calculations and allowed for vacancies, and in reality, we should be able to have it paid off in just over nine years. I want to check with Georgio and see how we can do it to get the best tax advantage. We'll want to pay you as manager and have the expense against the rental income."

"Well, that's great, but one little thing is on my mind. Where are we going to live?"

"That was the next thing! With the financing from the Bertollinis, we can pay off our mortgage with Ana and my uncle. So in reality, the Bertollinis will buy the two houses to be demolished for the new building. Then we can buy a new house and have our aunt and uncle give us a new mortgage for it. I'm thinking we should start looking sooner rather than later so we can be well settled in before the bambino arrives. Pasquali mentioned he might know of a house we can look at."

"That sounds great. I've been thinking that we should look around, maybe a little outside downtown. It would be great to have a nice family home with a yard and a good garden. I'll talk to some of the girls at work and see if they have any thoughts. I know a couple of them live a little further out but have no trouble getting in and out of the city. Word is that they are working on a new subway system that will run under Yonge Street from Union Station up to Eglinton Avenue. It should be finished in the near future. They are talking early 1954."

The following evening, when Clemente arrived home, Yolanda was waiting for him. Sitting down before they started on the dinner preparations, she said, "I talked to the girls, and they said there were some nice houses available a bit north, just off St. Clair Avenue West. I thought tomorrow we could go up and have a look around and see what we think. If we like the area, we can get a hold of Angelo Leonardelli and see what is available. Did you hear back from your boss?"

"Yep, and from what he said, it sounds like it is in the area your girls were talking about. I told him that we had a real estate agent we used to purchase our current house, but he says we should deal directly with the people and save on the real estate commissions. He says he knows the people and they will be honest and upfront. They are apparently related to him. He suggested that if we want to go and see them tomorrow, he'll set it up."

She nodded, and now that they had their own telephone, he called his boss.

A thunderstorm rolled through in the night, and as a result, the morning was clear and a touch cooler. The humidity that had hung over the city was gone for the moment. It was Saturday, and after a quick breakfast, Clemente and Yolanda headed up to St. Clair Avenue West in their company truck. Following the directions that Pasquali had given them, they ended up on a side street and, within a minute or two, pulled into the driveway of the house. It was very plain and unassuming, as was the neighbourhood.

As soon as they stepped out of the truck, the front door opened, and a man came down the porch steps to greet them. He was a friendly middle-aged man around fifty to fifty-five. He was short, stout, and balding. He had a warm smile and said, "I'm Pasquali Bertollini's cousin, Gino. Come in and meet my wife, Isabella. She's been busy."

They went in, following Gino to the kitchen. The smell was wonderful. There was a middle-aged woman who could have been his sister. She was wearing an apron, and they could see that she had been busy baking biscuits, which had just come out of the oven. "Hi, I'm Isabella. Welcome. Sit while I get us coffee." She brought coffee and a plate of the lovely-smelling biscuits to the table. She looked so much like Gino. She had short black hair, a warm, round face, and sparkling eyes.

They talked about the house and the neighbourhood. "We're moving to Downsview," Gino told them. "Now that we've had our coffee, why don't you go and look around? Don't hurry, we'll wait for you on the back porch."

And so the young couple worked their way from the basement to the main floor and then upstairs to the bedrooms and bathroom. They then visited the garage and the front and backyard. They were quite surprised to find a second kitchen in the basement, which was used for making wine, tomato sauce, and sausage. There was also a "cold room," which was uninsulated and located on an outside wall. It was primarily used for storing vegetables and curing meat. Of course, they knew this was very common for people from the south of Italy who were avid gardeners.

The house looked perfect, and Clemente knew they could make whatever alterations they needed to make it work for them. The front yard was small but nicely landscaped, while the backyard had a garden that he guessed was twenty-five square feet and a nice grassed area with a fence that separated the lot from the neighbours'. The kitchen was a good size. Adjoining it was a small but very comfortable dining room, which was an extension of the living room. It was very bright and open, with lots of windows and glass-panelled doors. It looked perfect for them, and with three bedrooms, it would certainly accommodate them going forward.

Joining their hosts on the porch, Clemente said, "It looks really good. Are there any problems we should know about?"

"No, we always believed in preventive maintenance and have kept on top of things," Gino replied.

"Great, we think it could work nicely for us. We are expecting our first child in late spring. What are you asking for it?"

Gino's look became very serious as he cleared his throat and said, "Pasquali thinks a great deal of you two, and he told me that he considers you a very important member of his management team. So, based on his wishes, we are offering the house for the lowest price we can live with and still make our plans work." He then told them his price.

Clemente immediately jumped up and shook Gino's hand vigorously, saying, "That is perfect. We accept." Pausing, he turned to Yolanda, who nodded in agreement. They had discussed what they were willing to pay on the drive over and had an amount that would work for them. The price they were given was nicely below this. Wiping the tears from her eyes, Yolanda embraced Isabella, thanking her.

By mid-June, they had moved into their new home and were nicely settling in. Gino had not done any planting in the garden but had told the young couple they were free to plant what they knew they wanted to grow over the next three or four months. So, they did.

The building and land next door to their old house were purchased in due order, the zoning approvals received, and the building permit issued. The demolition commenced in mid-September. Their baby daughter had arrived on schedule and without incident. She was beautiful, and she was named Marie, after Yolanda's grandmother. Their family was started.

The new apartment building was completed in a little under a year. The apartments were rented out quickly. As manager, Yolanda vetted applicants, collected the rents, paid the expenses, and ensured everything remained in good working order. They had included an office for her, where she kept files and did her work. There was a mail slot in the office door so the tenants could deposit their rent cheques. The cheques dropped into a secure box, which was attached to the inside of the door. There was also a small kitchen, a bathroom, and a bed in case the baby needed to lie down or needed changing. As manager, Yolanda enjoyed the interaction with the tenants and was happy to have something meaningful that she could do with Marie in tow.

A second baby arrived two years later in February. It was another girl, and she was named Ana, after Favio's spouse, who enthusiastically agreed to be the godmother. Clemente was a proud father, although deep down he had been hoping for a son. Everything was good. They worked hard and enjoyed their daughters and loved the home and neighbourhood. It was further away from downtown and on a quiet street in a nice residential area. It had a great backyard with lots of room for entertaining, a play area for the girls, and a garden for Yolanda. In the fall, she planted garlic bulbs after fertilizing and mulching the soil. In the late spring, the tomatoes were planted.

The apartment was working as planned. Clemente had thought about building another one but decided that he didn't want to overextend.

A year and a half later, they were delighted when Yolanda became pregnant once again. Nine months later, a son, Michael, was born in August. Clemente was on cloud nine. With Yolanda working as manager of the apartment, Georgio Cagnoni had done his magic and was writing off her expenses against the revenue generated from the building's rental income.

CHAPTER **TWELVE**

Y OLANDA AND CLEMENTE watched as their children grew and developed. Ana and Spiffy became regular Sunday dinner guests, and they played with and spoiled the children with gifts and love. On Marie's tenth birthday, they brought her a small box of dark chocolates. Her reaction was incredible. She became a changed young girl as she dived into the box without any thought of sharing, and within a few hours, she had devoured the entire box. It became her favourite treat as well as a family tradition when a special occasion was to be celebrated.

The apartment was a great investment and was paid off, as planned, in a little over nine years. Many of their friends were purchasing summer property in Wasaga Beach, which was a little over two hours north of Toronto. It had piqued Yolanda and Clemente's interest, as the children were at an age where a summer spot would be an amazing lifetime experience. Plus, as an added bonus, it would get them out of the city during their summer holidays. When they shared their thinking with him, Spiffy said that he was talking to a fellow who had told him about a beautiful sand beach on Lake Huron, not far from a town called Owen Sound. It was called Sauble Beach, and because it was about three hours from Toronto, it was not in the same demand as Wasaga. Cottages would be cheaper, and the beach, in his friend's opinion, was better.

They decided to check it out, so they rented a car, packed up the kids, and headed to Sauble Beach. It was May 1965. Yolanda packed a food hamper, and the family left early in the morning. They headed toward Brampton, where they took the highway to Owen Sound. From there, the map directed them to a tiny village called Hepworth, and from there, they followed the sign pointing to Sauble Beach. For what seemed to the kids to be an eternity, they drove on and on. They proceeded up a small incline in the highway, and as they reached the top, they couldn't believe the sight that met their eyes.

"Oh my God, look at that!" Yolanda exclaimed. They were looking at the bluest water that they had ever seen, and it stretched before them forever. It was sapphire blue with white crests as the waves rolled onto the very flat sandy shore. Proceeding toward the water, they drove past a go-kart track and a minigolf course and then several stores. As they got closer, they could see the sandy beach in more detail. The colour was like light brown sugar, and seagulls were circling overhead. The kids had not uttered a sound as they were totally in awe of what they were seeing.

The day was amazing, and even though it was the end of May and there was a cool breeze coming off the water, there were quite a few people around looking very relaxed in their shorts and T-shirts and hats. Lots of different hats. Clemente followed the signs to the tourist information office and parked the car. "I'm going to pop in here to get some maps. Why don't you guys get out and stretch your legs?" he suggested.

As he went into the small cabin-like building, Yolanda and the children got out to survey what was before them. They were fascinated with the water, the sandy beach that ran forever both ways, the birds, and the cottages. There was a small building near the road with a sign just under the roof, which said, "Crowd Inn." It was a snack bar serving fast food.

"Come on," Marie called to her sister, and they both started to run toward the water.

"Don't go too close to the water," their mother called as she and Michael walked hand in hand behind them. Stopping, the girls took off their shoes and socks and started running on the amazing sandy beach. There was not a stone to be seen, just miles of flat, beautiful sand. As the girls ran, the seagulls, which were standing at the water's edge, squawked at them before flying away. They seemed to be voicing their displeasure at having their peaceful surroundings disturbed. Squealing with delight, the girls ran faster. Michael let go of his mother's hand, took off his shoes and socks, and ran off after his sisters, calling, "Wait for me."

When Clemente returned after about fifteen minutes with a handful of brochures and a map, he was smiling to himself as he watched his family enjoying themselves without a care in the world. Placing the literature on the front seat of the car, he turned, calling to his wife, "Hi, darling, I'm finished. Should we be grabbing something to eat? You guys must be getting famished." Looking back at him, she smiled and nodded. She then called, "Come on, kids, we can come back after. Who's ready for lunch?"

Hearing that, the children wheeled around and headed toward their father, all talking excitedly to him at the same time. He smiled as they gathered around him and said, "Did you guys have fun?" They all answered in unison, each telling him in their own words how neat it was. "Okay, what about some food?" he asked. Again, they all started talking at once, saying, "Yes."

"What about going over there," Yolanda said, indicating the Crowd Inn with a nod, "and trying something from them?"

Knowing that they had packed food for lunch, Clemente was a little puzzled, but hearing and seeing the kids' enthusiastic response, he knew it would be part of their experience. Looking at his wife, he said, "Great idea, let's go."

"We can have the sandwiches for supper or lunch tomorrow," she added.

The snack bar was perfect. The kids had hot dogs and fries while the adults had burgers and fries. Sitting at one round table, the children ate quickly so they could go back to the water. With their shoes and socks still off, they tore off again, running up and down the beach. They chased each other and only slowed down to turn their attention to chasing seagulls. They ran, yelled, screamed, and otherwise had an absolute ball. They had never experienced such unrestrained freedom in their lives, and they obviously loved it. Each one, in turn, stood at the water's edge, jumping back when the waves rolled in and waiting to see how long they could hold out before the waves washed over their bare feet. The water was pretty cool, but they didn't mind.

As their parents sat and had a cup of tea from their Thermos, they were filled with joy. Watching the children have so much fun, Yolanda commented, "This is pretty amazing for them."

"Yes, and for us. The girl in the tourist cabin said that during the peak summer months, July and August, the water is perfect for swimming, and there are lots of people on the beach. Let's have a quick look around before we head home. It's already coming on to three, so we should get going."

Knowing he was right, she suggested, "Let's just give them a bit more time to wear themselves out before we leave."

About five minutes later, they called their children and loaded them back into the car after cleaning the accumulated sand off their feet. Clemente had studied the map and decided to circle to another road on their way home. He wanted to get a feel for the place and see how developed it was. Once they were loaded up, he headed along the beach road away from the commercial area and away from the main entrance. He drove to an area called Sauble Falls and then took another road back. There were side streets and cottages running in all directions.

They knew it would take them about three-and-a-half hours to return home, so after a quick restroom stop and one last look around the main street, they retraced their route back to the city. As predicted, the children fell asleep as soon as they hit the highway and slept all the way home, totally worn out from their activity and the fresh air. Yolanda and Clemente didn't talk much on the drive home, as they were both mulling over what they had experienced before Yolanda nodded off.

CHAPTER **THIRTEEN**

O N ARRIVING HOME from Sauble Beach, the children were quickly fed with the food they brought back, bathed, and tucked in for the night. They were still exhausted from their amazing day and drifted off immediately. Yolanda and Clemente sat down with a cup of tea each. Yolanda said, "That was quite a day. Have you ever experienced anything like that before?"

"That was a first," was his response. "What did you think of it? I mean the whole day, the drive, the beach, and the area."

"Pretty amazing. I've never seen anything like it and think it is well worth the drive. You?"

"Never, and yes." After sitting quietly for a few minutes, he continued, "Should we look into getting a summer place up there? I know it is further away than the place near Collingwood, but I don't see how anywhere could beat it. And if there are fewer people because it is a little further from the city, that's a bonus."

"Yeah, let's ask around and see what people are saying about the two beaches. I can talk to the girls from the hotel that I am still in touch with."

"One other thing I'm wondering is if we should be looking at getting a car. You could use it for going to the apartments, shopping, running the kids around. And it would be good for you and me if we decided to go out for an evening by ourselves."

"Let me think about that too," his wife responded.

The following day, after the kids were off to catch their school buses, Yolanda said, "I've been thinking about the car. We've been all right without one, but if we are going to get a summer place then it would be the way to go. We may want to have the kids and me spend a few weeks or a month at the cottage in the summer. You could drive back and forth on weekends, so we'll need a car to use when you are not there."

Smiling, he replied, "I see you are thinking ahead again. That's great. Let's get Ana and Favio to take the kids next Saturday, and then you and I can drive up to Wasaga Beach and check it out. I was telling him about our impressions of Sauble, and he said the only way we'll know for sure is to go so we can compare them. We will rent a car, but this time you come and see what appeals to you. We'll rent it, and that way we will kill two birds with one stone: renting and test driving."

"Do you think we could drop the children off on Friday evening? That way we can grab a quick bite before we go and look at the cars. When we find one that might work, we can bring it home and then head out first thing Saturday morning."

"I'll call my uncle and see if it works for them, and I'll call the dealer and set it up. I think he'll look after us pretty well, given all the business the company gives him."

Clemente arrived at work as usual on Monday morning and was looking at what needed his attention when the phone rang. He took the call. Hanging up, he went and told Pasquali's secretary that he was going to look at a new type of metal stud that their building supply company was offering and said he wouldn't be long. "Just in case the boss is looking for me," he added.

As he parked the car and started toward the store, a young-looking fellow approached him, asking, "Excuse me, are you Clemente Gallorini?"

"Yes."

"My name is Sonny Castelletto. Can we talk for a few minutes?"

"About what?"

"Well, I am associated with a building supply group in Montreal. We are looking to expand. Your name was given to us as the guy who does most of the buying for Bertollini Construction. I'm thinking we can offer you top-of-the-line materials for far below what you are paying these guys"—indicating the store Clemente was going to—"if we can reach an understanding. We can also make it well worth your time personally."

"Well, we are pretty happy with our current supplier, so you would have to be offering something really good."

"Okay, how about 25 percent less than you are paying now on most items, plus a 10 percent finder's fee, paid in cash directly to you every month? Interested?"

Clemente's instinct was telling him to walk away. It didn't make sense, business or otherwise, unless they were trying to unload stolen supplies and materials out of their province. He knew that each province had its own police and that the chances of a provincial force trying to track hot building material out of province were pretty slim—unless, of course, they had solid evidence that it was happening. So, looking at the fellow, he asked, "Who are you working for?"

"The Ruzzini family," was the response.

"Let me think on it and get back to you. You said 10 percent in cash monthly directly to me?"

"Absolutely. Hand-delivered."

"And how do I get a hold of you?"

"You don't. We'll contact you," was the answer.

"Okay, give me a few days to think about it," Clemente said, and he turned and carried on into the store.

On his return to Bertollini Construction, he headed straight for his uncle's office, where he relayed the story to him. After listening intensely, Favio said, "Come on," and they headed across the hall.

They entered the boss's office, where Favio asked, "Have you got a minute?"

After listening to the story, Pasquali nodded and picked up the phone. He dialled a number, and after a few seconds said, "It's me. I need to see you." After a moment's pause while he listened, he said, "Good, see you then," and hung up. Turning to his two associates, he continued, "You did the right thing, Clemente. We'll have to go carefully, though, so we don't put you, your family, or any of our families at risk. Tony will be here shortly, and we'll see what he says."

Back in his office, Clemente began to wonder if he did the right thing. *Should I have just said no and walked away?* he wondered. But as he thought about it, he knew if these Montreal guys found a couple of builders in Toronto to take up their offer, all the other contractors would lose business, and companies like theirs would suffer. What he hadn't thought of was the reality that they could come looking for him for exposing their intentions. As he sat mulling things over and thinking about his family, Pasquali's secretary tapped on his door and said, "They are ready for you."

Walking in and seeing Tony's menacing look, he nodded and sat down beside his uncle. "Tell him," Pasquali directed. So, he proceeded to tell Tony exactly what had transpired.

When he finished, Tony thought for a moment, and then, looking at Clemente, said, "You did good. I know the Ruzzini family. I'll talk to them and see how we can sort it out." With that, he turned, nodded to Pasquali, and left the office.

The three of them looked at each other, and then without a word, Clemente and his uncle got up and left. Going back to Favio's office and closing the door, his uncle said in a lowered voice, "That was exactly the thing to do. You just went up in the boss's estimation. And don't worry about it, I'm sure you'll never hear anything about it again."

Returning to his office and planning to get on with his day, Clemente thought, *I'll have to remember to tell Pasquali about those new studs. They may be the way to go with larger buildings.* He then picked up the phone and called the car dealer, telling him, "We'd like to get a car on Friday afternoon. We are thinking about buying one, so we'll pick one and take your demonstrator for a test drive to Wasaga Beach. I'll bring it back on Monday morning. Okay?"

"No problem," was the response.

# CHAPTER FOURTEEN

T HE FOLLOWING SATURDAY, they headed up Highway 27 to Wasaga Beach. There had been a thunderstorm during the night, but it had moved off. The air was cloudy and cool, but still, it was very pleasant.

The car Yolanda had chosen was a six-month-old Mercury Montcalm, dark blue with four doors. It was larger and more comfortable than the cars they had rented in the past, and she found it easy to drive. Clemente had suggested that they look at something more upscale. He suggested a Lincoln Continental would be more their style, but Yolanda said, "No. I want a practical family car, not a show of prestige."

Arriving in Wasaga in just over two hours, they realized that it was certainly a shorter and more direct route. This beach was located near the bottom of Georgian Bay. It was bigger and more developed than Sauble, and the beach was made up of darker sand. They could see why vacationers from Toronto favoured it. It was a shorter trip to get to, and the beach area was bigger and more developed. There seemed to be more and easier beach access. As they drove around, though, they felt that the warmth and friendliness of Sauble were missing. They also had the feeling, after continuing to look around, that their children would be safer at the other beach.

Yolanda, as the family treasurer, had advised her husband that with the apartment bought and paid for and the mortgage on their house almost paid off, they shouldn't have any trouble purchasing a nice cottage. "My idea," she explained, "is to add the cost of the cottage to the mortgage your aunt and uncle are holding on the house." Then, out of the blue, she continued, "I'm thinking that once we get a cottage sorted, we should give some thought to getting out of the city core and moving up to the Downsview area. With the kids heading to high school over the next few years, it will be better for them up there. There'll be more for them to do and more opportunity to meet a broader mix of people. It's not a bad thing, but most of the kids at their current schools are Italian. There's nothing wrong with that, but I think their growth and school experience will be broader in Downsview."

"That's great, but what about the money and the cost of buying another house?" was the reply. "Are you thinking that we can afford the cottage and a new house?"

"Well," she hesitated and then continued, "I haven't told you, but I have been putting a bit away in another account. It's in both our names, but you were so busy at work and taking on so much, I decided to forge your signature rather than get you involved."

He stared at her in disbelief. "What!" he exploded. "What were you thinking, forging my signature? Why would you do that? Don't you trust me?" He was so mad that his face had turned a deep red.

But before he could say anything else, she went on. "You were so busy and had so much going on at the company—I didn't think you needed anything else on your mind. I'm sorry, but we have enough to pay off the mortgage, buy the cottage, and purchase a new house, as long as we don't go crazy on what we buy. Oh," she continued, "and we also have enough to send Marie to college or university and buy the new car. I've saved all the income tax refunds that Georgio Cagnoni got for us."

That did it! He grabbed her and pulled her to him. She felt herself starting to shake. "Don't you ever leave me out of our family business," he said in a strong voice. "I am the head of this family, and I need to know what is going on."

Then he paused as what she had told him started to sink in. Realizing that she had acted in the family's best interests, he took her in his arms and held her for a few minutes until he settled down and gave her a huge, long, passionate kiss. He said, "That's why I was so lucky to find you and to ask you to marry me. You are amazing. I'll see if Pasquali can recommend a good, honest real estate broker in Sauble Beach."

She now felt warm and happy inside as she blushed.

$ $ $

"SIT DOWN FOR a moment," Pasquali said when Clemente poked his head in to ask him about a real estate agent in Sauble Beach. Calling out to his secretary, he said, "Ask Favio to come over for a minute." Favio arrived, and he, too, was shown to a seat. Then Pasquali joined them at the table.

"I wanted to tell you," he commenced, "Tony called me last night when he got back from Montreal. He hates flying, so he took the train both ways. Anyway, he had a meeting with Don Ruzzini, and it turns out that your instinct was right," he said, looking to Clemente. "Sonny was in Toronto on a fishing expedition. It seems he felt that he was not getting the respect he deserved from the Ruzzinis, so he decided to show them. He came to Toronto on his own, without them knowing. Apparently, he sought us out by going to the biggest Italian-owned building supply store in the city. He told them he was a buyer from Montreal and asked who their biggest and most respected contractor was. They mentioned us. He then asked who did the buying for them, and he was told you. He then paid the clerk to call you and tell you about the new studs he wanted you to see. The clerk described you to Sonny, and he waited in the parking lot for you to arrive.

"The bottom line is that Sonny is no longer associated with any family in Montreal. They appreciated the fact that you were smart enough to recognize that something wasn't right and do something about it. Tony said to give you their greetings, and if you are ever in Montreal, you are to look them up. You saved them from what could have become a very embarrassing situation if Sonny hadn't been stopped. I just wanted you fellows to know and to thank you"—again, he looked at Clemente—"for your instinct and for sharing it with us." He then stood up and shook Clemente's hand, nodding to Favio.

"That is good to hear," Clemente said. "And the metal studs they showed me at the supply store may be of some value when we are doing larger projects. Let me look into them a little further, and I'll let you know.

"By the way, I came in to ask you if you knew of a good real estate agent in Sauble Beach. We are thinking of looking for a cottage in that area. It's less busy than Wasaga, and we got a really good feeling about it."

"I'll ask around and let you know." Pasquali called Clemente that evening and told him about Peter Dixon.

$ $ $

TWO WEEKS LATER, Clemente and Yolanda once again imposed on Ana and Favio to take the children for the weekend, on the promise of a night out at the restaurant of their choice. Getting up early on Saturday morning, they got into the Mercury that they were still looking to buy and headed north. Again, Yolanda drove. The day was overcast and cool, so they had brought light jackets with them, not knowing what the weather would be like at Sauble Beach.

They were chatting about several things when Yolanda said, "As a follow-up to our conversation the other night, you do realize that we could certainly pay off Ana and Spiffy's mortgage? I get the feeling, however, that they are more involved in our lives with it being in place. After all, we are their only family here."

"Yeah, I think you are right. We came over on their recommendation, and things have worked out well. It seems they are proud and happy with what we are doing and really enjoy being involved in our lives. If it wasn't for them, we wouldn't be here."

Arriving around 11 a.m., they headed down toward the beach until they came to a building with a sign that read "Sauble Realty." The day was still overcast, and as they had driven through the commercial area, they saw the flags were blowing straight out from the west. Opening the car door to get out, Clemente very quickly reached into the back seat and grabbed both of their jackets. He handed his wife hers, saying, "We are going to need these."

Waiting for them was the broker Pasquali had recommended on the advice of a cousin. "Hi, I'm Peter. Come on in to where it's a little warmer, out of the wind."

He was a rotund fellow in his mid-fifties with a small moustache riding on his upper lip. He had an outgoing manner and was instantly likeable. "How was your drive up?" he inquired once they were seated in his office. "Here, I thought you might be hungry," he said, setting a tray with coffee and doughnuts in front of them. They chatted casually about their family, their life in Toronto, and their thoughts on the cottage they were looking for.

After about a half hour of talking, Peter said, "As it turns out, yesterday I got a new listing for a nice four-bedroom cottage on Fifth Street, three blocks from the water. There's also a separate listing for an adjoining lot, and I was planning to post them on Monday."

"What are they looking for?" Clemente asked. Peter told them.

"Are they flexible?" Yolanda asked. "It is more than we budgeted, but if you think it is worth a visit, we'll go and see it."

"Okay, we can talk in the car," Peter responded. He headed to the door and then held it open for them.

Within five minutes, they pulled up in front of a cottage that was painted white with dark green trim. Stepping out of the car, Peter turned and pointed toward the lake, saying, "As I said, the lake is three blocks away. Do you want me to take you through, or would you be more comfortable on your own?"

"We are good. Why don't you wait for us in the car and out of the wind? We'll be along after we've had a good look around." Peter nodded in agreement, and after he unlocked and opened the front door for them, he retreated to his car. Stepping inside, they found themselves in an old cottage, and to their surprise, it was fully furnished. "I wonder if the furniture is included," Yolanda wondered aloud.

There were four small but nice bedrooms, one of which was a little larger than the others. Then there was a living room with a wood-burning fireplace, a kitchen/eating area, and a bathroom with a shower located just before the back door. Yolanda commented that it was a good location for the bathroom, since the kids could come in the back door to use the toilet and not troop dirt through the main cottage. Looking out, they saw a barbecue/patio area and a nice growth of pine trees. They continued to check things out. Yolanda was looking at the flow of the rooms and the comfort of the interior. Her husband was looking at the beams, rafters, flooring, and the walls and windows. He saw that the building was not insulated, so he could see the structure, as everything was exposed.

"Let's go and look outside," Clemente said once they had finished examining the interior. As they headed out the front door, they saw that there was a small sitting area right across the front of the building, like a sun porch, but the depth only allowed room for one chair. There were four chairs side by side, all facing west.

Stepping out, they headed around the building. Clemente inspected the base, the beams, the roof, and the windows and doors, while Yolanda looked at the general layout and the trees and bushes on the lot. As they came around to the front again, she asked, "What do you think?"

"Well, remembering that it is a summer cottage, it's pretty good. I don't see anything that would be a problem, and there is an oil-fired heater, which would be good for cool days and evenings," he replied as they walked over and got into the car. It was warm, as Peter had kept it running.

"What did you think?" Peter asked. "Is it worth an offer, or do you want to look at what else is available?"

"Are there any issues that we should be aware of? We won't be happy with unpleasant surprises," was Clemente's reply.

"You should know that water is an issue for all cottages here. But this cottage has a decent well and a good filtration system," Peter added. "The water filter should probably be changed monthly, and the septic system has just been cleaned and works well. Most people use bottled water. I think I mentioned that the vacant lot right there," he said, pointing to his left, "has its own deed and is being offered separately."

"What about the furniture and kitchen dishes and pots and pans?" Yolanda asked. "Are they being sold separately?"

"No, they are all included. The only things you will need are bedding and towels." Hearing that brought a smile to her face.

"Let's go back to the office to talk," Peter said, putting the car in gear.

On the way back, Clemente inquired, "What are they asking for the adjoining lot?" Upon hearing the answer, he said, "We will talk about it later."

Peter assumed this meant they would like to get the cottage settled first. Reaching the office, he suggested, "I'll leave you to talk things over. Use my office and call me when you need me." Then, before leaving them, he again told them the asking price.

Shortly after, they called Peter back to his office and told him, "We are prepared to make a cash offer for the fully furnished cottage, and we would like occupancy as soon as possible." The offer was $5,000 less than the asking price. Continuing, Clemente added, "We want occupancy as soon as possible because there is some work we want to do before summer."

"Okay, let's give them a call and see what they say," the broker answered.

Yolanda and Clemente went to the kitchen at the back of the office and waited. Shortly, Peter came to tell them, "I've talked to them, and they have made a counteroffer. They are quite surprised to get an offer so quickly, but they will only lower the price by $2,000."

"And how much do they want for the neighbouring lot?"

Peter told them.

"Give us a moment to talk this over."

Peter left. In a few minutes, they called him back.

Clemente was looking at his wife, and then he turned to Peter and said, "Tell them we are prepared to purchase the adjoining lot for the full asking price. We'll make a down payment of half and pay the balance in five equal annual instalments. But it will only work if they are willing to accept $3,000 less for the cottage."

"Let's see what they say," Peter said, and, picking up the phone, he made the call. In a moment, after telling the party and getting their response, he thanked them. Turning to the couple sitting across from him, he said, "Congratulations. You bought yourselves a cottage."

The next weekend, Clemente and Yolanda trekked back to Sauble Beach with a certified cheque for the agreed purchase price, and after signing the necessary papers, they got the keys to their new cottage. They then drove to the cottage, went inside, and ended up making love in their new bedroom.

The following weekend, they packed up the kids in the newly purchased family car and brought them to their new summer home. And, of course, they stopped and had burgers, hot dogs, and fries at the Crowd Inn.

# CHAPTER FIFTEEN

THE COTTAGE WAS great, and the family came up most weekends until Canada Day. That weekend was the first long weekend of the summer. They knew the traffic out of the city would be crazy, so they left a little early and got to the beach just before suppertime. The kids unpacked while their father started the charcoal barbecue and their mother got out the meat and food she had brought. Because it was a beautiful, warm summer evening, they ate at the picnic table out on the little patio. Everyone was totally thrilled to be there and to have their first of many barbecues at the cottage.

They quickly established a yearly routine, with Clemente and Yolanda travelling to the cottage for the weekend of May 24. They had the kids stay with their aunt and uncle while they drove up and got things ready for the summer, including turning on the water, checking the septic tank, bringing bedding and towels, doing a thorough cleaning, and ensuring all traces of the winter residents—mice, spiders, flies—were removed.

On Thanksgiving weekend, when the cottage was closed for the winter, they brought everyone up. The refrigerator was emptied, cleaned, and unplugged from the electrical socket, and the door was left ajar. All bedding, clothes, towels, and face cloths were packed up and taken home to be washed and stored away, ready to be brought back the following spring.

The children made friends with kids from neighbouring cottages and spent their summers swimming, playing on the beach, and generally having a great time, enjoying the relaxed life at the cottage. As the girls grew older, they started sunning themselves on the beach.

Several times, when he had nothing to do or no one to play with, Michael would seek out his sisters and tell them, "I want you to play with me."

The girls almost always said, "No," to which he replied, "I'm going to tell Dad."

Invariably, Marie would tell him, "Get lost, you little turd," and then go back to whatever she and her sister were doing.

Clemente built a small cabin behind the main cottage for the kids. It was called "the Bunkie." The kids slept there when friends came for a visit from the city. Yolanda and the children came to the cottage a week before Clemente came up for his holidays. They stayed for an extra week when he returned to the city to go back to work. Spiffy and Ana were regular guests at first, and then they bought a trailer and parked it on the vacant lot. Barbecues, pasta, and lots of wine were the order of the day at the cottage. When the family was not using the cottage, they had an arrangement with their real estate agent to rent it out. As it turned out, the additional rental income allowed them to pay off the adjoining lot in three years.

$ $ $

A YEAR AFTER buying the cottage, Yolanda decided that the time was right to buy a new house in Downsview. She wanted to get the children settled in a new neighbourhood before they entered high school. The people from whom they bought their current home had moved to Downsview, and they had kept in touch over the years. When she mentioned to Isabella that they were thinking about moving to Downsview, she suggested that they come to visit and look around so they could get a feel for the area. She gave Yolanda the address and told her it was just off Keele Street.

Arriving at the house, Clemente and Yolanda were surprised at the size of the lot. It was quite a bit larger than theirs. They rang the bell, and Isabella opened the door and gave them a huge hello, followed by hugs. She had aged somewhat but was still herself.

As they entered and looked inside the living room, they were taken aback. There was an old man sitting in an easy chair. He looked decrepit. His face was wrinkled and drawn and looked blank. There was no recognition, and his eyes showed no signs of life.

Isabella asked him, "Gino, do you remember Yolanda and Clemente? They bought our other house just off St. Clair." There was no response. Turning to them, she explained, "He's having a bad day. I'm sorry. Come into the kitchen. Would you like tea or coffee?" They both said tea would be fine, and they followed her into the kitchen and took a seat at the chrome table.

"I'm sorry to tell you that Gino has Alzheimer's and doesn't know who anybody is, including me. I'm trying to look after him as best as I can, and we have a home care nurse who comes in twice a day to wash him and help me with him." She paused as the kettle whistled and poured the boiling water into the teapot that she had ready. She left the tea to steep and continued. "I am putting him into a care facility next week, and once I get things sorted out, I'll look for an apartment near him." She brought a dish of biscuits and teacups to the table. "You said that you were thinking of moving into this area. If you would be interested and it works, I'll sell you this house."

Yolanda and Clemente looked at each other, totally taken off guard. Yolanda spoke first. "This is quite an unexpected surprise. How about after tea we walk around and have a look? We'll have to see where the schools are and get a feel for the neighbourhood, but yes, we'll certainly give it some thought."

Having their tea, they told her about their children, the cottage at Sauble Beach, and how much the family was enjoying it. "Our oldest daughter, Marie, is now a teenager, and she will be entering high school next year. This is why we are looking for a house now—so we can get settled before she goes to a new school for grade 9," Yolanda explained.

After tea, they looked around while Isabella went and sat with her husband. Starting upstairs, they noted the three bedrooms, the small bathroom adjoining the master bedroom, the main bathroom, and the linen closet. In addition to what they had seen, there was a large dining room and a sun porch downstairs. The door from the sun porch went out to a raised deck, which in turn led to a ground-level patio. The basement was mostly unfinished, but Clemente saw the potential for a family room and another bedroom. The garage was big enough for two cars, and there was a workbench and a fair bit of shelving. The garden was quite large, and although it had been neglected for a few years, it looked promising. There was a nice, large front lawn, and it was nicely landscaped.

All in all, they thought everything looked quite good. They rejoined Isabella, telling her they quite liked it. "We'll have to give it some thought," Clemente told her. "We'll drive around the neighbourhood and get a feel for it before we head home. What are you going to ask for it?"

She told them what she wanted.

"No problem," he said. "We'll talk it over and let you know what we think. If we need to come and look through it once more, will that be a problem?" They were told it wasn't, so they thanked her, said goodbye to Gino, and left. They drove around the area, noting the schools, stores, parks, and general upkeep of everything.

"Well, I sure didn't expect anything like that," Clemente commented as they drove home. "Do you think it might work?" he asked, glancing over at his wife.

"I think it is promising. What a shame about Gino, though. God, I hope nothing like that ever happens to us."

"It won't."

They bought the home and moved in about two months later. Thanks to Angelo Leonardelli, they got theirs sold at a good price in good time, and everything went smoothly.

CHAPTER **SIXTEEN**

C HRISTMAS IN THE new home was great. Clemente had the family room done in the basement, and the Christmas tree was set up there. He also had a bedroom added downstairs, and as they expected, Marie jumped at the chance to claim it as hers. *Typical teenager,* they thought.

Clemente and Yolanda watched as their children grew and developed. Their characters and personalities gradually became more apparent. While their father saw them during dinner, in the evenings, and on weekends, it was Yolanda who saw and dealt with them every day. She was very pleased that they were able to move to the Downsview area before the kids entered high school. While they considered moving them to the public school system, it was decided, with input from the children, that they would remain in the Roman Catholic system for high school. One advantage was that they could walk quite easily to the Catholic high school, while they would have taken a bus to the public school.

Marie went to high school first. It was 1967, Canada's centennial, and she was fifteen just before she entered grade 9. While she didn't have any of her friends from her previous school, she was quickly accepted by her new classmates, as the school was new to all of them. They all adjusted together, and no one was thought of as a new kid. They were all Catholic.

Her sister was thirteen, and her brother was twelve. They both transferred to new schools in Downsview and seemed to fit in quickly and easily. Transferring within the Catholic system made it a little easier for them, it seemed. Once they had all settled in, their parents were relieved, especially their mother.

Watching them progress through the grades, their parents saw their personalities and interests continue to develop. Yolanda saw her oldest become a very task-oriented, business-minded, no-nonsense young lady. Marie had her father's looks and personality, and she was good at school.

Her sister, on the other hand, was more of a free spirit and was always on the lookout for adventure. Her mother felt that Ana was more like herself in personality, and she had a good, kind heart.

And then there was Michael. At age twelve, he was a carefree boy who loved life and didn't take things too seriously. He was mediocre at sports and school and didn't seem to have the concentration or desire to really excel at anything. But as he aged and developed, it became apparent that he had his father's constant approval and backing.

Clemente was always involving him in activities in which he thought his son should take an interest. While the girls loved sports and were quite successful in many, it was Michael whom Clemente took to see the Maple Leafs hockey games when the company tickets were available. The girls were never included. Michael had fun playing road hockey with the neighbour kids, and so Clemente bought him a complete set of hockey gear and signed him up to play minor league hockey. He took him to the office and showed him what he did and how the company operated. He had him do odd jobs around the company and paid him for his work.

One summer day, Michael was playing touch football in a park near their school with a couple of buddies. He realized that he had to go to the bathroom, and rather than go home, he headed over to the public toilets at the edge of the park. He had never been in the building and saw it was divided into two sections, with the women's facilities on one side and the men's on the other. As he settled into one of the stalls to do his business, he noticed that the closed door he was facing had been well-used by past visitors. There were several things etched into the door with sharp objects: "Harry was here," "Joe Jones Rules," and "Barry loves Margie" were some.

What caught his eye and fascinated him were two things, one beside the other. The first one read:

> No matter how much you jiggle and dance,
> the last few drops go down your pants.

Then right beside and a little lower was:

> A shithouse poet, when he dies,
> should have erected where he lies,
> a fitting tribute to his wit,
> a monument of solid shit.

He sat there, wondering why people felt the need to leave their marks and comments on the public restroom doors. He also wondered what kind of a mind would come up with these poems. He had never been a great fan of the English language but was very impressed just the same. He must have reread the poems three or four times, marvelling at how they flowed and rhymed. He knew he would never forget them.

Yolanda encouraged the girls to establish a little home-based business selling knick-knacks made from materials they came across in their travels around the neighbourhood and at the cottage. They took them to school and church picnics and yard sales. She also hired them to clean the common areas of the apartment buildings and showed them how to save their money using a savings account. She helped them establish the new accounts at the neighbourhood bank and explained the need to have a source of emergency cash at hand for unexpected things that cropped up. They also learned the concept of compound interest from her.

As they progressed through high school, with Yolanda's blessing, the girls became interested in music and each took up an instrument. Marie played the oboe, while Ana took up the trombone. They loved playing in the school orchestra, and Yolanda was thrilled and regularly attended their concerts. Clemente and Michael attended the major concerts, like the Christmas concerts, but were generally more comfortable with the girls pursuing their own interests. The girls also took up curling at school and spent Saturday mornings at the local curling club, where the school rented ice time and established a school curling club.

As soon as Michael turned sixteen, Clemente started teaching him how to drive. When the girls asked if they could be included, they were told that there wasn't time for their father to teach the three of them and that their mother would be their teacher.

Yolanda grew quite concerned with Michael and the fact that Clemente favoured him. She could see that Marie was not overly fond of her brother nor of the fact that their father obviously favoured him. Yolanda knew that she should have done it years ago, but she decided that she and Clemente had to talk about it.

She made arrangements for the kids to spend a weekend with their aunt and uncle. She then made a special supper for herself and Clemente, and after the meal, she suggested that they talk about the family. They were still sitting at the dining room table when she said, "I know that in the old country and in most of Europe, from what I am led to believe, the oldest son is considered the heir of the family, and he is groomed for that role and the responsibility that goes with it. That is probably why we came here, because your brother, as the oldest son, was in line to inherit the family home and business. I know that you were thrilled when we finally had a son who would keep the family name alive." She paused to let that sink in before continuing.

"Things are different here, and by giving Michael so much of your attention and time, I am afraid that you have alienated him from his sisters, especially Marie. I'm seeing that she is feeling slighted and unsure why you favour him over her, and I'm pretty sure that deep down she is harbouring resentment toward him. It is not healthy for either of them or the family and may cause issues in the future." She waited for it to sink in.

Looking at her, he hesitated before responding, "I never thought about it that way. I just knew that having a son was something I needed. When you say it, though, I see that you are right, and I'll have to try to set things right. Let me see what I can do, and I'd appreciate anything you suggest."

# CHAPTER SEVENTEEN

B Y 1970, THE company was flourishing, and it had become involved in a number of larger projects. Clemente and Favio's responsibilities continued to grow as the company did. It became obvious to Pasquali that he would not be where he was if it weren't for the efforts of his top two men. And so, when he asked them to join him for dinner in a private dining room of a very high-end restaurant called Mastro's one evening, they knew something was brewing. It was mid-October, and the construction business was still in full swing but beginning to gear down.

Not knowing what to think, Clemente and Favio arrived together at the appointed time. They left their vehicle at the front door to be parked by a valet. They were then shown to a private dining room, where their boss was waiting for them. To their surprise, there was another middle-aged gentleman in the room with him. Pasquali welcomed them like they were his brothers and introduced them to Angelo DeLuco, his lawyer.

As he shook DeLuco's hand, Clemente noticed that he had a stronger than usual grip and a very serious and grizzled face. His hair was long and wavy. He was dressed in slacks and an open-necked white shirt and a black sports coat.

They all sat down at the preset table, and a waiter appeared from behind a screen at the back of the room and offered them the choice of either something to drink from the bar or a glass of the red wine he was carrying. Each of them chose the wine, and when Favio asked about it, he was handed the bottle so he could see that it was a Brandini Cerretta Barolo from Piedmont. He handed the bottle back to the server, who then proceeded to pour a small amount into his glass. He stepped back as Favio raised the glass to his nose and smelled it before taking a sip. Favio held the wine in his mouth for a second or two before swallowing it. Turning to server, he gave an approving nod, and the server proceeded to fill everyone's glasses before returning to fill Favio's.

They had a wonderful meal, talking about their families in Canada and in the old country, their interests, and their lives in Toronto. When the table was cleared and the serving staff left and closed the door behind the screen, Pasquali said, "I wanted us to get together because we don't do it often enough. I have been thinking and wanted to share some thoughts with you. As you know, our business has grown quite a bit, and we have been very successful, in no small part because of you two. You are both very honest, very smart, and very loyal members of company management team. I have come to rely of you for your knowledge and your advice. I never want to lose you until it is time for us all to retire, so I've been giving some thought as to the best way to make this happen. I've shared my thinking and sought advice from Angelo. We've had several chats about this, and here is what we've come up with."

Turning to Favio, Pasquali continued. "I want to make you our vice-president and chief financial officer." Then, looking at Clemente, he said, "And I want you as our vice-president and chief operating officer."

He then paused to let it sink in before continuing. "Now, it's not just about titles. It is about having you both as partners in the company, and this is why Angelo is here. We will incorporate the company tomorrow. I want to pay you each a bonus each year, but rather than cash, I want to give you company shares so you can increase your ownership in the company. We can then pay you dividends, based on the company's annual profitability. Angelo can draw up the paperwork to formally have you become shareholders and partners in Bertollini Construction Incorporated. What do you think?"

Looking at each other and then back to Pasquali, they were speechless for a moment. Then, looking Pasquali in the eye, Favio said, "It would be an honour to become a shareholder in Bertollini Construction Incorporated. I respect you and admire your leadership, and again, I would be honoured." He was going to include his nephew but decided that Clemente was his own man, and it would be better to let him speak for himself.

After a minute, clearing his throat, Clemente said, "I can't believe how fortunate I have been to be affiliated with the company and you both. This is beyond my wildest dreams, and it would be an honour to join the ownership team."

On hearing this, Pasquali left the table and went to the back of the room. Returning a few minutes later, he was followed by their server, who was carrying a large silver tray, a bottle, and four glasses. He, in turn, was followed by another server who was carrying two smaller silver trays and two envelopes. The first server set the bottle down, removed the top, and poured and delivered a glass to each of them. Stepping back, the second server set a smaller silver tray and an envelope in front of each of the two new shareholders. Both servers left the room.

Pasquali then stood up and raised his glass, saying, "Welcome to our new shareholders." The other three stood and picked up their glasses and, in unison, said, "*Cin cin*," then all drank what turned out to be the finest of Italian cognac.

Sitting again, the two new shareholders picked up the silver trays that had been placed before each of them and saw that they were engraved with their names and "in recognition of your loyalty and service. bertollini construction. october 1970." Opening their envelopes, they saw cheques payable from the company to them in the amount of $25,000.

Clemente arrived home in a very good frame of mind, and when his wife asked him the purpose of the dinner, he responded, "Well, it was pretty amazing. Pasquali has decided to change the status of the company, so Spiffy and I are now shareholders. We are both vice-presidents and have new job titles. I'm now the chief operating officer, and my uncle is the chief financial officer. Here is what he gave me," he said, handing her the silver tray. "Oh, and he also gave me this," he said, handing her the cheque.

She looked dumbfounded, then surprised, and then ecstatic. She couldn't believe it. "Wow! I'm glad he realizes how valuable you are to the company. What do you think we should do with this?" she said as she held up the cheque.

"Well, I think you should put it away. As the kids leave high school, we can give them each $5,000 as a graduation present. You and I can keep ours to use for something special down the road."

"That's a great idea," she told him as she checked the reverse side of the cheque to ensure he had endorsed it. He had.

The following morning, Clemente, Pasquali, and Favio met at Angelo's law office and signed the papers to become shareholders and directors of the new corporation. As they reviewed the documents before signing, they noticed that Mrs. Bertollini was listed as the secretary on the new board of directors. They weren't surprised, as they knew that behind the scenes she was a huge part of the company's success.

Yolanda had had many chats with her daughters about their thoughts and plans for after high school. She knew they were two different personalities, and so she was not surprised and actually pleased that they seemed to be taking very different directions.

Marie had remained very serious, very focused, and very rigid in her thinking and mannerisms. She had gone out with a few boys in high school, but only occasionally and if there was a special occasion, like the graduation dance. There were no serious relationships in her life, although she had several friends who were boys, and they enjoyed each other's company.

Ana, on the other hand, had gone from being a young tomboy at the beach to growing up to be a very social, outgoing young lady who had lots of boyfriends and one or two serious relationships during her years in high school.

Yolanda discussed this regularly with her husband, and they both felt good about the directions the girls seemed to be heading. They decided that, when each child left high school, they would take them out for a dinner, discuss their thoughts and plans, and give them the $5,000 cheque that they had put away for them.

So, as graduation was approaching, they took Marie out to Antonio's for her dinner. While they were eating, they asked Marie about her plans.

Marie's answer was pretty well what they were expecting. "I am thinking that I would like to go to college and take a course in business administration," she told them. "When I finish, we'll see, but becoming a chartered accountant might be the way to go. It'll be a fair amount of work, but it would be a pretty interesting career. There's a five-year home study course that you do before taking the exam to get your CA accreditation.

You do the course while you are working and learning on the job, and I can get credits from some of the courses I take in the business program and so complete the CA course faster."

"That's great," her parents said together. Her father added, "We have a graduation gift for you." And he handed her the cheque for $5,000.

She was obviously surprised. "Wonderful. Can I use it for anything?"

"Of course. It is your gift from us," her mother told her, and as far as they knew, she put into her bank account and it remained there. Yolanda was curious but didn't want to interfere in her daughter's business.

Marie went to a local college that fall and started her studies. Her father had told her that over the summer she could work in the business office of the construction company. She was thrilled to have this opportunity, and she worked, filling in for vacationing staff and learning about the business side of the construction industry while being paid.

Two years later, it was Ana's turn, and again, they took her to Antonio's. During her last year of high school, she had volunteered at Sunnybrook Hospital as a candy striper. She loved the contact with the patients and enjoyed being in the hospital environment. It was no surprise then, when she, in answer to her father's question, replied, "I'm going to apply to become a student nurse, and hopefully they'll accept me."

"Well, we have no doubt that they will jump at the chance to get you," was her father's reply. Giving her the cheque, he added, "This is a graduation gift from your mother and me."

Unlike her sister, she looked at it and said, "Wow. Thanks." That was it. No other comment or talk about it.

She moved into the nurses' residence as soon as she finished high school and commenced her training. She found some of the training rigid and steeped in tradition, but on the whole she thoroughly enjoyed it and found the camaraderie of the student nurses invigorating. Her parents were very proud.

Michael struggled with high school, failing and repeating grade 11. So it was two years after Ana when he finished grade 13. When he was taken out for his graduation dinner, he knew from his sisters' experience what to expect. What they didn't tell him was the surprise gift he would get.

So, as dinner was concluding, his mother said, "So, Mikey, are you still looking to go to Ryerson and take business administration?"

"Yeah, I think it would be good, and I've learned a lot from Dad and working at the company."

"Well, here's a graduation gift from your father and me," she said, giving him his cheque.

"Wow! Thanks," was his response. They could almost see the wheels turning in his mind as he stared at it. A few days later, a used Ford Mustang appeared in the driveway. It was about seven years old and was white and blue. When his mother asked him if he bought it, he replied, "Yeah, I thought it would save me time going downtown to Ryerson. I won't have to worry about buses or the subway."

His course was a three-year business administration course. During his summers, he worked for Bertollini in a variety of jobs as a general labourer. He did the work happily and developed a nice summer tan, working with his shirt off. He was five feet ten and a little on the husky side. He made pretty good money. He was given several opportunities to try his hand at various trades, and while he picked up a bit of training, he really wasn't all that interested.

Yolanda felt quite happy that they had moved from the middle of the city to Downsview as she watched Michael joining a group of friends to play soccer during the beautiful summer evenings. Michael especially enjoyed the pizza and beer parties after the games. He was a very social person.

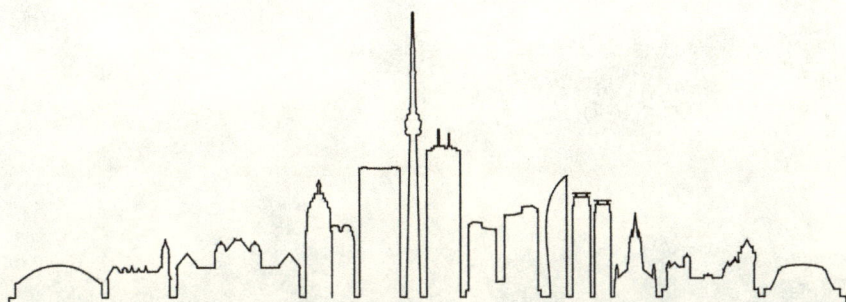

# PART TWO
## TAKING FLIGHT

CHAPTER **EIGHTEEN**

A FTER FINISHING COLLEGE in three years, Marie decided to work for a family named Romano who owned a local bookkeeping business. During her first summer at college, she had seen a notice on the bulletin board saying someone was looking for a summer student. Marie went to their office to apply, and she met Antoinette. It turned out that it was her business, and she hired Marie on the spot, telling her that everyone called her Toni. She joined two other girls who were full-time clerks, and upon graduation, she stayed on as the third clerk. They had been quite impressed by how quickly she adapted to the office routine as a summer student and didn't want to lose her. What they showed her was absorbed immediately, and she progressed rapidly from entering receipts and disbursements to keeping a client's books.

Within nine months, Marie was looking after the books for five different businesses. Not only did she keep the books, but she also administered their business loans, owners' loans, purchases, and telecommunications. She loved the work, and over the course of her dealings, she met and had interactions with several chartered accountants who prepared the year-end statements and filed the annual income tax forms for the business owners and their families.

One of the chartered accountants was very impressed with the work Marie did and her understanding of what she was doing. His name was Fred Sutherland. One Friday in early April, he asked her to join him for lunch. She assumed that he was doing it to show his appreciation for her willingness to assist him when he worked on clients for whom she kept the books.

Over the course of the meal, after a great deal of small talk about the importance of education and family, he began talking about the work of chartered accountants. "I am a manager and have three students working under my direction," he told her. "Would you be interested in joining our office as a chartered accounting student and working toward your designation on my team?"

Taken aback, she answered, "To be honest, I have been thinking about pursuing my CA designation and am aware of what is involved." She then added, "I would be thrilled to join your firm and commence working on my CA. I know I'll get some credits for my college business administration diploma."

Telling her employer when they returned that afternoon, Toni replied, "I was expecting this, as Mr. Sutherland told me what he was planning to do. We weren't surprised and are sorry we are losing you. We wish you the very best."

"Of course, I will stay on until we have wrapped up at the end of the month," she answered. "You and your staff have been wonderful to work with, and I have learned a great deal from you."

Marie made the announcement to her family that evening at dinner, and they were thrilled. Clemente was especially enthralled with the possibility of having his oldest daughter become a chartered accountant. He asked Yolanda, "What is the likelihood of Italian immigrants having a child become a professional?"

"When the child has good parents, anything is possible!" she answered, smiling.

Finishing her work at Romano's at the end of the month, she arrived at the offices of Ferguson and Associates Chartered Accountants on April 1, 1976. The company had purchased a large, old three-storey home. It looked very impressive, and they had added an addition to the rear of the house in the backyard and added a parking lot. The first floor housed a large reception area, where the receptionist welcomed clients and the clients waited for their appointments. There were two small meeting rooms and one large boardroom. Two of the junior partners had offices there, while the remainder were situated on the second floor.

Marie worked under the guidance of a manager and was on Fred Sutherland's team. He was the partner she reported to. After two days of orientation, she was introduced to "the Bull Pen." She learned that this was the name given to the large addition where eight CA students worked. They each had a work table, and there was a great deal of camaraderie and chatter in the room when there were no clients or partners about. The firm's senior partner was Robert McNair.

Marie had developed into a fairly strong-willed individual with a strict work ethic. She was a touch on the stocky side, with medium-length dark hair and many of her father's features. She loved working with numbers and dealing with clients' accounts. While she was a very pleasant and friendly individual, she became known in the firm as a no-nonsense individual, and as such, her social life was not particularly active. There were a few girls in the office that she joined for lunch on a regular basis, and once a month they went out for dinner. She did develop a friendship with one of the young accountants in the office, William Brown. Bill was a few years older, and like her, he was a fairly serious individual.

One day, Julie Henderson, one of Marie's co-workers and the organizer of the social outings, invited Bill to join them for one of their monthly dinners. Marie had been with the firm for about a year and a half. She had attended several meetings and audit reviews with Bill and thought of him as rather a bookish, tweedy sort of fellow. She guessed he didn't have a lot of excitement in his life. He was of medium height, with sandy-coloured hair and a slim build. His narrow, pointed face was not too noticeable, as he wore thick, brown-framed glasses.

At the dinner, at Julie's suggestion, they sat beside each other. Whether by design or random chance, no one could say. He hadn't been shy in joining the group conversations and talking with her when the time seemed right.

She felt very at ease with him, and at the end of the evening, when he offered to see her home, she agreed. Marie had been offered an apartment in her parents' new six-unit building, and when it was completed, she chose the three-bedroom unit on the top floor. This gave her an office as well as a studio where she could pursue her interest in starting to paint. She had a great collection of classical music and was beginning to collect a bit of art, although, on an accounting student's pay, she did not have a great deal of free cash flow for the purchase of non-essentials.

As he was dropping her off, they chatted for a few minutes, and Marie mentioned her love of classical music. Bill immediately responded that he, too, loved the classics and that he had a season ticket for the Toronto Symphony Orchestra's concerts. She told him that one of her goals, once she achieved her CA designation, was to purchase a season ticket. They said good night, and she went up to her apartment, thinking nothing more of the exchange.

When she arrived at the office the following Monday morning, she was surprised to find an envelope on her work table with her name on it. She opened it and was thrilled to find a ticket for the next TSO performance the following weekend. Enclosed was also a note from Bill, asking if she would join him for the concert and dinner afterward. She called to thank him and said that she would love to join him. That was the start of their relationship.

Marie and Ana had met and played with several boys at Sauble Beach. They had played spin the bottle and similar games. There had been kissing and groping, but nothing had ever amounted to more than that, although she had been propositioned many times. Marie didn't have a great desire or need to have sex with Bill, but she enjoyed his company. He was well-read and a good conversationalist.

One night in her apartment, they were sitting and listening to Chopin when Bill leaned over and kissed her, saying, "I think you are wonderful." It caught her off guard, but then she kissed him back. Before long, they moved into the bedroom.

They continued to live separately, and when Marie finished her courses and achieved her professional designation in 1979, their romantic relationship continued as best friends. Marie enrolled in art classes and took up painting as a hobby. She bought a few pieces of art when something really caught her eye and often sought Bill's opinion when she was deciding.

She loved her work and was a very good accountant. Her clients loved her thorough, forthright manner and had no hesitation recommending her to business associates. She visited her parents regularly and kept in close touch with Ana. She didn't have a great deal of time for Michael, whom she still considered to be spoiled and immature.

Continuing to work for the accounting firm, she was made a manager after three years. She took on her new role with enthusiasm and was very good at it. The clients loved her and valued the work she did for them as well as the advice she offered.

Marie and Bill continued to see each other, and their relationship grew. They talked off and on about their future plans, and at one point, they talked about moving in together when she was made a partner in the firm. After five years, she fully expected to be invited to become a partner, as one of the senior partners had semi-retired and there was a vacancy. Bill had been very supportive, so when the partners' retreat was held, she waited with anticipation for their call. It never came! It turned out a young fellow who had just finished achieving his designation was announced as the new partner.

Marie was devastated! Sitting down with Bill that evening when he arrived back, she said bluntly, "What in the hell is going on?"

Bill was obviously uncomfortable as he replied, "It's not good. George Jarvis got the nod. His uncle really pushed for him and told everyone that, as an Italian female, you wouldn't fit the image the firm was looking to portray. He was very persuasive, and everyone agreed."

She was shocked, hurt, and furious. "Did you stand up for me?" she demanded.

He replied, "Yes, of course, but George's uncle carries more clout."

"Did you threaten to resign if they didn't select me?"

"No," he said. "I told them that they were making a big mistake. They were passing on a far better and more capable CA. But they ignored me."

Standing up abruptly, Marie said, "I can't believe you didn't put your career on the line for me. I guess that tells me how much you really think of me. Obviously, you are a useless, gutless asshole, and I never want to see you again." With that, she stormed out, almost taking the door off its hinges as she slammed it.

When she got to her apartment, she threw everything of his out in the hall, then called the building superintendent to come and change the locks. Finally, feeling a little more composed, she sat down and wrote a letter of resignation to the partners. She drove back to the office and put the letter, along with her office keys, on the senior partner's desk. She then cleaned out her desk and left. Her resignation letter was civil but frank and to the point.

Bill felt sick. He knew in his heart that Marie was right, and he felt for her. It wasn't right. But he had reached his career goal. He was a CA in one of the best chartered accounting practices in Toronto, and he was a partner. He wasn't prepared to jeopardize his position. It was what he had striven for. It was his dream come true.

The following morning, the senior partner, Robert McNair, came to Bill's office. He was a large man with a heavy frame, a full head of black hair, and a large moustache, which was grown to hide a cleft lip. Sitting down, he looked Bill square in the eye and told him, "I am truly sorry for you, but surely you can see the partner's position. We can't have a wop's daughter as a partner. We would be the laughingstock of the city."

Bill replied, "I know you are right, but you really hurt her. Too bad we couldn't have made her a special associate partner or something."

"It is what it is," was the reply as McNair got up and left Bill's office.

After taking a few days to cool down and gather her thoughts, Marie called her uncle and told him what had happened. "Don't worry about it. It's not the end of the world. You are better off now that you've seen the true side of your boyfriend and his company. I'll do whatever I can to help you," he assured her.

With Favio's help, she found a new office on a busy street a few blocks from the heart of Little Italy. It was on the ground floor with a good view. There was a sitting reception area, a small kitchenette, and three rooms that would become the offices. She thought it was nicely painted, so she didn't have to do much before moving right in. At her uncle's suggestion, she ordered a new sign and hung a notice in the window advising that this was the new home of "Marie Gallorini, CA."

She then contacted Toni Romano and advised her that she was starting her own practice. After telling Toni what had transpired, she mentioned that she was looking for a receptionist assistant.

Toni replied, "Sorry things didn't work out. They lost a good person who would have made a great partner. I think I know someone who would be perfect as your administrative assistant." Within two days, Sonia Willis was hired on Toni's recommendation.

Next, Marie prepared and took out ads in the local newspapers announcing that she was now offering accounting services under her practice, Marie Gallorini, CA. Finally, she called Uncle Spiffy and brought him up to speed so he could get the word out to the people he had undoubtedly talked to.

She had managed her money well and had a very healthy bank account on which to rely until her business was up and running, but she didn't need to use much of it. Uncle Spiffy, true to his word, spread the word, and she had clients lining up at her office doorstep within days of opening her new practice. Most of them knew her from her days as a bookkeeper at Toni's. She knew then that between Toni and her uncle, things would work out in her favour.

In her first year, she hired two young people who were experienced and were contemplating enrolling in the CA course.

CHAPTER NINETEEN

A NA HAD DECIDED to enter the nursing profession as a student nurse and began working on her registered nurse designation. She was good at it and loved the work. She lived in the nurses' residence and didn't have to travel to get to work, so she could spend time taking the courses she needed to obtain her designation. She dated periodically, but nothing serious developed.

A few years later, she was a registered nurse and was trying to decide where she should live. She was thinking that, like her sister, she could arrange to get an apartment in one of her parents' buildings and maybe work at another hospital.

Finishing her shift one day, she was relaxing in the nurses' lounge, thumbing through that day's copy of *The Globe and Mail*. Scanning the employment ads, one from the Stanton Yellowknife Hospital caught her eye. She remembered a couple of Thanksgivings ago when her father's old friend Marco had visited. He had told them how the uranium mines had closed in Uranium City, Saskatchewan, and he and several friends who worked at the mine as hard rock miners had gone to Yellowknife to work in the gold mines. He had then regaled them with stories of the long, dark, cold winters and the wonderful, bright, long summer days, partying in a local hotel and curling at the local curling club. He said how warmly they had been welcomed by the local Italian community. Always having the desire to travel and see more of Canada, she answered the ad on a whim. She never thought for a moment that anything would come of it.

Within two weeks, she received a telephone call from the personnel department of the territorial government inviting her to attend an interview at the Royal York Hotel the following week. Arriving at the appointed time, she was welcomed by a personnel officer and Mrs. Todd, the head nurse from the Stanton Yellowknife Hospital. They reviewed the information on her résumé, delving into aspects of her work experience. They asked her what she knew about life in Yellowknife. She talked about her father's friend who worked at the Cominco Mine and the stories he had told her family. As the interview ended, they told her that someone would contact her in due course.

Within the week, she received a message to call them. When she did, she was offered a nursing position, with a nice increase in her annual salary. She accepted and was told that a formal job offer would be mailed to her immediately.

When Ana arrived home that weekend and shared her news, her parents were completely taken off guard. They had no idea where she was going or how she would fare. After giving it some thought, her mother said to the family, "Now I know how our parents must have felt when we decided to come here."

On Yolanda's suggestion, Clemente called Marco the next afternoon, seeking assurance that his daughter had made a wise choice and that Marco would look out for her. Of course, Marco was thrilled, and he assured his old friend that Ana would be fine.

On a September morning in 1977, Ana flew to the Edmonton International Airport and then took a shuttle bus to the industrial airport in the downtown. She overnighted at a nearby hotel and then left on a PWA flight going to Fort Smith and then to Yellowknife the following morning.

Upon Ana's arrival in Yellowknife on a beautiful mid-September morning, she was met by a young fellow, slightly built with black wavy hair and the start of what was obviously his first moustache. Approaching her, he asked if she was Ana Gallorini. As she replied, "Yes," he took her hand and, shaking it vigorously, introduced himself as Jimmy Boyd. He could not believe what he was looking at. Before him stood a beautiful, slim young woman with medium-length black hair. Her eyes were dark and very intriguing. She had high cheekbones and a lovely face. He had to pull himself together and not stare at her.

"I'm from the personnel department and will take you to the hospital. Welcome to Yellowknife," he told her.

Collecting her luggage, they left the terminal and headed to the parking area, where a light blue vehicle with the Northwest Territories crest on each door was waiting. Jimmy watched as Ana looked at the coat of arms and then said, "Check out the licence plate." Walking to the front of the car, she saw a white licence plate in the shape of a polar bear. "Welcome to the Northwest Territories," he said with a huge smile on his young face.

The drive from the airport was interesting, and Jimmy provided a running commentary on what she was seeing as well as the history of the town. He only paused to answer her questions. They arrived at the front of a building identified by a large sign as the Stanton Yellowknife Hospital. *Wow,* she thought, as it was hard to believe that she was here. As they had driven into town, she had noticed a large lake, lots of rock, and some very small evergreen trees.

"I'll drop your luggage at your new apartment," he said, pointing to a three-storey building just down the road. He then escorted her into the hospital. They arrived at what turned out to be the head nurse's office, and after gently knocking on the door, he opened it and beckoned Ana to enter. Ana immediately recognized Mrs. Todd from the interview in Toronto. With a warm and friendly smile, Mrs. Todd said, "Nice to see you again. Welcome to Stanton Yellowknife Hospital."

While Ana hadn't spent any time looking at her during the interview, now that she was looking directly at her, she saw that she was a small, thin lady with greying hair and a thin face with a few wrinkles developing. "I think the best and the most productive thing is for one of your colleagues to take you around and introduce you to the staff and show you our facilities. I'm sure you'll have a ton of questions." With that, she picked up her telephone, dialled two numbers, said "She's here," and hung up.

As they were chatting about the flight, a young woman about Ana's age tapped on the door frame and entered the office. Before the head nurse could say a word, the new arrival came to Ana, taking her hand and saying, "Hi. I'm Jill, and I'll be your guide dog." Laughing and glancing quickly at her boss, she took Ana by the arm, and they headed into the hospital proper.

Jill took her through the building, making introductions as they went. Unlike the Toronto hospitals, the Stanton Yellowknife was a single ground-floor building and was very compact and efficient. It turned out that Jill Leblanc was from Vernon, British Columbia, and had been in the Northwest Territories for a little over two years. When questioned, she told Ana that Vernon was a small town at the top of the lake in the Okanagan Valley in the interior of British Columbia.

After finishing their late lunch in the hospital cafeteria, they left and walked the short distance to the apartment building. She saw it was only slightly larger than the family's apartment building in Toronto. It was a very plain building painted light grey with dark grey trim. There were two nice birch trees that were starting to change colour, positioned on either side of the sidewalk leading into the building. As they walked over, they continued to compare notes about backgrounds, families, likes and dislikes, and the men of Yellowknife. Jill, who was quite attractive with long, dark brown hair, high cheekbones, and a very pretty face, told Ana that she had dated various guys, but nothing serious had developed. "There are lots of young eligible fellows around," she added.

Proceeding into the building and walking up a flight of stairs, they stopped at a door with a number 6 on it. Jill opened the unlocked door, ushering her in. "Welcome to your new home," she announced as she made a sweeping motion with her arms. Before Ana was a very compact one-bedroom apartment that included a living room, a galley kitchen, a bathroom, and a bedroom. A sliding door off the living room opened to a small deck, giving her a view of the side of the hospital and the lake that was behind it.

Jill waited while Ana unpacked and then called a taxi to take them downtown. Jill had told her that there were a few things to do, including getting her telephone hooked up and renting a post office box.

Once those jobs were done, they headed around the corner to pick up groceries and made a quick stop at the liquor store before returning to the apartment.

While Ana really didn't get a good look around, the city seemed quite different from anything she had experienced before. The buildings were not big, nothing more than ten storeys high, and all appeared to be fairly new.

The main street was quite wide, and the traffic moved along nicely. It was called Franklin Avenue. There were two sets of traffic lights. Everything in the downtown was contained within about four or five blocks, and it had a good welcoming feel to it. She felt right at home.

As they returned to the apartment, Jill said, "We have a surprise for you. Everyone in the building who is not on shift is coming to my place for dinner and to meet you." It was wonderful and left Ana feeling quite comfortable as she fit into the mix immediately. After the potluck dinner, it was decided by those who did not have an early shift that they would take her to the local watering hole called the Hoist Room for a few after-dinner drinks. They called a taxi and headed downtown. The taxi stopped about half a block from the post office, and they took a flight of stairs down from the main street to a fairly new, nicely decorated, and rather dimly lit bar. There was soft music playing and lots of chatter. The name, she was told, referred to the room at the gold mines where the miners took the elevator, or hoist, as it was called, underground to the gold deposits, which were found in veins of the rock well below the surface. Settling in with their drinks, they got to know each other and shared stories about what brought them to "the Knife." The bar was very lively, with a lot of people coming and going. They had a fun evening, and Ana met a number of interesting people from various parts of the country.

Returning to her new apartment, she was ready to crash after her long day. *There is one more thing I have to do,* she thought, checking that her new telephone was working. Hearing the dial tone, she dialled. When it was answered, she said, "Hi, Mom. It's me, and I'm calling from my new apartment. Everything is good, and I've settled in already and made several new friends. The hospital is new and quite nice."

"That is wonderful to hear," her mother replied. "Your father's not home yet, but I'll let him know. He'll be thrilled. Have you spoken to Marco yet?"

"No, not yet, but I will call him as soon as we hang up."

"Say hi to him for us. Thanks for calling. You must be exhausted after your long day. Love you, bye."

"Bye, Mom. Love you."

Pressing down on the receiver button, she got a new dial tone. Glancing at the piece of paper she took from her purse, she dialled the number. A man's voice said, "Hello?"

Ana asked, "Marco?"

"Ana," was the reply, and then Marco asked, "*Come stanno andando? When did you get in?*"

"This morning," she replied. "I've had a very busy day and am dead tired, but I wanted you to know I am here, safe and sound. The people at the hospital are wonderful, and they have made me feel right at home. I start work tomorrow but wanted to touch base with you. Mom and Dad send their regards."

"That's wonderful," he replied. "It is so nice to hear your voice again. Welcome to Yellowknife. I won't keep you now, but we want you to come for Sunday supper. I will call you before I come to pick you up, but we are thinking around two if that works."

"Yes, that would be wonderful."

"Great. Get a good night's rest. What is your number, so I can call you before I come to pick you up?" She gave it to him. He welcomed her to the north again and then hung up.

Her sleep was wonderful, and she woke up feeling refreshed. She met Jill at the front door after a bit of toast and coffee. Stepping out, she immediately noticed that the morning was fresh and crisp. It was mid-September and there was a hint of frost in the clear and bright northern morning air. That's when it really hit home. While she had not yet seen much of her new surroundings, she was here.

Ana went to Marco's for dinner her first weekend in Yellowknife and was overwhelmed by her reception. There were ten Italian couples, including Marco and his wife, Bella. She was treated like a long-lost friend. She was surprised to find such a vibrant Italian community in Yellowknife. She learned, as the evening progressed, that they had all come north to work in one of the gold mines—the Giant Mine and the Cominco Mine, referred to by the locals as "Giant" and "Con." Most of the wives had jobs in the community, and Yellowknife was certainly their home.

The food was amazing and seemingly endless. Everyone wanted to know about her family, what they did, and where her parents came from. Had she been to Italy? Did she have a partner or boyfriend? Was she interested in meeting some nice Italian boys? And it went on. She was blown away by it all. Marco sat back and smiled, taking everything in. She was given standing invitations to most of their homes and promised a good meal. "Don't be lonely," she was told over and over.

"I won't," she assured them.

As she joined the ladies in the kitchen, cleaning up and getting the dishes put away, she was given advice about doctors, banks, hairdressers, grocery stores, and the like. She was told which bars to avoid. She picked up a fair bit of local gossip, although she obviously didn't know the parties involved, and of course, she was given a thorough briefing on the city council and the territorial government. Finally—and most importantly— she was given the scoop on the local Roman Catholic Church, St. Mary's. Several ladies offered to pick her up in the morning and take her to the eleven o'clock Mass. She bowed out gracefully, saying she had a shift at the hospital. As she left, she thanked her hosts and all of the guests. Walking back to her apartment in the crisp night air, she decided to call her parents to tell them about the evening and extend to them the many greetings she had accepted on their behalf. Working on a nice cup of hot herbal tea, she made the call and chatted about her impressions and the people she met. Yolanda and Clemente were thrilled and asked all kinds of questions. Finally, she said good night and went to bed.

Ana was very interested in her new community, and she enjoyed meeting and talking to the other residents. She joined the local curling club, which was very close to her apartment, and met a cross-section of Yellowknifers. As she learned, the town had changed forever when the territorial government relocated from Ottawa. The town had originally been made up primarily of prospectors, miners, and a few merchants. The Territories were administered from Ottawa. In the 1960s, it was decided that the administration of the Territories should be located in the north. There was a great deal of speculation as to where the new capital would be located, and a task force was appointed to determine the best location. While all odds were on the community of Fort Smith, which virtually straddled the Northwest Territories–Alberta border, the task force decided on Yellowknife. It had an existing economic base and would not become a "one-horse government town," as one of the locals put it. The Government of the Northwest Territories officially moved to Yellowknife in 1967 and set up shop.

Ana loved nothing better than to drive around the city and outlying area. Luckily, several of her colleagues owned cars and were happy to show her around on their days off. One of the areas she found quite interesting was past Giant Mine on a road that went nowhere. It was called the Ingram Trail, and it left Yellowknife and went past several amazing lakes and recreational areas. It opened up to fishing, camping, and hunting areas. As a result, there were quite a few cottages and cabins on the lakes. The largest and most popular was Prelude Lake.

The weather, while remaining clear and crisp, was changing. The days were becoming shorter, and there was a notable change in the weather. Late fall was upon them. By Thanksgiving, which she spent with a friend she met curling, there was ice on the puddles and along the edges of the smaller lake in the mornings. Shortly thereafter, people began wearing heavy coats and jackets. Then, just as Halloween was approaching, the snow came, and the temperature dropped. Winter had arrived.

Coats were discarded for parkas and lined boots. Gloves, scarves, and wool hats became essential, as did block heaters, battery blankets, and oil pan heaters for cars. The temperature fell very quickly, and Ana experienced minus twenty-five degrees about a week later.

November 11 arrived, and she and a couple of her work friends decided to attend the Remembrance Day service in the Elks Hall. It was bitterly cold, and cadets, who were stationed around the cenotaph, were relieved every fifteen minutes so they could warm up. After the service, the girls decided to go to the Legion to join the celebrations.

Arriving and discarding their winter garb, they were invited to join a table for drinks. Most people in the room seemed to know they were nurses and gave them a warm welcome. There was a lot of reminiscing and storytelling. Everyone was having a great time. Ana sat back, taking everything in, as she did not know that many people.

A young RCMP constable with his tunic unbuttoned and hair a little dishevelled asked if he could get her a drink. "Sure, a rum and coke would be nice," she said, smiling.

He returned shortly, taking a seat beside her, and set her rum and coke in front of her. He had a drink that could have been scotch or rye for himself.

Sitting down, he smiled and said, "*Buongiorno.*"

She smiled back and replied, "*Buongiorno.*"

He said, "*Commena stai?*"

Laughing, she replied, "*Bene, molto bene, grazie.*"

Then he said, "That's all the Italian I know, but you could teach me some more."

Laughing again, she replied, "We'll see."

Pretending to be very serious, he continued, "Constable Kornichuk of the RCMP, at your service, ma'am." Then, smiling, he added, "Hi, I'm Dave."

Ana told him her name, and they spent the rest of the afternoon chatting. As the afternoon progressed, her girlfriends interrupted, saying, "We thought we would head out for dinner."

She was about to say she would join them when Dave asked, "Do you like Chinese food?"

Without hesitation, she replied, "I love it."

He answered, "Okay, we'll catch up with you girls later." As they got up to get their parkas, they were surprised to see that most of the guests had already left. The afternoon had gotten away from them. Leaving the Legion, he said, "You won't believe the size of the spring rolls they serve."

Walking about a block, they came to the Gold Range Hotel. Ana had heard about it from the Italian ladies who told her that it had a rough bar frequented by unruly locals. They bypassed the entrance to the bar and restaurant, and went directly into the hotel lobby, where David said, "Just a minute," and walked over to the desk clerk. He said something in a very low voice and then returned to her side.

Within a minute, a Chinese gentlemen appeared and said, "Hi. Please, come this way."

Within a few minutes, they were shown into a small room that contained a table and four chairs. The table was set for two, and as they were sitting, David explained, "They have this room for us to use. It's private, and our clients, the riff-raff of the town, don't know we are here. We consider it one of the perks of the job."

Within minutes, their host arrived, introducing himself as Clavin and giving them menus. He waited to take their orders. After a short wait, he returned and served them what Ana thought was the finest Chinese food she had ever experienced. As foretold, the spring rolls were almost a meal in themselves and were amazing.

Putting on their winter gear and getting ready to leave, they decided to walk rather than call a cab. They couldn't see each other, as the parka hoods extended well past their faces to protect against the cold and the wind. As they walked, they shifted the parka hoods to the backs of their heads so they could see each other's faces. It was a clear, cold night, and Dave told her they were fortunate that there was no wind. Her face was cold, and wanting to see the stars, she pushed the hood further back. She couldn't believe what she was seeing. The night sky was completely alive with soft pulsing and flashing multicoloured lights. As she stopped and stared, Dave said, "I guess you've never seen the northern lights before. They really are pretty amazing." They continued to her apartment, where they shook hands and said good night.

$ $ $

IT WAS NOW mid-December, and Ana hadn't heard from Dave for over a month. She didn't know why but didn't dwell on it. Through curling and friends, she had met and gone out with a couple of other guys. It was nice but nothing serious. There was no shortage of social activities in her life.

Then, out of the blue, she received a call, and it was him. "Hi there, sorry we haven't talked for a while. I have been on a course in Regina, and they really frown on you making personal calls. Hope you've been well."

"Oh, hi. I hoped I might hear from you but knew that something must have come up," she replied. "Yes, everything is good at this end."

"Great. We are having our Christmas party next Thursday. We generally don't have it on the weekend because at this time of year, our weekends can be a little hectic with all the parties going on. It keeps us pretty busy. Anyway, I wondered if you would be free to come with me. There's a dinner and a dance."

After a brief pause, she replied, "Sure, that would be lovely. What time should I be ready?"

"I'll pick you up at seven. It's at the Explorer Hotel, and we'll take taxis. It would be crazy to take your own car this time of year since, if you could get it started, it would take half an hour just to warm it up. I am really looking forward to seeing you again. Ciao."

She hung up with a good feeling. *Now, what will I wear? I'll have to get my hair done,* were some of the thoughts racing through her mind.

The taxi arrived just before seven. It was a clear and cold evening with the temperature hovering around minus thirty. Fortunately, there was no wind. David rapped on her apartment door at exactly seven o'clock. When she opened it, he said, "Wow, you look amazing." He helped her into her parka, and they headed off for the evening. As the taxi headed for the Explorer Hotel, he told her about the course he had been on and that it could lead to him becoming a detective down the road.

It was a wonderful evening. Everyone was very friendly and welcoming. She was a little surprised at the number of couples attending, but David explained, "It's the one time of the year that we include the members and their wives from the surrounding communities. They are all in our division, and several have flown down from the Inuvik detachment. They have their own Twin Otter." Reacting to her puzzled look, he explained, "That's the name of the aircraft they have."

They ate a wonderful meal, danced, sang, and chatted. Everyone, and especially the women, was interested in her, asking about where she worked, where she had come from, and what she was thinking about the future. It was very apparent that Dave was well-liked by all and highly thought of by the officers. Later, as they stood at her apartment door saying good night, David kissed her. She was not surprised and had actually been hoping that it would happen.

She thanked him, saying, "It is too bad the taxi is waiting because you could come in for a nightcap."

He smiled and said, "Don't go away." Turning, he left the building and returned a few minutes later. "I paid the driver off and told him I won't be needing him," he said as he followed her into her apartment.

The following morning, Dave got up early, kissed Ana passionately, and left, saying, "I'll call you later."

At around four-thirty, Ana had finished her shift and headed to the apartment. Shortly thereafter, Dave called and asked, "Are you up to going out for dinner, or would you like me to make you something here? I make a mean spaghetti with bolognese sauce."

"Spaghetti sounds wonderful. What time do you want me? I'll get a taxi. I found a nice Italian red at the liquor store. I'll bring it over."

To Ana's delight, Dave proved to be a perfect gentleman. He was almost six feet tall with short brown hair and a fairly thin face with a strong jaw and a moustache. He was well-built, thoughtful, and courteous. He always treated her with respect. His disposition was good-natured and happy. He had a good outlook on life but was able to take control of a situation when the need arose. He had served in Alberta before going to Baffin Island and working at the detachment in Pangnirtung. Then he transferred to Yellowknife, and most importantly, he could not believe his good fortune in finding Ana. It had all started innocently. Occasional dating and getting together over Christmas. More serious dating followed, and then a quick trip to Brandon to meet Dave's parents, followed by another quick trip to Downsview to meet Ana's family. Both sets of parents were thrilled with their offspring's choices of partner. Then, after speaking to a government buyer and getting a great deal on a diamond, he had the local jeweller mount it on an engagement ring, which he offered to her. She said yes.

They were married in St. Mary's Church on a cool, cloudy but pleasant day. Dave and his best man were in full RCMP formal dress uniforms. It was a quiet affair with only a few friends attending. But an unexpected surprise arose when, two days prior to the wedding, Ana's phone rang. When she answered it, a voice said, "Have you got a maid of honour yet?"

Recognizing her sister's voice, she answered, "Yes, I do."

"All right, call her and tell her she's now a bridesmaid," Marie replied. "I'll be there tomorrow morning."

Ana was completely surprised and thrilled. Marie arrived and stood up as her maid of honour. It was just the way they wanted it. Ana asked her father's old friend Marco to give her away, and he was honoured.

They moved quickly into a new apartment and then left for Hawaii for three weeks of rest and relaxation. One of the RCMP's civilian employees' parents owned a condominium just outside Honolulu in a place called the

Makaha Valley. The office staff had taken up a collection and rented the unit for three weeks, which they gave to Ana and Dave as a wedding present.

The morning after the wedding, they flew out of Yellowknife on the morning flight and, changing planes in Calgary and Vancouver, arrived in Honolulu at about four in the afternoon. As they collected their luggage and stepped outside to pick up their rental car, they were hit with the warm, salty, humid Hawaiian air. The day was sunny, and there was not a cloud in the sky. They were thankful for the warmth after their winter in Yellowknife.

Picking up their vehicle, they left the airport and headed to the Makaha Valley. It was about a thirty-minute drive. The condominium building turned out to be a long, thin, eight-storey building. There must have been over a hundred units, they guessed. As a result of the design, each unit faced the ocean. There was a large hill at the back of the building. The unit doors exited to the hillside, and the parking lots were on the hillside, leaving the front to face the palm trees, hibiscus hedges, green grass, and of course, the Pacific Ocean.

After parking and taking the elevator to the sixth floor, they entered their home for the next three weeks. It was a very nice unit consisting of a sitting room, a bedroom with a queen-size bed, and a kitchenette. There was a balcony that gave them an amazing view from the large swimming pool to the ocean. They were thrilled when they realized that the sun would set right before their eyes.

They spent their first week relaxing and enjoying downtime. They found a nice, protected beach that was great for swimming and sunbathing at Pokai Bay, just a short drive from the condo.

For their last two weeks, they toured the island and shopped after spending their mornings at the swimming pool. They usually ended up having dinner in Honolulu, trying different restaurants and eating establishments. While touring, they were impressed with the range of activities and places of interest on the island, noting the many pineapple plantations, the amazing beaches, including Waikiki and Diamond Head, and the Polynesian Centre. They were thrilled to find a luau where they experienced roasted pig.

One morning, as they entered the pool area, one of the residents looked up from his lounger and said to them, "Welcome to another shitty day in paradise." And that proved to be right on. Every day was warm and sunny. The peace and quiet were only disturbed by the occasional shrill call from one of the condominium's resident peacocks.

$ $ $

AT THE END of April, David and Ana returned from their honeymoon in Hawaii. It had been a very eventful three-and-a-half months, and it didn't seem real to either of them. It was as if they were both expecting to awaken from a dream as they entered their new apartment in Yellowknife. They arrived home rested and very happy that they had found each other.

CHAPTER TWENTY

A S HE WAS preparing to graduate from Ryerson Polytechnic, Michael was anxious to spread his wings and strike off on his own. He had a good personality and really enjoyed talking to people. There was a standing offer of a job with Bertollini, but Michael was itching to choose his own path. He had chosen a business administration course at Ryerson Polytechnic, a downtown college. As graduation approached, a number of career days were held in which employers looking for new graduates set up booths and gave talks on their businesses and the opportunities that awaited the new graduates. Investment companies, banks, insurance companies, large multi-faceted corporations, department stores, car dealerships—the list went on. Michael and his classmates attended each one, and they were very enthused about what was being offered to them as a stepping stone into the working world.

After taking in numerous presentations and attending a number of follow-up meetings, Michael was torn between joining a life insurance company and a financial services company. He was leaning toward the life insurance position because they were offering a small starting salary while he received education and training. Once he finished the training, they would provide him with what seemed to be endless lists of potential clients. All he had to do was contact them, determine what type of protection they needed, complete an application, collect a cheque, and most importantly, receive his commission cheque. It sounded very straightforward. He understood that as soon as his training was completed, he would be a licensed life insurance agent, and more importantly, he would switch from salary to commission. The people he talked to regaled him with stories about the monetary success of their companies' agents. It was very appealing to him, and after all, he loved talking to people. How could he go wrong?

And so, when he graduated, he joined the life insurance company that appealed to him the most. His trainers were all employees of the company who had started out as life insurance agents and, according to them, had become very successful. They regaled the trainees with insurance war stories. They talked about when they had started, how they had developed their skills and finally started selling big policies, and the good money they made. They talked about how the company rewarded them with foreign trips and conferences where they and their colleagues would be wined and dined and given further training from the industry's best. They were told that their goals should include achieving their Chartered Life Underwriter designation, or CLU. It involved courses of home study that zeroed in on the nitty-gritty of life insurance, taxes, and the like. The CLU designation would give them a prestigious status in the life insurance community. Only the very top agents achieved this, they were told.

Michael's training went well. While his understanding of the different types of policies was a little confusing at first, after being exposed to the business for a few days and having existing agents come and talk to new agents, it started to make sense. It became clear that the company wanted them to sell whole life insurance rather than term insurance. Of course, it was drilled into them, as trainees, that they would be working on commission. As a result, they would only be paid when they sold a policy and it was approved, and they would make significantly more money by selling whole life rather than term coverage.

As the training was concluding, the trainees were instructed to make a list of family members and friends who were working and whom they could approach to test their sales skills. Michael had no trouble preparing his list, and the first name on it was Favio, his Uncle Spiffy.

Michael had prepared his presentation for his uncle with great care. He had run it by his supervisor several times, fine-tuning it, and as a result, was ready with the answers to the anticipated questions. The proposal was for a $50,000 whole life policy.

Michael called his uncle and asked if they could have lunch. They met at a friend's restaurant, and Michael told him about his new job. After chatting as they ate, Michael proceeded to tell him about the training he had undergone and asked if he could show him something. Of course, Favio said, "Sure."

"Have you ever considered life insurance?" Michael asked.

The answer was, "No."

With that, Michael launched into his well-rehearsed presentation on the pros of life insurance and why everyone should have the protection it offered. He ended by telling his uncle that he could have that protection for his wife for only fifty-eight dollars per month.

Pausing, Michael said, "What do you think?"

Favio wrestled in his mind with how to answer his nephew. He didn't want to hurt Michael's feelings, and he really wanted him to succeed in his career. But he couldn't, in all good conscience, let him think that this was what he should do with the rest of his life. "Mikey," he said, "I think the world of you, and I would do anything to help you succeed, but I need to tell you something. You can do okay selling life insurance, but of more value, in my opinion, is the sales training that you have received and the experience you will gain in the life insurance industry. Once you have a couple of months or so under your belt, I suggest that you sit down and think, 'Is this really what I want to do with my life?' You could consider another sales position like selling real estate. While you are involved in this business, meet everyone you can and ask questions of everyone. Try to get as much knowledge about the industry as you can. It will help you later on. Now, where do I sign?"

Mike was thrilled. His first sale! His uncle didn't let him down. Spiffy brought out his chequebook and said, "I don't like this monthly stuff. I want to pay year by year." Favio gave Mike his cheque and told him to fill in the amount.

Back at Michael's office, his superiors were thrilled. They treated him as if he were a soldier returning from battle. They heaped praise on him, telling him he was a natural. They gave him a number of files that were "orphaned accounts," explaining that these were clients who held policies, but their agents had left the business, so they were not being serviced. They explained further that he should call them, introduce himself, and set up meetings so he could meet them. "Once you sit down with them, you can do a review, get to know them, and see if they should have an additional or different type of coverage. Their lives have probably changed, and this is an opportunity for you to get some new sales." Michael thought it sounded great, so he spent several evenings calling and introducing himself and proposing a review of their current coverage. About 20 percent of the people were interested, and about 2 percent purchased new or better policies. He also contacted old friends and business acquaintances during the day. So all in all, he was pretty busy, and he was making a few sales.

There was a life insurance trade show at a hotel near the airport, and Michael decided to go and check it out. He found that it consisted of several life insurance companies and agencies that had set up booths to facilitate meeting agents and introducing themselves and their products. There were also industry speakers presenting on many relevant topics, such as taxation, retirement products, and annuities. Attendees could earn credits toward their ongoing education requirements if they were qualified CFPs or CLUs, which were professional designations in the industry.

As he walked through the exhibit booths, he heard, "Hey, Mike!" He looked, and to his surprise, there was a fellow he knew from high school. They hadn't been particularly close friends, but they had been together since grade 9. His name was Johnny Deitch.

"What's up, Johnny?" Mike said as he walked over to see him.

"A friend of mine, Grant Bonesteel, and I decided to set ourselves up as brokers after we were licensed," Johnny explained. "We set up an MGA, so we are free to sell any life insurance company's products. We are looking for licensed agents to join us. What're you up to, Mikey?"

"Just plugging away with a company here in the city, and I'm enjoying it. What is an MGA?"

"It stands for 'master general agent.' It means we can do a lot better for you than you are probably doing with your current company. Let's meet for drinks and dinner tonight. You can meet Grant, and we'll explain everything to you."

"Great."

Rendezvousing after the show, Mike found Johnny sitting with a fellow who was a little older than him, Mike guessed. They were both heavy-set fellows. Johnny had very pale skin, straight black hair, a round face, and cheeks that would make a chipmunk envious. Grant was taller. He wore glasses and had wavy brown hair. He had a very serious face and piercing eyes. He came across as a different type of person to Mike. They were introduced, and Grant immediately took over the conversation.

"Johnny was telling me about you and that you are working for a company here in Toronto. We did the same until we realized that there was a better way, and we make more money. You're in a closed shop now, so you only have their products to sell. We, in our MGA, can source all companies' products to get the best and cheapest for our clients. We are here looking for agents who want to get out of their closed shop and expand their horizons. You can make more money and be your own boss. You hungry? I'm starved. Let's order dinner and talk while we eat. You want a drink first?" Mike nodded yes. "Wine or hard stuff?"

"A single malt with ice wouldn't go amiss."

Their drinks came, and they ordered their meals, then ate and continued chatting.

"We're paying," Grant announced as the meal came to an end. "Having our own business, we can write it off as a business expense," he explained. "After what I've told you, are you interested in joining us?"

"I'll really have to think about it, but yes, I am very interested," was Michael's response. "Great to see you again, Johnny, and to meet you, Grant. I'll give you a shout when I make some decisions." Michael left it at that.

$ $ $

THE NEXT DAY, Mike went for a long drive in the country, stopping to sit under a huge maple tree on the side of a farmer's field. It was just on the other side of Brampton. He thought over what he was doing and what lay ahead for him. He remembered what his uncle had told him: "With your personality, you may want to take your sales training and put it to better use, like working in real estate." He had realized that selling life insurance was a tough go, as very few people actually believed they needed the protection it provided. It was usually young mothers who wanted it for their families should something happen to their husbands. *I think Uncle Spiffy is right,* he thought.

Arriving back at his parents' house, where he was still living in the basement, he called his uncle. "I've been thinking about what you told me, and you are right. I can't see myself spending my working years trying to sell life insurance. You mentioned real estate. Do you know any real estate brokers that I could talk to?"

"Of course. I'll ask around and call you back tomorrow."

$ $ $

WAKING THE NEXT morning and waiting to hear from his uncle, he decided to go for coffee after breakfast. He didn't want to quit the life insurance business until he had fully explored and was comfortable with the real estate angle. That wouldn't happen until he heard from his uncle, so he headed out.

Wheeling into a neighbourhood restaurant, he was just opening his car door when he heard someone call his name. Turning, he saw Sarah, a girl he had met and shared some classes with at college. He waved and went over to see what she was up to. In the process, he was introduced to her friend, Rose Habowski. He invited them to join him for coffee.

They ordered coffee, and Sarah told him about her adventures. He was listening with some interest, but he kept glancing across the table at Rose. She had fairly short light-brown hair bordering on red and a nice smile, and she was a couple of inches shorter than his five feet ten inches. She had a lovely oval-shaped face and a pug nose. They continued chatting about things in general, and when their coffee was done, the girls told him that they had better get going.

"Gee, that's too bad," he said. "I'm considering a career change and wanted to see what you thought. I was going to get us another coffee."

"I have to go and meet my mother," Sarah told him. "She is waiting for me to take her shopping."

Rose looked over, smiling at him, and said jokingly, "Well if you are buying, I'm good to stay."

"Sure, I'll buy," he answered.

They ended up talking for two hours, and as lunchtime was approaching, Michael asked, "Would you like to have lunch?"

Rose had told him during their conversation that she was working part-time for a veterinarian. "I'm working at one, and I have to go home and change, so I'd better pass," she told him.

"Okay, you can take a rain check if you like. Can I drive you home?"

"I don't want to put you out. I can catch the bus."

"No problem, I'll take you and then drive you to work to be sure you won't be late. I don't want anyone to think that I made you late," he said, laughing.

After dropping her off, he drove home and made himself a peanut butter sandwich. There was a note from his mother saying that his uncle had called and was waiting to hear from him. Upon returning the call, Favio told him, "I've spoken to a friend of mine who has his own real estate company, and he will meet you at three this afternoon." He then gave him the broker's name, address, and telephone number. "I suggest you call and confirm. Okay?"

"That's perfect. Many thanks. You are an amazing uncle," he added before he made the call.

Arriving at the address just before three, Michael saw the National City Realty sign on the small building. He entered and was greeted by the receptionist and shown to the broker's office. "Vincenco Genova, Broker" was on the sign on the door. Entering a large office, Michael was greeted by a short, slightly overweight middle-aged gentleman. He was balding and was trying to hide it by combing the hair from the side of his head, which he had let grow long, over the bald area.

"Hi. Have a seat. You can call me Vinnie," he said, pointing to a chair on the other side of his desk. "Your uncle said you were thinking about a career in real estate. Tell me about your selling experience."

"I'm currently in the life insurance business as an agent, and they trained me" was the reply.

"Have you sold anything?"

Mike told him about the policies he had sold and how it made him feel. They continued talking for a good hour, discussing Mike's plans and ambitions, the real estate market, how good agents succeeded, how the commissions worked, and what Mike could expect working in Vinnie's office.

For the second time that day, Mike really felt good about what lay before him. He had a really good feeling about his time with Rose but had put it to the back of his mind and focused totally on his current meeting. Vinnie covered everything from advertising to commissions. They finished at six-thirty, and Vinnie asked him to return at nine the following morning to meet the team and get himself enrolled in the real estate agents' course if he decided to proceed.

As they shook hands, Mike said, "You won't be disappointed. I'm really looking forward to this as my professional career."

Heading home on a high, his mind went back to Rose. *She is great, a good conversationalist, very level-headed, and from a Polish background,* he thought. She had graduated from high school in the city and had found a job with a local vet as his helper. She was working part-time but had commenced taking night school courses with a view to becoming a veterinarian's assistant. She was nice looking. She dressed well and seemed to be very interested in him. She laughed at his jokes, and they had obviously hit it off.

Mike took his real estate agent course and passed with a good mark. He joined Vinnie's brokerage and started his new career. He had heard somewhere in his travels that he should try to make himself stand out from all the other real estate agents. Giving it some thought, he decided to start wearing a black western-style hat as a visual trademark. His hope was that people would relate the hat to him and thus remember him.

Vinnie took out ads in a couple of local papers, announcing that Mike was joining the office, welcoming him, and inviting people who were looking to buy or sell to call him. In the photo they ran, he was wearing his new hat. Mike ordered his new business cards and some flyers that could be slipped into the mail slots of homes in the neighbourhoods where he and Vinnie had decided he should concentrate his marketing. Everything featured a photo of him wearing his trademark hat. He also took as many opportunities as he could to be the agent on duty in the evenings and on weekends. This gave him an opportunity to meet potential clients who walked into the office.

His first sale came within a few weeks when a young couple came into the office on a Saturday morning, looking to purchase their first home. Mike had done what he had been taught to do: establish a rapport with them, determine if they had good credit and what they could afford, determine what they were hoping to find and which neighbourhoods they were interested in, and finally, start showing them homes that fit their criteria. It worked beautifully. They fell in love with the second house he showed them. They put in an offer, and it was accepted. Spiffy was right: selling real estate was much more rewarding than life insurance.

The next day, he made a point of calling Johnny Deitch out of courtesy and telling him that he had made a career change and what he was doing. Johnny told him he was surprised and happy for him. He went on to suggest, "Once you get into the swing of things, the three of us should get together for a chat. Grant has been exploring an idea that could provide an amazing opportunity for us, and it is right up your alley."

Rose didn't have a car, so Mike would pick her up after work and give her a ride home. This invariably resulted in going for dinner and spending an evening together, which was his plan. He really liked her, and she was very interested in and supportive of his plans. He realized that she was not overly social and was not looking for an overly active social life. Rose told Michael that her family had Polish roots and that her grandparents had left just before the First World War, settling in the Kitchener area. Her grandfather had been in the printing business in Kraków and had no trouble getting a job. When he and his wife arrived in Canada, they had two children: a son, Rose's father, and a daughter. Her aunt had moved to the US after she finished her schooling and had hoped to get work as an actress in Hollywood. While she had had the occasional bit part as an extra, her day job was as a waitress in a restaurant near the Strip. Her father had stayed in the Kitchener area and taken an apprenticeship to become a plumber. He was a single parent and had little contact with her mother. He tended to be somewhat stubborn and pigheaded and had trouble working with other people. Starting his own business, he made a living, but apart from owning his own home and his vehicle, he did not accumulate any significant amount of wealth.

Rose's mother, on the other hand, was a primary school teacher, and over the years, she had kept in touch with her daughter. Her name was Mary McNeil, and she lived and taught school in Downsview.

When Rose had been finishing primary school, she had been invited to a graduation dance. Her heart had been set on going, but her father had absolutely forbade it. This had led to a serious fight in which he'd threatened her. Not knowing what to do, Rose had telephoned her mother the next day while her father was at work. Upon hearing what had happened, her mother had driven to Kitchener and brought Rose back to live with her. Her father had not seemed to mind, as it had taken the responsibility of raising a teenage daughter by himself off his shoulders. They had virtually no contact with him. Under her mother's influence and guidance, she had grown up to be a very well-adjusted young lady.

She had also told Michael that she had always had a pet cat when she was growing up and loved it immensely. While in high school, she volunteered at the local humane society after school and on weekends. During her last year, she met a local veterinarian who came to look after the shelter's animals, and Rose asked him if he needed someone to help him in his practice. She was an attractive, well-spoken, and outgoing young lady. Her love for animals was very apparent. He liked what she was doing at the shelter and offered her a job on weekends. When school was over, she started working as a summer student for him, and this developed into a full-time position. She was now looking for a new position, as her current employer had told her that his practice did not generate sufficient income for him to afford a full-time assistant, although he wished it did. He said he would give her a good recommendation.

She had a feeling that Michael was going to do well in the real estate business, and in three months, their engagement was announced. Rose saw how supportive his parents and his aunt and uncle were of her husband-to-be. She was impressed by the family's accomplishments.

When they talked about their marriage, Rose told him that she would be happy to go to a Justice of the Peace and have a civil marriage. She told him that she would be embarrassed because the bride's parents usually hosted and paid for at least part of the cost of the celebration. She went on to say that her mother did not have that kind of money and that her father would have no interest in anything to do with her wedding. When Michael told his parents, they would have none of it. They had the young couple set the date, and then they organized and paid for the celebration. And so, five months later, in September of 1976, they were married. As a wedding present, Clemente and Yolanda gave them a honeymoon in Italy and an apartment in one of their buildings.

As neither of the young newlyweds had been to Italy, they were totally surprised and thrilled by what awaited them. Michael's Uncle Luigi met them at the Florence airport and took them home, where they met his father's parents, who were his grandparents. There was a great celebration and an amazing meal. After spending a few days touring around Tuscany and getting a feel for the area, they returned to Florence, and after a few days, they took the train to Venice. Then, after marvelling at the canals and the ancient buildings, they took the train down to Rome, where they spent an additional three days. They then flew back from Rome to Toronto and moved into their new fourplex apartment.

Rose, with her current employer's help, soon found a vet assistant position in a large vet practice a few miles from the apartment. She was quite happy. Mike gave her his car and leased himself a new BMW. He told Rose it would be good for his image to have a prestigious car, and he could write it off, being a self-employed real estate agent. Wanting Michael to become successful, she didn't object to his new purchase, although deep down, she thought it was frivolous. She asked him if they could afford it, and he assured her it wasn't an issue.

His exact words were, "Don't worry about it."

So she didn't.

Mike did okay in his job. He loved talking to people and sharing his stories and experiences with them. He joined a Rotary Club and enjoyed participating in the various projects the club undertook. He had a tendency not to follow through with clients, however. After showing them a property and deeming that they were interested, he would ask if they wanted to discuss it themselves or think it over before deciding to make an offer. As a result, it seemed that his sales only came about when his clients asked him to complete the transaction. He did not seem comfortable guiding them through what they had done and reinforcing their decision to close the deal. It was almost as if he didn't want to put them on the spot by suggesting that they take the final step, whether it be making an offer or signing a new listing. As long as his uncle and father were sending people to him, things were okay, but certainly he was not meeting the expectations that Vinnie had for him.

# CHAPTER TWENTY-ONE

ERTOLLINI CONSTRUCTION CONTINUED to grow and was now recognized as one of the top medium-sized construction companies in the Toronto area. Clemente headed the very busy construction division and had a large staff working under his direction. He was viewed as a very good and fair boss. He demanded quality and made a point of spending Friday afternoons in the field, randomly inspecting the work that was in progress to ensure it was up to the company standards. Some of the workers did not appreciate him checking their work, but most accepted it and were pleased when he gave them a positive "thank you" for their efforts.

Yolanda, having left the hotel, was now working from home, managing the family's finances and the apartment buildings. They had added another six-unit apartment and a fourplex. The children were now on their own, working in their chosen careers. They were doing well. While they would have liked Ana to be a little closer, they knew she had grown to love the north. She was happily married and was enjoying her career as a nurse. They could not have asked for more.

In 1995, Clemente felt that he and his wife needed a break from their busy lives in Toronto. It was the year of their forty-fifth anniversary, so he had, as a surprise for her and inspired by his son and daughter-in-law's experience in Italy, booked a transatlantic repositioning cruise from New York to Venice. They were scheduled to depart in early May, and upon their arrival in Venice, they would rent a car and visit their families in Bucine. As neither of them had really seen that much of Italy, he decided they could tour the old country for three weeks before flying home from Rome.

He thought they could decide where to go once they were on the ground. He gave Michael the task of looking after the buildings and arranged with Marie to look after the financial side of things. He then took Yolanda for dinner at Antonio's to spring the surprise.

When he told her, she didn't know what to say, as her mind filled instantly with a jumble of thoughts. Then, looking at him, she started saying what she was thinking. "We've never been on a ship before, and what happens if we don't like it? What about your job? What about the apartments? What would happen if one of us gets sick while we are travelling? How much did it cost, and can we afford it? What if something happens to the kids or their families while we're away?"

Clemente heard her out and laughed. He had fully expected that reaction from his wife, as she tended to be a worrier when she was facing uncertainty. "I've looked after everything," he assured her. "The ship can carry twelve hundred passengers and has medical staff on board. There are lots of restaurants and activities if we wish to participate. There will be shows and entertainment every night. It's a holiday, so we can do what we want when we want. We'll only be on the ship just over a week." Then he went on to tell her of the arrangements he had made with Michael and Marie to look after things while they were gone.

Knowing her husband would have everything looked after and well-thought-out, she smiled and said, "You are the best. I can hardly wait to go. Thank you for being so thoughtful. That's why I love you." And with that, she gave him a great big kiss. They were caught a little off guard when the staff and owners of the restaurant all started to clap.

The children were happy and excited for them. They knew that their parents had worked hard building their lives in Canada. Apart from their summers at the cottage, they had never done anything solely for themselves. As the trip approached, Yolanda became more at ease with it and started to show her enthusiasm.

Before they knew it, they were in New York. They had booked a hotel room for the night and would board the ship at their leisure the following morning. Boarding commenced at 10 a.m., so they took time for a quick look around a bit of the city before heading to the ship. She departed at three that afternoon, and Yolanda and Clemente were thrilled to get pictures of each other with the Statue of Liberty in the background as they sailed past.

Sailing across the Atlantic was nice. The sea was choppy and the wind a little cool, but the ship was equipped with stabilizers, which resulted in a very smooth crossing. The days were generally sunny with a few clouds, and the sunsets were amazing.

As promised, there was entertainment and movies every evening and lots of wonderful music from which to choose. To Yolanda's delight, a group of five young Polish musicians played classical pieces every other evening, and they attended every performance. She could not get over how much she was enjoying this time away with her husband with no obligations or interruptions. Just the two of them enjoying their well-earned holiday and each other.

The meals were good and offered a nice variety, and while the drinks were mostly overpriced, Clemente found a nice red house wine that was fairly reasonably priced. They found themselves sitting in the sun on parts of the deck that were protected from the wind. The ship made stops at the Azores, Lisbon, Cádiz, and Málaga before arriving in Venice. They took tours at each stop, enjoying the sights in each of the different cities.

Sailing through the Strait of Gibraltar at night, they saw lights from both Europe and Africa on either side of the ship as they entered the Mediterranean Sea. The following morning, they awoke to a bright, warm, sunny day with no wind. They, and most of the other passengers, headed to the upper decks after breakfast and spent the rest of the day lounging in deck chairs under the sun. The weather remained constant until the voyage ended in Venice.

Disembarking, they were totally surprised to find Luigi waiting for them. He had added a few pounds and lost a little hair, and he looked a little older, but it was undoubtedly Clemente's older brother. "*Ciao, benvenuto a casa. Come state il viaggio?*"[9] he said in greeting.

---

9  "Hello, welcome home. How was the trip?"

"*Assolutamente meraviglioso,*"[10] they replied in unison and then laughed, saying, "*Come stai?*"

"*Eccellente.*"[11] Then Luigi went on to tell them that the two families got together and decided that he should meet them and bring them home. "Give me your luggage," he said to his sister-in-law and loaded their luggage into the back of the vehicle.

They drove off, heading for Highway A13 toward Florence. Luigi had non-stop questions for them. Driving along, they noticed how different it was to drive in Italy. The drivers seemed much more aggressive. They were happy to be home and told Luigi how much they appreciated him collecting them. Then it was their turn to ask him questions about the families, the farm, his life, his wife, and their family. They couldn't believe how different the land and buildings were from Canada. As they drove, Luigi explained that they had arranged for a rental vehicle for them to use while they were visiting and that he would drive them to the Rome airport when they were going back.

The visit was everything they could have wished for. The weather was great, with only one rainy day. They were thrilled to feel the vibe in Tuscany with its grapevines, olive orchards, cypress trees, hills—several with their old castles—and beautiful stone houses and buildings. The air was very special, and they felt right at home, although things had certainly changed over the past thirty years. Family, friends, visits, food, great wine, food, travel, and more food and questions were the order of the day. They fielded lots of questions about Canada and their life there.

They had three weeks, and they made the most of their time. It was wonderful for them to see everyone again and tour their old country. They had been to Florence and Rome on school visits, so they travelled south to Sicily, stopping in Abruzzi to visit Pasquali's family and then back up to Venice before visiting Milan and Turin. They then returned to Tuscany.

On their last evening, when they were alone, they wondered what their lives would be like had they stayed in Tuscany. They wondered about the

---

10  "Absolutely wonderful."

11  "Excellent."

opportunities their children would have had, had they remained. They both agreed that, while they loved Italy, immigrating to Canada had been the right choice.

They were sure that they had gained ten pounds each. The food had been non-stop. As she was packing her suitcase, Yolanda felt a small twinge in the left side of her chest. *Hmm,* she thought. *I must have pulled a muscle lifting the suitcases these past few weeks.*

# CHAPTER TWENTY-TWO

Y OLANDA AND CLEMENTE watched with pride as their family continued to grow and develop.

Marie was well settled, and her practice was thriving. She kept in touch with her friend Julie from Ferguson's and so was kept informed about the happenings at her former employer. During her first week of opening her doors, several local business owners dropped in to welcome her to the neighbourhood. One Thursday, a middle-aged lady came in and asked if she could see Marie. In answer to Sonia the receptionist's question, she replied, "I'm Monica Penny, and I'm the manager of the local chamber of commerce." So Sonia knocked on Marie's office door and said, "There is a Monica Penny here who is the manager of the chamber of commerce to see you."

"That's fine. Show her in," was the answer.

Sonia returned and said, "Ms. Gallorini can see you. Would you like a cup of coffee or tea?"

"Coffee would be nice with a little cream," was the reply, and Sonia stepped aside so the visitor could enter the office.

Marie smiled at the visitor, saying, "Hello. Please have a seat." She showed Monica to the meeting table that sat to the left of her desk. As they sat, her assistant brought in a tray with two cups, a jug of cream, and a carafe of coffee and set it on the table.

"Thank you," Monica said to Sonia before turning her attention to Marie and telling her, "My name is Monica Penny, and I am the manager of the local chamber of commerce. Are you familiar with our organization?"

"I've certainly heard of the chamber, but I'm not exactly sure what you do. I know your membership is made up of local business people."

"Yes, most are owners, and we advocate for them. As an example, you have just established your new business, and as things move along, you find something in the neighbourhood that doesn't meet your expectations or needs. Say the parking for your clients is not adequate. So, if you are a member of our group, you can bring it up with your fellow business owners at our next meeting. As a group, we will listen to you, explain to you why the parking is what it is, and if, during this process, we can see that your thoughts or concerns are valid and things need to be improved or altered, we will undertake to study the situation with the objective of developing a presentation that we can take before the local council to address the matter. We have dealt with a number of things, from the timing of street lights to garbage collection on the main business streets. We don't just deal with the local council—it could be any organization in the community, like the Police Services Board or the YMCA."

"I see," Marie answered. "How many businesses are represented?"

"Well, we have sixty-four members, and from that number, we select six representatives to sit on our board. We meet monthly, and if required, we can schedule extra meetings. The cost to become a member is seventy-five dollars per year for a small business like yours."

"Well, you have certainly given me something to think about. When is your next meeting?"

"Actually, it is this evening at seven. That is why I wanted to see you this morning—to invite you to come as my guest and meet the board. Will that work for you, Ms. Gallorini?"

"Yes, and call me Marie. I think that would be great, and I appreciate you thinking about me. I'll just stay here for a bite of dinner and then come to the meeting. Where is it being held?"

"We hold it in the Bank of Nova Scotia boardroom, just down the street. Why don't I pick you up at, say, a quarter to seven, and we can go together?"

"That will be fine, and I look forward to it. Now, tell me about yourself while we have our coffee," Marie said as she poured them each a cup. She was thinking, *this will be a great way to meet the local business owners and see if any of them might need our services.*

They chatted for about three-quarters of an hour, and then Monica left. She returned at a quarter to seven, and they proceeded to the local Bank of Nova Scotia, where a security guard let them into the building and to the boardroom. The members of the board were there, and after introductions, the chair, Thomas McKay, called the meeting to order and officially welcomed Marie. They certainly made her feel welcome, and she was interested to see the interactions among the various members. There was a convenience store owner, a druggist, a building contractor, a lawyer, and a beauty salon owner. During a coffee break, each member came and introduced themselves to her and welcomed her to the district.

Once they met her and learned of her background and experience, it was only a matter of time, and with Monica's encouragement, she joined the board of directors. Several of the businesses became clients, and a number became friends. A couple of single men invited her out for dinner, and she accepted their invitations in the interest of grooming them as clients. She brought a new sense of authority to the board, and it certainly paid off in their relationship with the municipal officials with whom they worked. When, for example, the chamber brought the idea of forming a citizens' patrol organization to the Police Services Board, it was implemented almost immediately. They proposed having volunteer citizens do routine patrols and door checks for businesses, thus freeing up police resources to focus on more pressing issues. Marie had provided a cost-benefit analysis for implementing it. Of course, the citizens were equipped with police radios so they could be in touch with the dispatcher, and they never involved themselves in what they saw. They observed and reported.

An annual provincial meeting was held in Ottawa, and at the urging of several members, Marie agreed to attend. It provided her with the opportunity to meet and mingle with the provincial executives and members from other parts of the province. A dinner was held on the second night, and she met several people during the pre-dinner reception. At one point, a gentleman introduced himself, and they were chatting when they were called to dinner, so they went into the dining room and sat together. He was a single fellow in his early forties. He had short brown hair and a rather large nose. His name was Jim Quirk, and he was from Windsor, where he ran a private business school. As they talked and shared stories, they were very uninhibited and comfortable with each other. She enjoyed his sense of humour, and he enjoyed her forthright approach to life. After the dinner, they had an after-dinner liqueur, and as the evening was winding down, he invited her to his room to have another liqueur from his mini-bar. She agreed, and they ended up spending the night together. In the morning, she returned to her own room to shower and change. She felt good that there were no ongoing obligations or commitments by either party as a result of their encounter.

Marie stayed involved with the chamber of commerce for several years, and each year she attended the provincial annual meeting. She was pleasantly surprised to meet up with Jim again, and afterward, she joked, "We have to stop meeting like this," as they again visited his room for a nightcap from the mini-bar. She was starting to feel like it was time to move on from the chamber when the president asked if she would be willing to sit on the provincial board. After giving it some thought and determining the time commitment, she agreed.

Marie Gallorini, CA, became Gallorini and Company, Chartered Accountants, when one of her juniors, Danilo, received his designation. The practice grew and developed, as did her standing in the community. When she and her former co-worker Julie met for their regular lunch together several years later, her friend told her how she got the feeling that the partners, on the whole, were impressed and some a little envious of her success.

$   $   $

DAVE AND ANA had two children: a boy, Leo, and a girl, Suzie. They were both born in Yellowknife. They left the north in the spring of 1993 after spending fifteen very enjoyable years in the Northwest Territories. Dave transferred to the E Division in Surrey, British Columbia, as a detective inspector in the criminal investigation department. He loved the work and soon settled into his new surroundings and job.

They bought a house in Richmond, and Ana decided to continue working, so she applied and was welcomed by the Vancouver General Hospital as the new head nurse of the ICU. The children, who were fourteen and sixteen, attended a junior high school close to home, and a

Filipino nanny was hired to be in the house for them until their parents returned home. She also did the housekeeping and quite often prepared meals for the family. With both parents working, it turned out to be a wise decision to hire her. She was single and in her mid-twenties, and her name was Wendy.

Dave loved his new job and was happy to get involved with the force's work in the lower mainland. His reputation preceded his arrival, and he was immediately accepted as a key member of the CID team. He loved the work, and his methodical, disciplined approach was respected by his colleagues. Ana had taken over as the family money manager and, thanks to her mother's training, was very good at putting money away. She enjoyed her work in the hospital but looked forward to the day she could retire and pursue other interests. She had always thought it would be nice to learn how to knit beautiful sweaters for herself and her family and to do some serious gardening.

$ $ $

ONE FRIDAY AFTERNOON, after Dave had been in his new job for a few months, his telephone rang. Picking it up, he answered, "Hello?"

A voice asked, "Dave, is that you?"

"Yes," he responded, "who's this?"

"It's Cal, Cal Alexander. How are you doing? I heard that you left the north and settled here, and I thought I'd better touch base."

Dave's mind immediately flashed back to the Eastern Arctic, where he and Cal worked together running the RCMP detachment in Pangnirtung for a couple of years. They had become good friends and knew that they could rely on each other if the need arose.

"Where are you, Cal? Can we get together? We have to catch up, and I want to introduce you to my family."

"Well, we are now living in a small town in the interior of the province called Naramata, just a few miles north of Penticton. We are about four and a half hours from Vancouver. We'd love to see you and your family. Any chance you could come up for Thanksgiving? Kathy would love to meet you and your gang, and we can put you up here. We have lots of room, and the kids can sleep in the lower level, where we have two bedrooms and a family room."

"Sounds great. Let me talk to Ana and make sure she has nothing planned. She's working at Vancouver General, and I don't know if she's set anything up with her colleagues."

"Okay, I'll give you my number. Let me know when you find out. We have a lot of catching up to do." David took down the number, thanked his old friend, and hung up. Over the years, the family had taken many holidays, and the children were always included. They returned to Hawaii several times and went to Disneyland, Knott's Berry Farm, and Universal Studios in California. Dave loved fishing and had done it at every opportunity in the north. The fishing was particularly good near the community of Pangnirtung, where the Arctic char were amazing. Quite often, the pilots of the Northern Division took training days. This undoubtedly involved a trip to an obscure lake, and several off-duty friends would be included.

Arriving home, he found Ana already there and getting dinner organized. Friday nights were always casual, with the least amount of preparation possible. He was greeted with, "Oh, hi. You're home. How about ordering a pizza for supper?"

"That would be perfect. I'll call. You wouldn't believe who called just before I was leaving." Ana looked at him and shrugged. "Cal Alexander. You remember I told you about our time in the Eastern Arctic together? He and his wife are living just outside Penticton, and they've invited us to spend Thanksgiving with them."

"The kids too?"

"Yep. They would have their own rooms on the lower level, just off the family room."

"Sure, why not? It would be fun to see a little more of the province and great for you to hook up with an old friend."

Dave was thrilled, and after he ordered the pizza, he called Cal and told him they accepted their invitation. Dave had taught the kids to fish, and they loved camping out with him. While Ana was always invited, she usually passed, saying she preferred to stay at home and, as she said, "sleep in my own bed." Dave had heard of the Penticton area and knew it was at the bottom of Okanagan Lake. He thought it could be a great place to go fishing and was interested in checking it out.

Ana was a little apprehensive about the upcoming trip. For years, she had seen Dave go out with the boys and come home drunk. It seemed that when he got together with his buddies, the alcohol flowed freely, and Dave inevitably drank too much. When this happened, they were smart enough to call the detachment for a ride home, but it bothered Ana to see this side of him. As they were leaving Yellowknife, she had confronted him because she was pretty sure this behaviour in his new position would not be tolerated. So she had told him, "Over the years, I have seen you go out with the boys and come home drunk. I didn't like seeing you do this but tolerated it because I thought it was some form of release. But when you start your new job, I think you should look at yourself and decide that you are not going to let this happen again. I don't think it will be tolerated, and if it is, I'm sure your career will suffer."

Thinking about it for a minute, he had looked at her and said, "Yes, you are right. I don't know why I did it, but it must have been some mental idea that I could do it with my buddies and no one would judge us or care. Obviously, I was wrong."

"Well," Ana continued now, "I guess I'm worried that if you get together with Cal and start reminiscing about the old days, that you might start drinking again."

"Well, you would be right to think that, except there is one thing that will keep it from happening." He paused for a moment before continuing. "Cal is an alcoholic. I've seen him at his worst when we were together in the Eastern Arctic. Then he met a young fish and wildlife officer who worked for the government, and he, too, was an alcoholic, but he had joined AA. After meeting and getting to know Cal, he took him under his wing. He introduced him to the program and became his mentor, or as they call it in Alcoholics Anonymous, his sponsor. It was a bit of a trick since the meetings were held in Frobisher Bay, so they attended them when they could but otherwise participated over the radio telephone. Cal confided to me that it saved his career and probably his life, so you don't have to worry. And," he paused again, "I hereby give you my word that I will never let that happen again."

Then, wrapping their arms around each other, Dave added, "I would be a fool to do anything that could harm you or our family."

He and Ana both made arrangements to take the Friday before the Thanksgiving long weekend off so they could use the extra day to drive to Naramata. They arrived just after four and were welcomed with open arms by Cal and Kathy. They had an amazing visit, and Dave's family and Kathy were totally engrossed by the stories the two old friends shared about their time with the Inuit in the Eastern Arctic. Dave had asked Cal about the fishing, and as a result, they and Leo took a trip just south of Penticton to check out Skaha Lake. Dave was very impressed and quite interested when he learned that the fishing was good.

The following summer, the family rented a cottage off Skaha Lake for three weeks. It turned out to be an amazing experience with fishing, campfires, swimming, and hiking. Ana had a large deck on which she could sit and read while having a full view of the lake. They fell in love with it.

Leo had joined the local Air Cadet squadron as soon as they arrived in BC, and he attended a two-week cadet camp in Alberta. He left a week before his parents and sister headed to the lake and was thrilled to join the family at the cottage when it was done. He was studious and outgoing. He was just under six feet tall, with black hair done in a brush cut. He had many of his mother's features, and Ana could see her father in him. Leo enjoyed the cadets, which was an organization that encouraged the young members to think for themselves. The older and more experienced cadets taught and trained the younger ones. As they developed within the organization, they were given military ranks. All cadets had the opportunity to attend a summer camp somewhere in the country.

After four years, Leo became a Flight Sergeant, and that summer he went to a summer flying school, where he earned his private pilot's licence. He was a good student, and while he was never the class leader, he was a hard worker and did quite well. Upon graduation, he enrolled in engineering at the University of British Columbia and graduated four years later. He commenced work with a civil engineering firm and soon received his designation as a professional engineer. He loved flying and would quite often rent a plane and travel around the province during his time off.

Suzie, on the other hand, was on the quiet side. She was a nice-looking young woman with her mother's black hair but her father's looks. She didn't mind being by herself; although, at her mother's encouraging, she joined Brownies and Girl Guides. In her second year of high school, she took a summer job washing dishes in a local restaurant. The following summer, she started working in the kitchen. Her parents had taught her how to cook the fish they caught, and she became quite good at it. It soon became apparent that she had a knack for cooking, and upon her completion of high school, she took a culinary skills course at a local community college. Upon graduation, she was hired to work as a junior chef in a major hotel's kitchen. She loved the work and developed into a very good chef. After several years, she was hired as the head chef of a new restaurant that was opening in Vernon.

After his talk with his wife about drinking, David never had more than one drink on any occasion, be it a party or a quiet dinner with his lovely wife.

Ana and Dave saw their families periodically. They went to Toronto every other year for a family visit and visited Dave's parents in the alternate years. Because Dave's parents were closer, they visited Ana, Dave, and the kids two or three times a year, so the relationship was stronger than with Ana's family. Ana found his parents very welcoming and friendly. Dave had explained that his father, Dennis, had been in the military, so they had moved around over the years. He held the rank of Major upon his retirement and had served in an infantry regiment. He had risen through the ranks and had been promoted from Sergeant Major to a Second Lieutenant. He enjoyed being commissioned but never forgot his roots in the rank and enjoyed meeting and getting to know people. Dave's mother, Wilhelmina, was known as Minnie. She was from an Irish background, and her maiden name was O'Sullivan. She, like her husband, enjoyed people, and she loved her grandchildren. She and her daughter-in-law also became very close.

CHAPTER TWENTY-THREE

WITH THE THREE men running the company, Bertollini Construction Ltd. had grown and flourished in the steadily growing city of Toronto. They continued to do what they knew and did best: building homes and small- to medium-sized apartment buildings. The management team worked well together. The construction division was headed by Clemente and was very large. It was deemed prudent to contract engineers and architects when they were needed rather than hiring them as staff. The company was very profitable, and the shareholders were doing very well.

It was just a matter of time, however, until a larger construction group contacted Pasquali and invited him and his wife to a meeting in Palm Springs, California. It was the winter of 2000, and it was a good break from the Toronto winter. They were flown down first class, given a suite in the best hotel, and wined and dined while they got to know their hosts, Giuseppe and Lorenzo Salvador, also from Toronto. The Bertollinis learned that the Salvador family had come to Canada in the early 1930s, and like Bertollini Construction, their company had flourished and grown. Their speciality was building high-end executive homes. They were now looking to expand their business while staying in the residential market where they were known and respected.

Pasquali loved and was very proud of his business. He had built it himself over the years. He had hired the right people and trusted them to do their jobs. It had worked well. They put in long hours to keep things running profitably and smoothly. They had built a good name for themselves. Pasquali was, however, getting up in age. He was just about to turn seventy-five. His wife had suggested that he should look to sell the business so he could retire and enjoy the fruits of his labours and his garden. He knew she was right but needed to find a buyer who would not only pay what the company was worth but also have a good reputation.

In the late afternoon of the second day in Palm Springs, Pasquali was invited to sit down with his two hosts. The purpose of this meeting was to make him an offer for his business. His hosts were heaping praise on him and the company he had built. They highlighted all the positive things he and his team had done and the good reputation they had in the industry. Then they showed him what they intended to do with his company and why it would fit nicely into their organization. They told him that all the staff and middle managers would be kept, but of course, they would install their own management team. They then presented him with their offer.

Pasquali was thrilled with the offer, but being the shrewd businessman he was, he didn't show any emotion at all. He sat without saying anything for a few minutes, then frowned and said, "Before I give you an answer, I have to discuss it with the company directors."

Smiling, Giuseppe replied, "We expected that, so if you go next door, you can do so."

Not quite understanding but not wanting to show any sign of not being on top of things, Pasquali said, "Oh, good." He got up from his chair and went to the room next door. He was not sure but assumed they had set up some type of conference call back to Toronto. As he entered the room, he was dumbfounded. Sitting there waiting for him and smiling were his wife, Favio, and Clemente. Laughing at his surprise, Favio explained, "We were flown down this morning. The girls were taken out shopping, and we have been shown around by Lorenzo. He brought us to this adjoining room, told us what was happening, and then left."

Pasquali was pleased and impressed by the way the brothers had organized this. He told his partners about the offer and the fact that they would be installing their own management team. The four directors were in agreement that it was a very good offer. They decided they would be happy to leave the company in good hands and retire. That being done, Mrs. Bertollini and the three men returned to the adjoining room, and Pasquali announced, "We find your offer acceptable."

Then, they all stood and shook hands with the two brothers, and for the first time since they had started the process, the major shareholder, the president of the company, and the chair of the board all broke into gigantic smiles.

That evening, the three couples went for a private dinner at the best local Italian restaurant in town. Spiffy had made a few calls and set things up. There was a great deal of wine consumed. Many stories were told. There were laughs and there were tears.

It was over!

Clemente's family decided to have a surprise retirement dinner for him. They wanted to get it done quickly before Favio and Ana left. Marie called her sister Ana to see if she and her family could attend on fairly short notice, and Ana assured her that they would all be there. The arrangements were made with Antonio and Julie to book the entire restaurant for the evening two weeks hence.

They had told their father it was a farewell dinner for his aunt and uncle, so he was totally caught off guard when he arrived with Yolanda and was informed that it was for him. It was a lovely evening with great food and drink and lots of stories and memories shared. When he stood to thank everyone, he said how proud and happy he was to have not only an amazing wife, but an absolutely wonderful family. Then he added, "However, it would have never happened had it not been for my Uncle Favio and his amazing wife. Not only did he encourage us to come to this wonderful city, but he sent us the tickets as a wedding present. Once we arrived, they took us under their wing, looked out for us, and made sure we were looked after at every turn. We cannot thank them enough for what they have done for us and our children. We cannot begin to say how supportive and absolutely amazing they are. Would you fill your glasses, stand, and join me in saluting Favio and Ana?"

As everyone stood, he continued. "To the absolute best relatives anyone could ever ask for. Cheers." With that, everyone saluted the couple, drank a toast, and then the whole room broke out in clapping and offered their best wishes, including to Julie, Antonio, and their staff.

Favio and Ana departed for Italy the following week as planned. His parents had passed away a few years earlier, and his father had left the family house and a small vineyard to him. He and Ana sold their property in Toronto, gave their trailer in Sauble Beach to Clemente, and returned to Italy for their retirement. Pasquali and his wife decided to remain in their house in the city, where they had developed an amazing garden over the years. Clemente stayed on the job for two more weeks while he completed a detailed project-by-project briefing for the new chief of operations and his staff.

Clemente was now seventy-one years old, and he was starting to feel his age. He and his wife had a nice amount of cash invested in GICs and treasury bills. Their plan was to sell the apartment buildings and keep the money for retirement and, at Yolanda's suggestion, share some of it with their children. He had discussed it with Pasquali and Favio during their last dinner out.

While Yolanda had enjoyed managing the apartments, she too was beginning to feel her age. Clemente had noticed that, since their holiday, Yolanda was looking more tired than usual. She seemed to be resting more and going to bed earlier.

One night, while they were going to watch television, he said, "I'm wondering if we should be thinking about selling and moving up north."

She hesitated before replying, "Well, prices are good, and we could get something smaller with some land so we can garden. Where are you thinking? The Sauble Beach area? The land around Owen Sound looks nice. Spring is coming, and it would be a good time to start looking."

"Well, no, I was thinking that Collingwood would be closer for the kids to come and visit and for us to slip down to the city. I am thinking we should go have a look around to get a feel for the place. We really don't know anything about it. People that do have told me it is a very nice community, and it is on the water, which I think would be nice."

That weekend, they had Michael and Rose over for dinner. After dinner, while Rose helped her mother-in-law clear the table and wash the dishes, Michael joined his father in the family room and was told about their plans. He was excited for them and enthusiastic. "I'll get you an evaluation for the apartments and this house," he said. "I think you are going to be happy. The market is pretty good these days."

The girls joined them, and they discussed the Collingwood area and what property values were doing there.

First thing the next morning, Mike got to work on completing the evaluations and gathering the information needed to list his parents' house and apartments. That evening, he dropped in at his parents' house to show them the results of his work. They were quite pleasantly surprised and told him to proceed with the listing of their property. In answer to his mother's question, he told them that it could take a couple of months before the sales were completed.

The following morning, he briefed his boss on what was going on. To his total surprise, Vinnie said, "I think that my brothers and I would be interested in buying these. We were looking at setting up a partnership, and this would be a perfect fit. And, since we can do it all in-house, we would pass on the commissions to keep the price down. Of course, you will still get yours."

And so it was done, quickly and efficiently. When Marie was told, she knew she would have to decide if she wanted to remain in her apartment and start paying rent or move somewhere else.

Shortly after, Vinnie had a meeting with Mike and told him that things in the office were not working out the way he had hoped. He then suggested that Mike might fare better in a small town. He said that Mike was a great guy, and he thought he would flourish in a location where "the people could get to know you and you could quickly establish yourself in the town's real estate market."

Talking it over later, Mike and Rose decided that with his parents looking to leave the city, they would probably be better off leaving too. They had the fourplex and could rent out their apartment when they left. Mike said, "I think I could slip into the city once a week to check on things and get the rent cheques at the end of each month." He never did tell her about his conversation with Vinnie, as he wanted to avoid any hint that he had not been successful.

After looking around southern Ontario, their search took them to Fergus, a small town just north of Guelph on the Credit River. One of the local realtors had advertised in a real estate magazine that he was looking for an experienced agent to join his firm. The town had been settled by Scottish immigrants who chose a location where a river narrowed, resulting in water flow that was perfect for a woollen mill. The local rock was granite, and the Scottish masons used it to build houses and the mill. It was a very pretty town, and they decided to rent rather than buy so they could be sure it was right for them before investing in a house. Rose told him that when the time came to buy, she wanted a classic old stone home that she could renovate to her liking.

CHAPTER **TWENTY-FOUR**

IKE VISITED THE real estate firm and found it appealing. It was a small independent firm called Apex Realty, owned and operated by Jim Dielle. There was one other part-time realtor, and Jim was the broker. They were delighted to welcome a new agent who had city experience, and they hoped that he could use his contacts to bring more folks from the city to their town. When asked where he was planning to live—Jim was obviously looking for a sale—Mike answered, "We are thinking that we will rent until we get a feel for the community and know our way around. Can you recommend anything?" After a brief discussion about their likes and dislikes, Jim recommended a nice little two-bedroom house across town. It worked out for them, and the price was right, so they took it.

Rose visited a local veterinarian, Dr. Hickling. Once he checked out her references, he offered her a job as his assistant.

With everything in place, the move was made. Mike was the family money manager, and he informed Rose that there were a few things he needed to settle before they left the city.

All she or anyone else knew was that Mike had met a few times with the two fellows he had run into at a life insurance trade show a while back: Johnny and Grant. As a result of these meetings, he had invested in their newly formed discount mortgage company.

The concept was that their company used funds from a private lender, whom Mike suspected was primarily Johnny's grandmother. The money was, in turn, loaned out as mortgages to young couples buying homes. As the rates they offered were a touch better than the banks were offering, business had been brisk. Mike had invested some money in the scheme and was now recommending the cheaper mortgages to his clients. He was failing, however, to disclose his involvement in the company.

As he and Rose were in the process of leaving the city, the two partners had advised him that the business was in trouble. The private lender had pulled their money out. The problem was that the company couldn't meet its obligations to its clients, and there was a distinct possibility that they could be taken to court. If that happened, it would come out that Mike had steered clients to them without disclosing his interest in the company, thus exposing himself to the risk of being sued. They had borrowed what they could from the bank, but that still did not cover things.

Mike was faced with the task of covering his share of the company's shortfall. Being desperate and not wanting his family, and especially his wife, to know, he decided that his only option was to use all their money and assets to bail themselves out. This was what they had in savings, plus the commission he made from the sale of his parents' buildings, as well as the money he had received from the sale of the fourplex that they had given him as a wedding present. When all was said and done, they went to Fergus virtually broke. He had to give up his BMW because he could no longer afford the payments. He had to find a vehicle that was respectable but with a very low sticker price. His choices narrowed down to a five-year-old Ford four-door sedan or a ten-year-old Cadillac. He opted for the latter because he reasoned that the Cadillac name would make a better impression on potential clients.

When the vehicle swap happened, Rose knew something was up. "What aren't you telling me?" she demanded. Sitting down with her, he proceeded to tell her what had transpired. She was devastated. He attempted to justify it by saying, "It really looked like a great business opportunity, and I thought I could trust them. After all, I've known Johnny for quite a few years, and he seemed like a decent guy. How was anyone to know that when his grandmother died, Johnny would be left right out of her will? That was what they were counting on to keep things running."

Rose was not impressed. "As of this moment, I am going to start looking after the family finances, and you will give me every cheque you get."

Reluctantly, because he loved Rose and didn't want to threaten their marriage, he replied, "Yes, dear." He knew that he had disappointed Rose and that she had lost some respect for him, and he vowed to set things right.

Rose's job with the vet went very well, and with her past experience, she soon proved herself to be invaluable to his small animal practice. Dr. Hickling was a tall caring man with brownish curly hair and a bushy moustache, which distracted from his long face. Rose was great with clients, and their animals loved her as she was soft-spoken and always had a treat waiting for them. A few days after Rose started, Dr. Hickling invited the young couple to a welcoming dinner at a nice local restaurant. They chatted and shared stories and family backgrounds. It turned out that the doctor's family had come from the island of Islay, just off the coast of Scotland. When he found out that Mike was a scotch drinker, he introduced him to the pride of Islay Laphroaig single malt.

"It has a very peaty taste because the water of the island passes through miles of peat bogs. But," Dr. Hickling assured him, "after your first sip registers on your taste buds, subsequent sips feel like an old friend has dropped in for a visit." Chuckling, he continued, "The trick to enjoying any malt whisky is to add a few drops of water to open the flavours and to hold it in your mouth for a few seconds before you swallow." Mike asked about using soda or ice in the drink, and he was told in no uncertain terms that this was sacrilegious. That was that. Mike became a Laphroaig convert.

Mike joined several groups in Fergus, including the local Kiwanis club and the chamber of commerce. He found the pace of a smaller town quiet, and he always volunteered to be the agent on duty for Friday evenings and Saturdays. His training and experience served him well, and he started making a few sales. Rose told him again, "When there is enough in the bank for a down payment, I still want to get a nice, big, stone house that I can redo."

Smiling, he answered, "Yes, dear."

# CHAPTER TWENTY-FIVE

C LEMENTE AND YOLANDA talked it over and decided that they would look for a new property with a bit of land in the Collingwood area. They could build a new house if they couldn't find an older home that suited them, but their priority was the land. They wanted to be able to grow their vegetables and hoped they could find something with a few fruit trees. The Collingwood area was known for its multitude of apple orchards, and it wasn't that much of a drive to either the city or Sauble Beach. They didn't tell either of the girls about their plans, and while they had hinted to Michael that they might be looking at a move, they knew he and Rose had settled nicely into their new situation in Fergus.

Over the spring and early summer, Clemente and Yolanda took several trips to Collingwood and the surrounding area to the south and west of the community to get a feel for and learn about the area. It was obvious to Clemente that Collingwood used to be just a sleepy community with great ski hills just west of the town. Now, for people looking to retire from the Toronto area, this was a place that was very appealing to them.

During the last week in June, Clemente and Yolanda headed up to Collingwood. It was a cool day with a northwest wind. White clouds were scurrying across the sky like puffs of cotton balls. Clemente and Yolanda wore light jackets to give them a little protection from the wind. It was a little over an hour's drive from their house, and arriving late in the morning, they stopped to have coffee and pick up a local paper. Clemente was reading the real estate section of the paper when he noticed a ten-acre parcel with a century farmhouse and a few outbuildings just a little southwest of Nottawa. Turning to his wife, he said, "Listen to this," and he read it to her. "What do you think?"

"Sounds like it could be promising," she replied, and finishing their coffee, they decided to go and check it out.

They drove south and, just past Nottawa, turned left at the first intersection. They carried on for fifteen minutes until they came to the "For Sale" sign. They saw that the selling brokerage was Century 21 and the listing agent was Lois Hunter. Parking the car in front of the house, they got out and looked at it from the road to determine if it might warrant a further look. It was an old, two-storey stone house. It looked fairly well-maintained, judging from the condition of the painted outside trim. The grounds also seemed to be well maintained. There was a front porch leading to the front door. There was a small flower garden in front of the veranda with daffodils in full bloom. The front door was off-centre, and there was a large window to the left. The second storey had three windows across the front. There was a stone chimney on the east side of the house, and the front of the house faced north.

"What do you think?" Yolanda asked. As Clemente was about to reply, a medium-sized sandy-coloured dog came bounding around the house, barking, tail wagging, coming straight for them. They were just about ready to jump back into the car when they saw that it was followed by a man. He wore coveralls and waved to them, saying, "He's okay. He's friendly."

As he approached them, he greeted them with a smile and said, "How do you do? Can I help you?" The dog was running excitedly around them, looking for attention.

Clemente smiled, saying, "Oh, hi. We saw the house listed in the local paper's real estate section and thought we would have a quick look to see if it was something we wanted to explore further with the listing agent."

The fellow, after telling the dog to come and lie down, introduced himself as George Stonehouse. He was an older fellow with a full head of brown hair, which was now turning white. He was of medium height and weight and had quite a few wrinkles on his well-tanned face.

George then went on. "My wife and I have lived here for fifty-seven years. It was her parents' home. Our family has all moved on, and we are thinking it's time to give it up and move into a condominium in Collingwood. That way, we can be closer to them. I worked for the township and wasn't really interested in farming, so we sold off all the land except for ten acres. I'd take you inside, but the wife would shoot me," he said, chuckling. "But we can have a look around the outside if you like."

Clemente and Yolanda both readily agreed, and George walked them around, the dog in tow. First, there was an old driving shed, and as they continued, they came to a large garden that had been planted and was just starting to show growth. Clemente calculated that it had to be close to thirty feet by fifty feet. Along one side were some grapevines, and behind them, Yolanda counted ten apple trees. The soil looked good. "Thank you for taking the time to show us. It looks quite good, and we'll go and talk to the agent. Oh, I noticed your little tractor in the shed. It looks like a Kubota. Does it come with the property?"

"No, but it could be purchased separately," was the reply.

Thanking him again, they left, and as they were driving back, Yolanda said, "That looked interesting. Let's grab a bite of lunch and then go and see if the agent is around. I would like to go back and see inside the house."

After lunch, they drove to the local Century 21 office and inquired if Lois Hunter was available. The receptionist advised them that she was out, but if they wanted to take a seat, she would call and see when Lois could come and meet with them. She made the call and advised them that Lois had just finished a meeting and would be back in ten minutes. She offered them each a coffee, tea, or water. Yolanda had tea while Clemente passed.

Lois Hunter was a tall lady, about forty years old, with sandy blond medium-length hair and a nice smile. She welcomed them warmly. After telling her of their plans to relocate from the city, they told her they had come across her ad for the Stonehouse property in the local paper. "We decided to drive out and see where it was, and as we were looking, the owner came and introduced himself and walked us around the outside of his property. Oh, by the way, you should know that our son is a realtor, and he will be our agent."

"That's certainly not a problem, and I'll give you a copy of the listing for him. The house has been updated over the years, and it is structurally sound." She gave them a copy of the listing and her business card. They thanked her and left.

Returning to their vehicle, Yolanda said, "Let's go and have another peek. I never looked to see if you can see the water from it." They did, and she could not.

They called their son that evening and told him about their trip and the house. They then gave him Lois's phone number and told him they had a copy of the listing for him. "Can you arrange a viewing in the next few days?" they asked.

"Consider it done," was the reply.

Michael contacted Lois, asking her to set up the viewing. Within fifteen minutes, her assistant called back and confirmed the appointment for two o'clock two days hence. Thanking her, he immediately called his parents. They were thrilled and agreed to meet at the property at the appointed time.

Mike went to Collingwood a little early and got the keys from Lois's assistant. He arrived at the house as his parents were pulling up. They went in the front door and found an immaculately cleaned house with oak floors and matching oak wainscotting. It gave a very good first impression. While dated, they found the house was well-maintained. It had three bedrooms and was a perfect size. Clemente thought that with a few modifications, it could be their perfect retirement home. As they walked back outside, Michael said, "I think the asking price is a bit high and suggest we offer $5,000 less." His parents agreed.

They did as Mike suggested. The offer was accepted, and they had their retirement home.

CHAPTER TWENTY-SIX

CLEMENTE AND YOLANDA took possession of the house on August 1, 2001, and made a few modifications at Yolanda's suggestion. These included an additional bathroom downstairs and a new south-facing sunroom. They were very happy with their purchase and were thrilled to find what the Stonehouses had planted and left in the garden for them to harvest and enjoy in the fall. They had been fairly busy since Clemente's retirement, and while they felt a little tired, they were pleased with what they had accomplished within half a year of his retirement.

The neighbours dropped by to introduce themselves and welcome them to the area. Marie and Mike and Rose visited regularly and were happy to see that their parents had settled in quickly and were quite at home with their new surroundings. The thing Yolanda and Clemente noticed the most was how quiet everything was. After their years in the city, they had just accepted the steady din from traffic, vehicle horns, fire trucks, and ambulances. The quiet here was amazing and very peaceful.

As autumn turned to winter, the days became shorter, and the wind from Georgian Bay grew colder. They were surprised and caught a little off guard when they saw how much snow they were receiving. It was easily four or five times what they saw in the city, and it stayed. At first, they quite enjoyed it. Shortly after they had settled in, one of the neighbours had come over and offered to blow the snow from their driveway over the winter. They had agreed, and they were certainly happy that they did.

The whole family arrived and stayed for Christmas. It was wonderful to have them all together again. While Mike and Rose joined Marie in staying with their parents, Ana and Dave got a room in a Collingwood hotel. Ana and Dave gave them a copy of *Northern Cookbook* as a gift, and Marie had given them a copy of *The Old Farmer's Almanac*.

Living relatively close to the water, they experienced lake-effect snow—and plenty of it. Several mornings, they woke up to a foot of new snow. While it had been beautiful and very picturesque at first, by early in the new year, it was starting to lose its novelty. Clemente purchased a new walk-behind snow blower so he could keep the sidewalks clear. The weather varied from beautiful, clear, cold days to cloudy and sunless days, usually with a west or northwest wind. The days were noticeably shorter, and both Yolanda and Clemente had gone into town to purchase new winter parkas and boots.

In February, the seed and plant catalogues from the various nurseries started arriving in their mailbox, and as the days gradually got longer, Yolanda and Clemente started turning their attention to spring planting. They found their *Old Farmer's Almanac* very informative and useful while planning their new garden.

As spring gradually appeared, the robins, red-winged blackbirds, and bluebirds arrived on schedule. Clemente had arranged to have their apple trees pruned well before the sap began to run. One of their neighbours had asked if he could tap their maple trees, and they had said yes. To their utter delight, the neighbour arrived one day in mid-March with a couple of large jugs of fresh maple syrup that he and his family had made from the sap they had collected from their trees. It was delicious. Life was good, and everything was showing promise. They ordered their seeds and starter plants and had a fellow come in to rototill and fertilize the gardens. When the *Almanac* told them to plant, they planted. Living in the city, they had never experienced or given any thought to this way of life. They did not have the very specific seasons in Italy that they found in Canada. They were totally happy and enjoyed their newly discovered lifestyle: retirement in the country.

One day, early in the summer, Marie received a telephone call from her mother. "Oh, hi, darling. Would you mind taking me to the city to visit my doctor?" she asked. "The traffic is crazy. I haven't seen him in about five years, and I'm long overdue."

"Of course," Marie replied. "Let me know when you get an appointment, and I'll move things around on my calendar."

Clemente wasn't in on the conversation, so the day she was going, she told him, "I'm going to see the doctor for a checkup, and Marie said she would drive me. I haven't been since before our holiday to the old country, and I'm not happy being so tired no matter how much sleep I get."

Not giving it any more thought, Clemente continued working in the garden. When Marie arrived to take her mother, he called out to them, "Drive safe," and they left. He assumed that Yolanda's age was catching up with her but wisely kept that thought to himself.

Arriving at the doctor's office right on time, Yolanda was immediately shown into the examination room. After a brief chat and catch-up, the doctor, a young woman of about forty-five, had her change into a gown and commenced the examination. During this procedure, she felt the sides of her breasts and immediately felt the lump on her left one. Yolanda flinched. The doctor asked her about it.

"I think I pulled something when I was handling luggage on our trip to Italy," she explained. "It hasn't bothered me, so I really haven't given it much thought."

"Okay," the doctor replied. "I'm going to order a mammogram just to make sure it is nothing more than that. I'll have my secretary call and see if we can do it today so you won't have to make another trip down." She went out and spoke to her staff, then came back in, finishing her examination and taking blood samples.

Within a couple of minutes, there was a knock on the door. "Yes?" the doctor answered.

Her secretary poked her head in, saying to Yolanda, "They will take you as soon as you get there."

The doctor then added, "That's good. I am going to call a surgeon and arrange for them to see you right after the procedure when the results are known. I don't want to speculate on what the growth could be, but I think we need to be absolutely certain so we can start treatment immediately if it is needed. But it is probably nothing."

They left the office, and Marie drove Yolanda to Sunnybrook Hospital. After entering and reporting to reception, they were escorted to the imaging department, where Yolanda was given a gown. Once changed, she went to the waiting room, where her daughter was waiting. About ten minutes later, she was taken to the mammogram machine. There, a technician applied pressure to the breast, and they squeezed it before taking an image of it. Finishing in a matter of minutes, Yolanda changed back into her street clothes and returned to the waiting area. As she was describing what had happened to her daughter, a volunteer came and took them upstairs to Dr. Harjit Gupta's office. Again, they waited in his waiting area for about twenty minutes.

A tall, slender fellow wearing a bright yellow turban, who was probably in his early fifties, greeted them, inviting them to join him in his office. As they were sitting down, he said, "I'm Dr. Gupta, and I'm a surgeon. We've had a radiologist review the mammogram, and I'm sorry to tell you that you have a growth on your left breast. I'm recommending surgery so we can see what it is and remove it if necessary. It could be cancerous." Neither Yolanda nor Marie could believe it. They both broke down in tears, hugging each other.

The doctor gave them a few minutes before continuing. "We'll need a CAT scan to determine if it has spread to your lymph nodes. If it has, you'll undergo surgery to remove the tumour, possibly the breast, and any affected lymph nodes. Once that's over, you'll be referred to an oncologist. They will start chemotherapy to kill any remaining cancer cells and stop the spread to other parts of your body."

Yolanda was totally shell-shocked. What had started as a routine visit to the family doctor had turned into a serious, life-threatening nightmare. The surgeon then said, "We'll do the CAT scan immediately."

They did, and it was confirmed that the cancer had not spread yet.

With the CAT scan behind them, they headed back home. Yolanda felt totally devastated, doomed, and defeated. *Cancer!* She couldn't believe it. She felt that her life was threatened by something she couldn't do anything about. She was shattered and depressed. She had never experienced such feelings in her life. *Is this how my life is going to end?* she wondered.

Arriving home, they went directly into the house, where Clemente was waiting. "How'd it go?" he asked, and looking at them, he knew immediately it wasn't good. He had two scared, tear-filled, sobbing women telling him at the same time what had happened. Remaining calm, he said, "Whatever is going on, we'll beat it. Things will be okay." Going over to the sideboard, he poured three glasses of wine, saying, "Let's sit down, and you tell me exactly what happened."

Composing herself, Yolanda started telling him what had happened. He listened, asking questions to clarify. He then suggested to Marie that she stay and make a light dinner for them "while your mother goes and has a good soak in her tub. I'm going to make a few calls."

Of course, with his uncle back in the old country, he decided to talk to Pasquali. Over the years they had worked together, Clemente knew that his old boss and business partner was very conscious of his health and had good contacts within the medical community. Clemente was determined to get the very best people to look after his wife immediately.

Placing the call, he got right to the point. "Sorry to have to tell you this, but my wife was diagnosed with breast cancer this afternoon at Sunnybrook. We are afraid and not sure who we should be talking to." Pasquali listened and thought for a minute after digesting what he had heard and then said, "Don't worry, and tell Yolanda everything will be all right. Let me talk to my doctor. He's a good man and knows a lot of really good people. I'll call you back after I've spoken to him. And don't worry."

"Many thanks, old friend. I appreciate it," Clemente responded, hanging up.

Marie was busy making a family favourite for supper, a simple pasta with marinara sauce. Clemente refilled her wine glass, saying, "Don't worry. We'll get Mom the best treatment that's available. I should have known something wasn't right when your mother started slowing down and feeling so tired all the time. I could just kick myself."

Yolanda arrived back downstairs looking a little more settled, and as they were getting ready to eat, the phone rang. "Hello?" Clemente said, answering it.

"It's me," the familiar voice said. "Understand that my doctor is no bullshitter. He says that time is of the essence, and if he were facing the situation, he would get his wife to an American hospital ASAP. He recommended one in Ohio, which he says has the most advanced equipment and best staff of any cancer hospital in the world. He says our medical insurance won't cover it because there are good facilities here, but as far as the medical community is concerned, these guys are the best. Here, if you have a pen, I'll give you the number." Picking up the pen on the telephone table, he wrote it down.

"Many thanks, my friend. We really appreciate it," Clemente said and hung up.

Returning to the table, he told the girls what Pasquali had told him. After a brief discussion, the call was placed to the hospital. The young lady on the other end of the telephone was amazing. She immediately set Clemente's mind at ease, telling him, "We know exactly what you and your wife are going through. We are committed to doing everything in our power to get you through this ordeal successfully." It seemed that, within minutes, she had taken all the pertinent information. Then he was talking to a doctor, who reinforced that time was of the essence.

Clemente told him, "We will get a flight as soon as possible."

"Call me back when you have finalized your travel arrangements," the doctor said, and then they hung up.

Calling Pasquali back, he brought him up to date, telling him they were going to find a flight and book it. To Clemente's surprise, he was asked, "When will you be ready to leave?"

"We'll head to the airport as soon as we have a flight," Clemente answered.

"Okay, be ready to go with your passports in hand at ten o'clock tomorrow morning. I'm arranging for a car to pick you up and take you to the airport. And don't worry. Try to get a good night's rest. Tomorrow you'll be in for a long day. Best to Yolanda. Good night." The line went dead.

Clemente relayed the information to the girls, and while Marie cleaned up the kitchen, he and his wife organized and packed their suitcases. They decided that Marie could stay the night. They got to bed after Marie made them some Sleepytime tea. It was not a restful night, as their heads were spinning with the events of the day and the uncertainty of what was to come.

Yolanda, Clemente, and Marie had finished breakfast and packing when, at nine forty-five, a black Lincoln Town Car arrived in their driveway. The driver knocked on the door and said, "I'll take your luggage first and then come for you." Driving down Airport Road, Yolanda and Clemente arrived at the airport just after eleven, and the driver took them directly to what turned out to be a private hangar. They boarded a private jet, and within a little over an hour, they landed in Ohio. After clearing US customs, they exited to find another driver waiting for them. They arrived at the hospital, where they were welcomed and taken to a private suite where Clemente would stay until his wife was able to join him. Yolanda was then taken by wheelchair while her husband went with the hospital administrator to complete the necessary paperwork.

Once everything was done, Clemente called Marie to tell her where they were and give her their contact information. She told him that Pasquali had already called her and brought her up to date with what was happening. "He told me that he considered you part of his family. He said that if I had any questions or needed anything, just to let him know. Oh, and I've let Ana and Michael know."

"Great. Can you let Yolanda's doctor know so she can inform the staff at Sunnybrook Hospital? Thanks, dear. I'll keep you posted. Talk soon. We love you." As he was ending the call, a man dressed in formal attire entered and set down a tray.

"You must be hungry, sir. Here is some dinner. Dial extension 2 on the telephone if you require anything else." And with that, he turned and left the suite.

Clemente was totally exhausted. The day seemed like a blur. After eating, he sat and relaxed, wondering how his wife was faring.

He must have drifted off, for the next thing he knew, there was a rap on his door. It was dark outside, and upon opening the door, he was greeted with, "Hi, Dad. I came as soon as I heard. I just checked, and Mom is fine. They are just finishing the operation, and they will give us an update when they are done. Oh, David and the kids send their best wishes, and they are sure everything will be fine." And with that, Ana entered the suite, gave Clemente a great big hug, and set her suitcase down.

They talked and caught up while they waited. Within the hour, there was another knock at the door, and Ana answered it. It was an older, bearded gentleman dressed in green scrubs. He approached Clemente, saying, "Everything is fine. We got everything, and your wife is resting in recovery. We'll come and get you when she has been settled in her room. Oh, I'm

Dr. Skinner, by the way, and I was the lead surgeon. Any questions?" He looked from Clemente to Ana and back. When they didn't say anything, he nodded and left.

$ $ $

YOLANDA RECOVERED NICELY, and her strength returned. It was decided that she could return home and commence chemotherapy at the Princess Margaret Hospital, as it was considered to be a leading cancer hospital in Canada. Saying goodbye to Ana and thanking her for her support, they flew back to Toronto on the same private jet that had brought them. Ana flew back to Vancouver. While Marie had wanted to pick them up, Pasquali insisted that he would have her brought to the airport so she could welcome her parents when they got off their plane and accompany them back home.

Yolanda was exhausted but happy when they finally arrived home. It felt like she had been living in a dream, but when she entered her house and settled into her own chair, everything seemed to come together for her. She commenced weekly chemotherapy sessions after being home for five days, which lasted for seven weeks. Toward the end, she noticed that her senses were not as they should be. There was a tingling numbness developing in her fingers.

CHAPTER **TWENTY-SEVEN**

MICHAEL AND ROSE had settled in and were enjoying Fergus. While Michael was selling enough to get by, he wasn't doing what Jim had hoped. Jim saw that, while he had the personality to be a great agent, he seemed to lack the motivation or inspiration to close sales. He could and did talk to people for hours about life, the outdoors, cars, and whatever else cropped up. He loved his involvement in the various clubs and groups he had joined, and he had no problem devoting time to the various projects they undertook. Unbeknownst to his wife and colleagues, Michael had started buying lottery tickets, which had led to the odd visit to the casino whenever he could work it into a trip without his wife knowing. He loved gambling and playing poker. He had convinced himself that "the big win" would happen in just a matter of time.

One day in 2003, when they finished supper and were loading their dishwasher, Mike said, without looking directly at his wife, "I've been thinking and wondering if we should be looking at moving to Collingwood." He paused and waited.

"What! Why?" Rose responded.

"This town doesn't seem to be going anywhere, and from what I am hearing, there are a lot of people selling in the city and then moving and buying for a lot less in Collingwood. With our Toronto experience, I think we could really do a lot better there."

Rose was extremely happy working in Dr. Hickling's practice, and he was very pleased with her and treated her with respect. While she was making good money, she could see that Michael was faltering. She was still hoping that he would get his act together and, deep down, had the feeling that it wasn't going to happen here. He continued to talk a good game, but when push came to shove, he just didn't seem to have that edge he needed. She had been able to put a little bit of savings aside, unbeknownst to her husband, but it was not enough to allow them to buy or even put a decent down payment on a house. She also knew that if he had known about it, he would come up with a hundred ways to spend it.

So, after a moment's thought, Rose replied, "If I can find a good job there, and it will make you happy, we should do it. After all, we don't seem to be getting anywhere here."

Surprised and thrilled, Michael said, "I've been researching firms in the Collingwood market and have decided on two that I can approach."

In 2003, after Yolanda's bout with cancer, she and Clemente were settling nicely back into retirement. They had a lovely, big garden and were growing tomatoes, zucchini, carrots, beans, peas, potatoes, asparagus, beets, and corn. Clemente never told anyone, including his wife, what her treatment at the American hospital had cost, but it had taken an enormous bite out of their savings. He knew it was well worth it now that it was over and her health was fine. She had visited the oncologist every six months, and everything was good. When Michael and Rose told them that they were looking to move to Collingwood to be nearer to them, they were pleased.

Marie's accounting practice was doing well in Toronto. She had kept her apartment and had built up a healthy investment portfolio, investing primarily in blue-chip, dividend-paying stocks and bonds. She had never developed another serious relationship, although she had many friends and acquaintances. She had taken up painting as a hobby years before and had now restarted it again. She had come across work by Canadian artist Roland Fenwick and was very impressed with his style. A gallery owner told her that Fenwick was from Owen Sound and that the local art gallery, the Tom Thomson Memorial, had a large selection of his paintings. Many had been done at locations on the Bruce Peninsula. Marie quite liked his landscapes and especially what he did with trees. She obviously had acquired some of her mother's talent. She was quite good and was enjoying working in both watercolours and oils.

Every year on her birthday, Marie received a birthday card from Bill Brown, and every year she deposited it unopened in a desk drawer. She was still bitter and disappointed in the way he had let her down. She just couldn't put it behind her. When her parents moved to the Collingwood area, she began to think about retiring and relocating closer to them. She always took time to look around and get a feel for the town when she visited. She liked the small close-knit community and thought that if she came across a nice lot, she would buy it. It could be an investment, or when she did retire, she could build her retirement home on it. Keeping this to herself, she carried on with her life in the city.

Marie noticed that she got a little light-headed from time to time, and when it happened, she would eat a banana and have a cup of tea. That seemed to settle things down. She was spending considerable time every weekend in Collingwood looking after her parents. When her mother was undergoing her chemotherapy treatments, Marie always took her to the hospital. Now she was taking her for follow-up appointments.

Yolanda was using a cane because of the lasting side effects from the chemotherapy. Her balance was not great. The doctor advised them that, while the chemo process had done its job and halted the cancer, it had also damaged some of her nerves and muscles, especially in her lower legs and feet. The resulting condition was called peripheral neuropathy. Yolanda attended balance classes at the local hospital and did some physiotherapy there as well. They made slight improvements, but she still had to be careful when she was walking, as she tripped and stumbled very easily.

In the autumn of the year following the end of her mother's chemotherapy treatments, Marie found a nice large lot on the outskirts east of Collingwood, in the area just off Poplar Sideroad. It was on the south side of the road and had been part of a nursery. She bought it, paying cash, and decided that she would hold it until she was ready to retire. She told her parents about her plans, and they were very pleased and happy.

# CHAPTER TWENTY-EIGHT

As MARIE'S DIZZINESS persisted and recurred more frequently, she made an appointment to see her doctor. She underwent a number of tests, and finally, they ordered a CAT scan. It revealed that Marie had developed a heart murmur, so she had medication prescribed. Her doctor also suggested that she consider slowing down, as she was still working long hours, especially during tax season. Taking this advice, she commenced planning her exit from the business. By this time, she had several young assistants, and one, Danilo, a younger fellow, had attained his CPA professional designation. When the time was right, she called a staff meeting.

"I have developed a medical condition, and it has been suggested that I should consider retirement," she informed them. "I'll be looking for someone to take over the practice and wanted to give you a heads-up." They talked a little more and left it at that.

The following morning, three of the senior staff requested a meeting. "Of course," Marie answered and invited them into her office.

Sitting around the rectangular meeting table in her office, Danilo, the more senior of the three, told her, "We got together last night, and after talking it over, decided that we would like to buy you out and take over the business. I will become the senior partner, and they"—motioning to the other two—"will finish work on their CPAs. Once we agree on the value, we will pay you out over three years. We can give you a lump sum now and a third of the remainder at the end of each fiscal year. Will that work for you?" he asked, looking anxiously at Marie.

"That's wonderful and is all I could hope for," Marie said, rising to shake each of their hands. "Once my lawyer has reviewed everything and drawn up a purchase agreement, I will formally announce my retirement. I'll also do a letter to our clients first, keeping them in the loop and letting them know that I have every confidence in you going forward."

Within two months, everything was done. Marie turned the keys over to the new associates and left. During the time she was exiting the business, with her father's help, she had found a contractor. The contractor had worked with her to draw up plans and was now ready to commence construction on her new house. It would be a three-bedroom stone-clad house with a second floor containing a well-lit room that would be the art studio. When Ana asked her why she was building what appeared to be a large house, Marie answered, "I am looking ahead to the resale value, and a three-bedroom home will have more family appeal and should therefore sell for more."

Marie moved in late autumn of 2004. As soon as she had moved in and had everything organized, she invited her parents for supper. They arrived, telling her that it was only a twelve-minute drive, and they then presented her with an armload of vegetables from their garden. Yolanda thought the house was great—"Nicely designed and nicely decorated," she added.

Clemente agreed. He never told anyone that he had visited the house regularly while it was under construction, ensuring that everything was done to his standards. He had introduced himself to the contractor and advised him that he would be inspecting the crew's work. He didn't want Marie to know anything about it, and the contractor had agreed. Clemente gave him $500 to make sure his daughter didn't find out.

The trees had turned and were starting to lose their leaves as the nights were getting close to sub-zero temperatures. The days were generally bright and pleasant, so Marie thought she could get some of the yardwork started now. She asked the contractor if he could recommend a landscaper, and he told her that a fellow named Jorge Gomez was pretty good and reasonable, so she called him.

The next day, Marie and Jorge met at her place, and after introducing themselves, she told him, "I'm not looking for anything fancy, just a nice lawn, some shrubs, and a couple of nice spruce trees."

He was a short, slender fellow with an accent that sounded like it could be Spanish. He had a head of thick but short curly black hair and long sideburns. He had a thin face, large eyebrows, and dark, piercing eyes. His nose was fairly prominent, and he spoke with a hint of a lisp.

"No problem," Jorge told her. "We'll get the topsoil down first and get the trees planted. We should probably wait with the shrubs and grass until the spring. I could build you a storage shed now for the lawn mower, tools, hoses, and fertilizer. If you decide to put in a garden, it will be good to have a potting shed."

"That sounds perfect," she responded. "Would you happen to know who I could get to look after the grass cutting and weeding once everything is done?"

"I've got just the guy. His name is Carlos, and he is good and reliable and reasonable. When they deliver the topsoil, I'll have him introduce himself to you."

"Thanks, that sounds perfect."

The four loads of beautiful black topsoil were delivered three days later, and a crew of five men arrived to spread it. As Marie was leaving to go to her fitness centre, one of them tapped on her car window. She lowered the glass, and a tall, thin fellow with a long face and a head of black, curly, and somewhat unruly hair said, "Hi, I'm Carlos. Jorge said you needed a gardener, and I'd be happy to do it for you. I charge twenty dollars an hour, and if you like, I will come and look after it when we have it in."

"Nice to meet you, Carlos. It sounds like your mother tongue is Spanish. *Buongiorno.* That sounds good. Come by in the spring once the grass is down and the shrubs are in, and we can talk. Have a good day." And raising the window, she drove off.

$ $ $

MICHAEL AND ROSE had made their move in the late spring of 2004, and while it had been Mike's intention to join a local real estate firm, things changed. Jim Dielle had contacted him, suggesting that they open a branch in Collingwood and that Mike could run it. Mike thought it would be an ideal fit, and within a few weeks, he had the office up and running. He got his broker's licence, which allowed him to become the branch manager.

This gave him a higher commission as compensation for the administrative duties he was now obligated to perform.

Rose, in the meantime, had visited the veterinarians in the area and had no trouble finding a good job. It was a larger practice with two younger vets and a staff of three. It was located just out of the downtown core. Starting as an assistant to the vets, she soon settled in. Mike and Rose had found a house to rent in town, and it was close to the new real estate office, so they were well settled in and working by the time Marie was able to move into her new house.

$ $ $

THINGS WENT ALONG smoothly for quite a while, and Yolanda continued to visit the oncologist every six months, but now Clemente was driving her down. Their routine was to leave their car at the Yorkdale Mall and take the subway to the hospital. After she saw the oncologist, they would return to the mall and have lunch in the food court and then do a bit of shopping before heading back home.

The plan was that she would continue with the semi-annual checkups for five years. On her first visit of year four, however, things took a turn. It was late spring. The doctor told her that he was seeing something, and he wanted her to return for further testing. She wasn't overly worried and came back in two weeks. She underwent a series of tests and was advised that the results were not good. The cancer had returned to her liver. Keeping her in the hospital overnight, they did a biopsy of the liver and found that the cancer was spreading quickly. They gave her four months to live.

Yolanda and Clemente were absolutely dumbfounded. Returning home, they immediately called the children and gave them the bad news. Within three months, Yolanda was bedridden, and they set up a hospital bed for her in the dining room. Ana took a leave of absence from her job in Vancouver and came and moved in. She and Marie worked in shifts to look after their mother. They bathed her and made sure she was comfortable and fed her, but they could see that she was noticeably deteriorating as the cancer spread rapidly through her body. They were devastated, not only at watching their mother decline but at seeing their father's reaction. He became a lost soul as he witnessed her slipping away.

Five weeks later, Yolanda was moved into the hospice, and within the week, she passed away peacefully in her sleep. Her family was by her side. The daughters clung to each other, crying. Michael and his father wrapped their arms around each other, and then they spontaneously moved and took the girls into their arms. They were heartbroken. Wiping a tear from his eye, Clemente said, "She was the best thing that happened to me."

Plans were made to have a funeral Mass and her burial in Toronto. Clemente was totally beside himself with the loss of his lifelong partner. The family saw his hurt and saw him developing a lack of focus. His daughters were concerned and didn't want him to be left on his own. Then, out of the blue, with no prior consultation, Michael and Rose announced that they were moving in with him. Marie was immediately on high alert.

David and the children had come for the funeral, and the family returned home together. Marie had spoken to Ana and David before they left, expressing some concern about Michael and Rose moving in with their father. She wasn't completely convinced of their motivation. When she shared this with her sister and her husband, David replied, "Yes, we understand, but at least they will be there over the winter, and your father won't be on his own."

Marie reluctantly agreed.

$ $ $

CLEMENTE WAS FEELING like a part of his insides had been removed. He felt like he had lost his right arm and left leg. He was physically fine, but mentally he felt sick and depressed. He couldn't tell his children because he knew that they would worry, and he knew there wasn't anything they could do to make things better. She was gone!

The nights in bed, when he had nothing else to occupy his mind, were the worst. Then, one night as he lay there thinking about her, she appeared to him. He didn't know what to do. "Where are you? Are you okay?" he asked without giving it any thought because he knew she was there.

"Don't worry," she replied. "I'm in a good place, and I am fine. I am here with you, and I will stay as long as you need me. Don't worry."

So, he began by telling her how much he loved and missed her. She answered, and so it started. Every night before he drifted off to sleep, she appeared, and they discussed what was happening in her family's life. He asked her questions and her opinion. She shared with him what she thought. Sometimes the conversations went on until the rising sun began to make the eastern sky red. Some nights the children heard him talking and assumed that he was dreaming and talking in his sleep. In the mornings, he seemed happier and most at peace with himself and everything around him.

CHAPTER **TWENTY-NINE**

**M**ARIE WAS TORN! On one hand, she felt obligated to protect her father's interests now that he was on his own and vulnerable. On the other hand, she was pleased that her brother and his wife had moved in with him. Deep down, however, she suspected that it would only be a matter of time before they started using his money for themselves. Marie viewed her sister-in-law as a very ambitious individual who, it seemed, had taken a degree of control in the marriage. Marie also suspected that her brother's actions were, to some extent, being manipulated by Rose. As a result, Marie made a point of visiting and spending time with her father regularly. Soon, she could not help but notice his gradual lack of enthusiasm and outlook. She decided it was time to act.

On a cool mid-November day with dark grey clouds quickly scurrying across the sky, propelled by the brisk wind blowing in from the water, Marie picked Clemente up and took him for a drive. As they headed east toward Stayner, she started to explain the legal steps she recommended to ensure that he was protected should he become ill or otherwise incapable of making decisions for himself. He seemed to understand what she was telling him and appeared more positive and more like his old self.

"You know," said Marie, "I've seen some pretty disturbing things over the course of my career. I recall an older, well-to-do gentleman who was living on his own after his wife passed away. He had no close contact with his son, and his daughter had died somewhere in South America. They weren't a close family. He didn't want to leave his home and had no desire to go into a retirement home, so he hired a caregiver to look after the housework and assist him. Soon, the caregiver brought her mother with her to help with the cleaning of his house. He was in his nineties and had outlived most of his friends and acquaintances.

During their visits, the caregiver and her mother soon realized how lonely and vulnerable he was. They would bring cookies and have tea with him. They would often discuss his life and then shift the conversation to the contents of his home. They would show a particular interest in a certain piece of furniture or collectible and start quizzing him about its history and how he had acquired it. During the conversation, they would tell him how nice it was and how lucky he was to have found it. They would then go on to say how they would love to have such a piece, asking if he knew where they might find one. Inevitably, he would get caught up in their story and tell them that they could have his piece.

Of course, their reaction was one of, "Are you sure? Oh, we couldn't." And finally, "Well, if you are sure. You are so kind and thoughtful." And then would come the coup de grâce: "This will keep your memory in our hearts forever." This went on for a few years until he was living in a largely unfurnished home with only a few basic sticks of furniture left. Of course, they sold everything for whatever they could get and took the money and ran." She paused, letting that settle in before going on.

"Things came to light one day when the son of one of his old friends dropped in and, finding his hearing aid malfunctioning, offered to go and pick up new batteries for him. Upon returning, he came in for a cup of tea, and during the subsequent conversation, he inquired about a nice carriage clock that had caught his eye a few years earlier. He was thinking that he would offer to buy it, but it was nowhere to be seen. Looking around, it struck him that the rugs and the bulk of his furniture were also gone. The old gentleman told him, when he inquired, that he had given them to his caregiver's mother. Not wanting to upset the gentleman, his friend's son changed the topic of conversation, and they chatted about hockey and the loser Maple Leafs for the remainder of the visit.

"Upon leaving, the fellow called a lawyer friend, telling him what he had experienced. The lawyer responded that without a complaint from the victim or his family, there was nothing that could be done. The caregiver had not received anything herself, and there was nothing to stop him from giving his things away."

Clemente was totally engrossed in the story and asked, "Do things like that happen often?"

Marie said, "It's hard to know because people don't talk about it very much. I think they're probably embarrassed, and once it has happened, there is nothing they can do about it. The people who cheat seniors say, 'Of course, that the item was given as a gift.' If the senior's family tries to dispute this, what proof would they have? It would be their suspicions versus the word of the caregiver, and with no proof, nothing could be resolved. The one way that does offer a degree of protection would be to have a power of attorney drawn up. This," she explained, "would appoint a person of trust to look after their affairs when and if they became unable to make decisions for themselves. But the power of attorney can only be activated when a doctor or a lawyer recognizes that there is a problem and declares the individual incapable of making his or her own decisions."

"What exactly is a power of attorney, and how does it work?" Clemente asked.

So, Marie explained it to him as they drove home, eventually asking, "Would you like me to set up an appointment with a lawyer so they can discuss it with you?"

"Yes," Clemente replied.

Once she returned home and dropped him off, she called Raymond James, a lawyer who had helped her with her real estate project, and made an appointment. She knew that her father and mother had drawn up a revised will just before they had left on their cruise to Italy. Yolanda had suggested that they do it in case something happened to them while they were travelling.

They arrived at the lawyer's office the following week. After introducing Raymond James to her father, Marie explained that her father was looking to have a power of attorney in place in the event that his health deteriorated in the future. Clemente saw that the lawyer was a short fellow with a round face and a prominent dark brown moustache. He was balding and had a pair of reading glasses hanging around his neck.

The lawyer then explained, "There are two types of power of attorney that should be considered. The first is a power of attorney for general property, while the second is a power of attorney for personal care. If that is clear and you understand the difference, then I will talk to you," he said, nodding to Clemente, "privately in my office, and when we are finished, I will come and get you, Marie."

As Clemente and the lawyer sat down in his office, Mr. James stated, "We must be clear that the powers of attorney are only valid while you are living. Upon your passing, the powers of attorney cease to be in effect, and your will becomes the valid document. Do you have an updated will?" he asked.

"Yes," he was told. "I have just had a new one completed."

Hiding his surprise, because Marie had not mentioned this, Mr. James proceeded by asking, "Who would you like to appoint as your attorney?"

"Marie," was his response.

The lawyer then asked, "If Marie is unable to act, who would you like to take her place?"

"My other daughter, Ana."

"That's fine. Excuse me for a moment while I have your daughter join us." Mr. James then left the office and asked Marie to join them. Once she settled in, he explained her father's wishes.

"Would you be willing to act in that capacity?" he asked.

"Yes."

"That's fine. I'll contact Ana and determine if she is willing to accept the appointment. If she agrees, you will both be appointed jointly and severally as his attorneys for personal care in one instance and for property in the other." Then, turning to Marie, he said, "Your father advised me that he has recently updated his will."

While this caught Marie totally off guard, she tried not to show her surprise.

$ $ $

ROSE WAS DEEPLY disappointed in her marriage to Michael. She had grown up in a family of three. Her father had been a tough taskmaster and a very demanding head of the Habowski household. She had inherited a degree of this. While Michael was a pretty nice guy, she saw that he lacked drive, ambition, and direction. She had kept her feelings to herself, thinking there was nothing to be gained by telling him this if she wanted the marriage to last.

When Michael's mother had passed, however, Rose had seen an opportunity. Knowing that Michael was his father's pride and joy—and seeing that his father had a nice house, a great cottage, and, she guessed, a pretty fair bank account—she had suggested that they could move in with his father and help look after him, his home, and his property.

So, she had told Michael, "Not only can we look after him, but it will save us rent. And," she added, "now that your mother is gone, it would be prudent for him to update his will. We wouldn't want anything to happen to him if his will is not current."

On her suggestion, they had visited Clemente the following day and taken him out for brunch, after which they took him for a ride before returning to the house. They went in, and on Rose's prompting, Michael asked his father, "Would you like us to move in with you? We don't want to leave you all alone, and we could certainly help by doing the shopping, making the meals, and taking you to appointments. We will help with running the house and looking after the property too."

Clemente had been thrilled and replied, "That would be the best thing that could happen to me, now that your mother is gone."

So, within four days, in early November, Rose and Michael had given notice, packed up, vacated their rental, and moved in with Clemente. Rose wanted to suggest that, because there were two of them, they take the master bedroom and move Clemente into one of the other two smaller ones. But, knowing her husband would say no, she let it go.

Sitting and talking a few days later, Rose said to Clemente, "My father always told us how important it was to have a current will."

To which Michael added, "It might be a good idea for you to visit a lawyer and have your will updated now that Mom's gone."

As Clemente was mulling it over, his daughter-in-law piped up, saying, "It would be important for you to get your wishes down on paper. You never know when something could happen."

Michael then added, "Rose and I would love to have both this house and the cottage. Marie has just moved into her new home and so would have no interest in this house, and of course, Ana and her family are settled out west and would never move here. If we had the cottage, both Ana and Marie would be welcome to use it at any time."

A few days later, Clemente had asked Michael to arrange an appointment with a local lawyer.

$ $ $

MICHAEL HAD ASKED around and then called a recommended lawyer, Kenneth Scholtz. After a brief chat, he set up an appointment for his father. When they arrived a few days later, the receptionist directed them into a meeting room, where a thin, slightly balding middle-aged man wearing thick, dark-lensed glasses was waiting. Standing up, he introduced himself to Clemente first and then to Michael.

Michael spoke first, explaining to Mr. Scholtz, "My mother recently passed, and it seems prudent for my father to make a new will."

Turning to Clemente, the lawyer asked, "Is there an existing will?"

"Yes," Clemente answered, "but with my wife's recent passing and our move from Toronto, I'm not sure where it ended up. I can give you the lawyer's name. He's in Toronto," he added.

"That will work. Give me his name and phone number, and I'll give him a call if I need to talk to him." Then, looking at Michael, he said, "You can wait in the reception area while your father and I discuss his wishes."

Michael left and sat down in the reception area, where the receptionist offered him a cup of coffee and a doughnut. He said yes and thumbed through the local newspaper, checking out the real estate listings and advertisements.

Within about half an hour, the lawyer called him. "Your father has given me his wishes, and I will call him when the new will is ready to be reviewed and signed."

They drove home in silence, as Michael did not want to quiz his father, assuming he would find out the details when the will was ready.

Clemente was mulling over in his mind the conversation he and the lawyer had had about the new will. He had told Ken Scholtz what he wanted regarding his assets and his children. The lawyer had said to him, "Of course, you can do what you wish, but as your lawyer, it is my responsibility to make you aware that what you are proposing could result in problems down the road."

He was on the verge of telling the lawyer to proceed anyway but then had second thoughts. "Let me get back to you, then," he said, thinking to himself, *I'll discuss it with Yolanda tonight.*

$ $ $

IT WAS ANOTHER gorgeous autumn day in Penticton, although the days were becoming noticeably shorter. Dave had forgone his usual second cup of coffee to go fishing. They had bought the cottage that they had previously rented on Skaha Lake and renovated it completely. It was now their home.

Cleaning up after breakfast, Ana thought she would go to a protected area on their deck, out of the wind, and spend a few hours in the warm sunlight. She had just slipped on a light jacket and headed out with a new book when the telephone rang. Picking it up, she heard her sister's voice. Marie was obviously upset, and without any niceties, blurted out, "That no-good turd of a brother and his no-good wife have talked Dad into writing a new will. They didn't tell me. Did they tell you?"

"No," Ana replied, taken aback.

"Why would they do that unless they were trying to cut you and me out?" Marie said.

"Surely not," Ana replied. "Dad wouldn't go for that. Let's wait until we know for sure, and if we think we are getting screwed, I'll come down and help you get things sorted out. I will get Dave to join us since he has experience in these things. Don't forget, we are the powers of attorney."

Marie listened and then responded reluctantly, "Okay. I just don't understand why Dad hasn't called a family meeting to share his thinking with us and get our input."

Ana replied, "Because Mom is not there commenting and suggesting things to him, and as the only son, Dad has always favoured Michael. I think it's an Italian man thing."

After chatting about the weather and what their children were doing, Ana said, "I'll talk it over with David and see what he thinks."

"Okay," Marie answered, and then they hung up.

$ $ $

RETURNING WITH A couple of nice trout for supper, David heard from Ana about the phone call and her sister's concerns.

"Yeah, I'm not surprised," he answered. "It has always seemed to me, from what I heard, that your father was disappointed that his first-born had been a girl. Of course, his disappointment was felt by Marie regularly, although she didn't understand it. When you came along, it was not as disappointing for your father because there was not the same expectation that there was with the first-born. Then when Michael arrived, your father's dream came true. He finally had a son who would keep the family name alive and who could be groomed to be the head of the family."

Giving this some thought and looking back on her memories, Ana could see what her husband was saying. Then she thought, *No wonder Marie was so resentful of Michael and the way Dad treated him.*

Ana really appreciated David's common-sense approach to things like this. *He has a great analytical mind,* she thought. She was especially appreciative of the fact that he always kept his opinions to himself and only expressed them when he was certain that it was appropriate to do so. She knew that was why, when he retired from the force, his colleagues had suggested that he obtain a private investigator's licence. They wanted to be able to call him when they faced a situation where his special skills were needed.

# CHAPTER THIRTY

N O SOONER HAD they arrived back at the house than Rose pulled Michael aside and said, "How did it go?"

"Well," he explained, "Dad and the lawyer met by themselves. I have no idea what they did or didn't do, but from his body language, I get the feeling that it has not been finalized. We'll just have to wait. Dad wasn't offering information, and I didn't want to push him, so I just let it go." He could see that she was not happy. She stewed and fussed for the rest of the afternoon.

Then she made Clemente's favourite meal for supper, spaghetti with bolognese sauce. After pouring the wine, she asked, "Did you have a good meeting with the lawyer?"

Her father-in-law replied, "Oh, yes, it was fine. Mr. Scholtz was very friendly and helpful, although he was concerned with my thinking on the distribution of the assets. I'll have to give it more thought before I discuss it with him further." Michael quickly changed the direction of the conversation, and they finished the meal and settled in to watch television.

The question of who was named executor remained unasked. Michael and Rose were unaware that Marie had been named and that Ana was also named in the event that Marie was unable or unwilling to act. Finally, if neither of the girls were able or willing to act, the job fell to Mr. Scholtz. Of course, Clemente's first choice was Marie because of her financial background and experience. He was also sure that, as the older sister, she would look after the interests of her younger sister and her baby brother.

$ $ $

MARIE BIDED HER time as her sister had suggested, but she was not at ease. She worried about what was going to happen. The worry and pressure she was feeling were starting to take their toll. Marie didn't feel great but put it down to not eating properly. Also, building a new house, moving, and her appointment as her father's power of attorney all added pressure. But she waited.

Within a week, after receiving further instructions from his client, Ken Scholtz had finished drafting the will. His office called and advised Clemente it was ready to be picked up. After receiving it and settling his account, Clemente drove over to Marie's house and delivered a copy to her. She invited him in for coffee, but he said that he had another meeting and left.

Sitting down with a cup of tea, she read and then reread the new will. Then she picked up the phone, called Ana, and proceeded to read the will to her. As she finished, she told her sister, "There's no way Michael is going to get that cottage. It's worth a fair bit of money, and it should be sold and divided equally between us after the capital gains tax is paid."

Ana wasn't 100 percent sure what the capital gains tax was or how it was involved, but she didn't want to get into it now. "Let me discuss it with David," she suggested. "He has a pretty good handle on these things. And then we can decide how to proceed."

As Ana was about to hang up, Marie added, "I'm thinking of asking Dad to move in with me, so we can get Michael and Rose out of the house. The longer we wait, the harder it will be." Marie had thought long and hard. She had to get her father away from her brother and his wife because she was sure they were using his money, as neither of them seemed to be doing any kind of work.

So, she called him. "Hi, Dad, it's me. Just checking in to see how you're doing. Are you going to any medical appointments soon? Oh, I see. What time is the appointment? Okay. Everything else is all right. Great. Love you and see you soon. Bye." With that, she hung up the phone.

$ $ $

MARIE'S HUNCH WAS absolutely right. Michael, at his wife's urging, was constantly asking his father for financial assistance, under the guise of driving Clemente to appointments, running errands for him, and doing the grocery shopping. Both Rose and Michael had stopped working when they moved in with Clemente, and Michael was seriously contemplating giving up his licence and retiring from the real estate business.

One day, Clemente was scheduled to have some blood work done at the hospital.

Once they dropped him at the lab and he was registered, Michael said, "We are going to have a coffee in the cafeteria. Come down when you're finished and join us. Okay? You'll be getting pretty hungry since you have been fasting."

"Yes, I'm starving, but they told me not to eat until they took the blood. I will see you down at the cafeteria when I'm finished."

Michael and Rose got their coffee and sat, chatting while they drank. When they finished their coffee, Mike looked at his watch and wondered out loud, "I wonder what is taking Dad so long. Save my seat, and I'll go and check." He got up and headed back to the lab.

When he got there, his father was nowhere to be seen. "Excuse me," he said to the technician at the check-in desk. "My father was here for some blood work. Is he finished? His name is Gallorini."

Checking the computer records, the technician said, "Yes, I remember him. He was surprised that his daughter was waiting to pick him up. They left about fifteen minutes ago."

Michael didn't know what to think. He went back, telling Rose, "I don't know what is going on. The nurse said that Marie picked him up about fifteen minutes ago."

"What the hell!" she responded.

"Marie must have needed him for something and not known where we were," he speculated. "I'll call her when we get to the house."

He did, and there was no answer. Rose was not happy, as her instinct told her something wasn't right.

$ $ $

MARIE HAD CALLED Raymond James to see if she could bring her father in for a consultation, but Mr. James was in court and unavailable. On his secretary's recommendation, Marie had contacted J. R. Aldershott and made an appointment to see him that afternoon.

The first thing her father told her when they settled in her car was how hungry he was. "I had to fast before I had the blood taken, so I haven't eaten yet," he told her.

So, leaving the hospital, they went to a favourite restaurant. She had coffee while Clemente ordered grape juice and a western sandwich. As he was eating, she told him, "It's not good for Michael and Rose to be living in your house. If something happens, we may have to sell the house, so they should leave and get themselves resettled now. We don't want you to live alone, so I would like you to come and live with me. I've got lots of room, and it won't be a problem. And to make sure there are no problems going forward, when we are finished here, we'll go and see another lawyer. His name is Jason, and I think we should see him to make sure everything is being done properly." As his power of attorney and the executor of his will, Clemente had complete faith in Marie and her judgment.

As they were shown into Jason Aldershott's office, they saw a serious-looking fellow in his mid-sixties with thick, black, somewhat unruly hair and long, distinctive eyebrows. After the introductions, Marie proceeded to tell him, "Raymond James did some work for us but wasn't available, so his office suggested we talk with you." She then provided him with an overview of the family and her father's situation. "I want to have my father come and live with me so I can look after him and his affairs. I was a CA with my own practice in Toronto."

Listening and then thinking for a few minutes, Jason told them, "Family matters can become fairly sticky when it comes to wills and property. While there could be several issues in play here, the first and most important is the care and custody of your father. As his power of attorney, you will have no problem having your father, as an aging widower, in your home and under your care. Has your father had home care nurses involved with his care yet?"

"No. It is something I want for him and thought I should discuss it with his doctor first. I've noticed a few little things starting to happen with his balance and memory," she replied.

Jason then said, "I suggest that you line up the home care nurses first and then speak to his doctor to ensure that he is in agreement."

Marie was quite pleased and thanked Jason, adding, "There is one more matter that perhaps you could help me with. My brother arranged for our father to see Ken Scholtz and have a new will prepared. My sister, who lives in BC, and I weren't involved in any way. We are concerned that my brother convinced our father that my brother and his wife should have the family cottage at Sauble Beach over and above his share of the estate. That's what the new will states. I have a copy if you would like to see it."

"I know Ken Scholtz quite well and am pretty sure that he would have ensured that Clemente's decisions about his estate were his own," Jason replied.

"For our peace of mind, would you meet with our father and determine if there was undue influence on him to make the decision he did?"

Jason paused and then replied, "Collingwood is a small town, and all the lawyers know and respect each other. I'm hesitant to question another colleague's work. I could meet privately with your father and videotape the meeting to determine if anyone tried to influence him in this matter."

"That would be great. Thank you. Once my father has settled in, we'll make an appointment for him to come in."

Marie went home and made arrangements for a home care nurse to come assess her father. She then made an appointment to meet with his doctor. The meeting went well, and after hearing her concerns and telling him what she had done, the doctor agreed that having home care involved was the thing to do. Marie then called Jason's office and made an appointment for their private meeting.

The meeting was held within the week, and the upshot was that Jason Aldershott found no indication that Clemente had been subjected to any kind of influence or pressure when making his new will.

# CHAPTER THIRTY-ONE

THE HOME CARE nurse arrived the next day and brought a colleague. Sitting down with Marie and her father, they explained, "We will assess you first, and depending on what we determine, we can decide on a course of action." It was agreed, so they started the assessment. One nurse focused on Clemente's cognitive skills, while the other focused on his physical capabilities. The nurses were very thorough, and at the conclusion, they suggested that Clemente lie down and take a rest, since the testing had obviously taken a toll on him.

Marie was concerned to see her father so worn out. As he went to lie down, the nurses discussed their findings and observations with her. The first nurse said, "He is showing symptoms of early Alzheimer's disease. His memory is starting to slip, and it will have to be monitored. Has he had any dizziness?"

"Not that I'm aware of," Marie responded.

The second nurse stated, "I noticed the start of balance and muscle weakness, and if that continues to decline, your father could experience some falls that could cause him serious harm."

The nurses then inquired about his diet and personal hygiene. The first nurse asked, "Is he having trouble urinating?"

"I honestly don't know. I'll start monitoring him carefully and see if there is anything evident."

"You were right to call us. Things seem to be just starting to deteriorate, and we will work with you to ensure it is closely monitored." They got up to leave and then added, "We'll be sending his doctor a complete report, and we'll arrange for the start of regular visits by a home care worker."

The doctor called the following day, asking Marie to bring her father in for an examination. When it was concluded, he prescribed a mild medication for his Alzheimer's and recommended therapy and another medication for his balance loss and declining motor skills. The nurses called in every week to check on him. It was clear that his condition was deteriorating.

Shortly after her first visit, the nurse asked, "Would you be interested in having your father housed in a nursing home?"

"Definitely not—he is going to keep living with *me*," was her answer. "He and my mother raised us and looked after us while we were growing up. It's only right that we look after him, now that he needs help."

The nurse smiled and left.

$ $ $

MARIE KEPT ANA in the loop. They talked every week on Sunday evening, and usually the call was on speakerphone so that David and sometimes the children could be included. Marie told them, "One of the nurses asked if we considered putting him into a nursing home, and I told her no."

Ana replied, "We are in total agreement, and if you can't or aren't able to look after Dad, we certainly will."

That gave Marie peace of mind.

$ $ $

MICHAEL AND ROSE continued to live in Clemente's house, and Michael telephoned his sister periodically to get an update on their father. It was not a happy time. Neither he nor his wife had saved any significant amount of money, although Rose had a little bit stashed away. They had both stopped working, and now that Clemente was not living with them anymore, they had to look after their groceries and the house expenses as well as keep gas in their car. They had applied for early Canada Pension Plan benefits and had just started to receive them. But they knew they would have to wait until they turned sixty-five before they would start receiving the old-age pension. They had to manage their expenses carefully, and Rose was not very comfortable with this. She finally told her husband what she was feeling.

After hearing her out, Michael replied, "This is just temporary. Everything is going to work out. With our share of Dad's assets and the cottage at Sauble Beach, we won't have to worry. We can do some travelling and even spend winters in Florida if we like."

"That's well and good, but it would be nice to have extra money now as things are pretty tight. Do you think, based on what we are going to inherit, we could arrange for a loan now?" she asked.

"I doubt a commercial lender would consider it without proper secure collateral."

"How about a private loan? Could we ask one of your dad's old friends?" Rose inquired.

"Well, it's too bad that our uncle is gone because he would do it in a minute. I know Dad has kept up his relationship with Pasquali Bertollini. He might entertain it."

So, Michael and Rose put their heads together and drafted a nice letter detailing the situation. They mailed it to Pasquali. The letter requested a private loan of $100,000. Michael had initially thought they should ask for $50,000, but Rose suggested $100,000. They could certainly use it. So that was what they did.

CHAPTER **THIRTY-TWO**

I T HAD BECOME Marie and Clemente's routine to watch television in the evening before having a mug of hot chocolate and going to bed. Once Marie had her father settled and was in bed herself, she read a couple of chapters of the book she was working on to help clear her mind before she drifted off. It seemed that she had just closed her eyes when a loud crash and a thud brought her back with a start. Sitting up, she listened. Her heart was pounding, but the house was quiet. Getting out of bed and putting on her housecoat, she went to investigate.

She couldn't think of anything that could have fallen and made that much noise. She looked around the bathroom, kitchen, and dining area and saw nothing. Then she saw that the door to the basement was open. She turned on the light and looked into the basement. There, at the bottom of the stairs, was her father. He was lying prone on the floor, face first, awkwardly spread and totally still. There was blood trickling from a cut on his head.

Rushing downstairs, she called out, "Dad, are you all right?" He was unresponsive. She panicked for a second, not knowing what to do.

Again, she screamed, "Dad!" She shook him. "Can you hear me?" No response. "Don't worry, I'll get help," she assured him. Running back upstairs, she grabbed the telephone and dialled 9-1-1.

"This is nine-one-one. What is your emergency?" said the voice at the other end of the line.

"My father has fallen down the stairs, and we need an ambulance. He's not moving."

"All right, what is your location?"

She gave her the address, adding, "It's just off the Poplar Sideroad."

"The ambulance is on its way."

Hanging up, she switched on the outside lights and unlocked the front door before running back downstairs. She sat beside his lifeless body, cradling his head in her lap, rocking back and forth, sobbing and telling him, "Daddy, oh, Daddy. Help is on its way. You'll be all right. I'm here, Daddy. Stay with me."

While it seemed to take forever, the ambulance arrived in just under ten minutes. A police constable had heard the 911 call on his radio and had arrived a few minutes earlier. "What happened?" he asked.

Marie told him, "I had just drifted off when I heard a loud noise and went to investigate. I found my father at the bottom of the basement stairs, unconscious and bleeding."

"Was he well?"

"He has been diagnosed with Alzheimer's, and a couple of times recently, he asked about his wine in the basement. I told him that there was no wine cellar in this house and that the one he had was in the basement of his Toronto house." And then she added, "He has been having dizzy spells, and his balance is not good, so he is using a walker regularly."

The ambulance attendants loaded him onto a stretcher and rushed him to the hospital. The policeman took her in his cruiser, and they followed.

At the hospital, Clemente was rushed into the emergency room. Marie waited with the constable.

In a matter of minutes, a young doctor came out. He told her that he was sorry, but they were not able to revive her father. Marie immediately broke down in tears, and the constable took her in his arms and comforted her.

Arriving back home, the policeman asked, "Is there anyone I can call for you?"

"No, thank you," she replied. "That's all right. I'll call my family. I want to thank you for your support and understanding."

"No problem. Here is my card with my number if you need anything or think of anything else. I'm truly sorry for your loss. I'll see myself out," he said, turning to leave.

Marie put the kettle on, made a cup of tea, and then called Ana. Of course, with the three-hour time difference, Ana and Dave weren't in bed yet. Marie told her sister what had transpired and assured her that she was fine now that she was over the shock of what had happened. Ana replied, "We'll be there the day after tomorrow," and then hung up.

*It's late, but I'd better let Mikey know,* Marie thought, so she dialled his number. It was 3 a.m., and Michael sounded groggy as he answered the phone, saying, "Yes?"

"Sorry to wake you, Mikey. I'm afraid it's bad news." She went on to tell him what had happened and that his father was gone. He was silent as he let what she was telling him sink in. Marie continued, "Ana and David will be here in two days, and I'll look after things until then. Sorry to wake you, but I thought you would like to know. We will talk tomorrow. Bye." And with that, she hung up.

Marie knew she wouldn't be able to sleep, so she made a second cup of tea and kept replaying what had transpired over in her mind. Then she made a mental note to call Pasquali Bertollini in the morning and make an overseas call to her father's uncle.

$ $ $

ROSE WAS WIDE awake when her husband finished the call, and she asked, "What's going on?"

"It was Marie. Dad was sleepwalking and took a fall. He's dead."

"Oh my God!" she responded. "I'm so sorry. He was a wonderful man and a good father. We'll miss him."

"Yeah," Michael replied as he turned out the light and got back into bed.

"You all right?" his wife asked.

"Yeah, just a bit shaken." And with that, he rolled over and started to remember the great times he had had with his dad over the years. *Guess it's better for him to go like this than turn into a vegetable not knowing who he is or anyone else for that matter. At least he'll be with Mom now.* He slowly drifted back to sleep.

Rose's mind was also working, and she remembered how nice her father-in-law was to her and his son. *I wonder how long it will take for the will to get settled,* she thought. *It will be nice to have some money so we can do the things we want. I'm sure Michael won't mind selling the cottage and the lot.* And with that, she started to return to sleep.

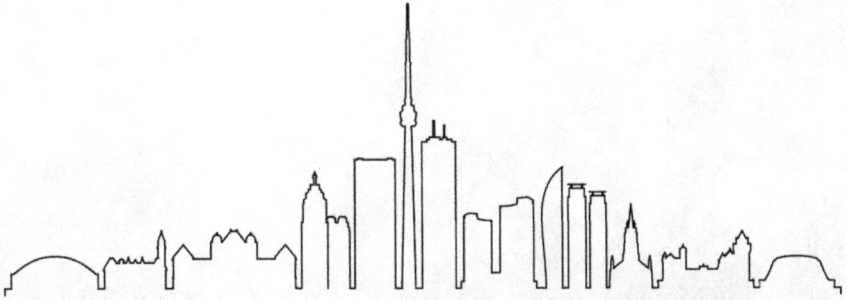

PART THREE

ON THE WING

CHAPTER **THIRTY-THREE**

ANA AND DAVID arrived two days later on July 14, 2008. Their children remained in Vancouver while Ana and Dave flew from Penticton to Calgary and then to Toronto, where they rented a car and drove directly to Marie's house in Collingwood. The funeral was scheduled for the following day, and it was agreed that it would be a quiet, family-only service. After settling in with her sister, Ana suggested, "We should call Michael and Rose and get together for a family dinner."

"I know the perfect place," Marie responded, calling the restaurant and reserving the private dining room.

The five of them met and spent the evening recalling their childhoods and telling stories about their parents. They shared memories of Sauble Beach and how impressed they were on that very first visit. Everyone agreed how nice it was for them to be back together as a family.

They saw each other again at the funeral home, and after the service, Clemente's body was transported to Toronto to be interred beside his wife. They were surprised to see Pasquali Bertollini at the service. He offered his condolences.

The two sisters and David had travelled to Toronto to attend the burial and say their private goodbyes to their father. On the way back home, they stopped for dinner at an Italian restaurant in Vaughan that Marie remembered. It was called Ristorante Positano. The server arrived, told them about the specials, and then took their order. They ordered wine, and while they sat and waited, the server overheard them talking about their father and the funeral. When she went to the back to place their order, she mentioned what she had overheard to the owner.

Arriving at their table, the owner smiled and said, *"Buongiorno,"* introducing himself as Santino Scaini. The girls conversed with him in Italian, telling him, "We are just returning from burying our father."

"I'm terribly sorry," he responded. "What was his name?"

"Clemente Gallorini," they told him.

"While I never had the pleasure of meeting him, I certainly knew of him. He was well respected in our community. May I recommend the mushroom risotto and brasato al Barolo for your main course?"

"Yes, thank you. That sounds perfect."

While they drank their wine and waited for their meal, Marie told the others, "I've been thinking we should find a good lawyer—one specializing in family law—who would work with us in challenging Michael's entitlement to sole possession of the cottage."

Ana and David thought for a moment, and then Ana replied, "Do you think it is really worth it?"

"Well," Marie continued, "Mom's breast cancer operation and treatment really cost a lot. Looking back, Dad wanted the best for her. It was Pasquali Bertollini who recommended the American private hospital. He told Dad they had better doctors and the best equipment, which made them a better option than a Canadian public hospital. In reality, the care and treatment Mom received would have been every bit as good in Canada. Her life was not prolonged by having treatment in the US, but the cost was huge." Then, going on, she told them, "Dad has about $200,000 left in investments and savings. His house is probably worth something in the $400,000 range, and the cottage would probably fetch between 250 and $300,000, including the adjoining lot Uncle Spiffy gave us. So, in rough figures, we would each receive about $200,000 as the will is currently written. If the cottage is divided between us, we will each receive 75 to $100,000 more. If a lawyer's costs are $100,000 and we divide that between us, we should come out about $25,000 to $50,000 ahead."

Ana and David nodded in understanding, but David cautioned, "I've seen quite a few lawyers in action over the years, and we would be better off to agree on a set fee rather than them taking a percentage of the settlement. When they worked for a piece of the settlement, it seemed some of them put their interests ahead of the clients."

"I've talked to Jason Aldershott, and he doesn't think any of the lawyers in Collingwood would be interested. He said that in a small town, the legal community would not want to be in a position of challenging a colleague's work. If you agree, I'll make some inquiries and see if we can get recommendations for someone in the Toronto area who would do the job for us," Marie replied.

They nodded their agreement, and shortly after, their meal arrived, which was amazing. Marie wanted an update on her niece and nephew. By now, they had graduated and started working. She was also curious about their lives in beautiful British Columbia.

When the meal was over, they told Santino that they were too full to even consider dessert.

"I'm glad you enjoyed it," he said, adding, "The meal is on my wife and me, in memory of your father."

They were speechless.

# CHAPTER THIRTY-FOUR

With ANA AND Dave leaving, Marie set about going through her father's belongings, sorting them and washing everything. She had consulted with her sister and, as agreed, dropped them off at the local thrift store. Her next undertaking was to call several old family friends and associates and tell them about her father's passing. During the conversations, she indirectly sought their recommendations for good lawyers. She didn't get into any details but said, "Ana and I are joint executors and need someone we can talk to if a complication arises."

After spending several hours catching up, conversing, and discussing lawyers, she had received a number of names. One name that had come up three times was a younger fellow practising in Markham named Gerardo Morelli.

Marie then called her old friend from her time at the accounting firm, Julie Henderson. They hadn't spoken for quite a while, so after sharing news and generally catching up, they agreed to get together for dinner and a Toronto Symphony concert. As they talked, Marie asked, "We are looking to engage a lawyer and need someone reasonable and good. We've had an issue crop up with our father's estate, and Gerardo Morelli has been recommended. Do you know him?"

"Not off the top of my head, but let me check around for you," Julie replied.

The next morning, after leaving the thrift store again, Marie proceeded to the local courthouse and found out that civil trials would be scheduled to take place at the Superior Court of Justice in Barrie, which was the county seat.

Stopping for a bite of lunch, Marie headed to the local women's fitness centre and introduced herself to the owner. As there were no classes at the time, the owner was free to talk to her. "I've worked as an accountant and had my own practice in Toronto," Marie explained. "I've been thinking that I should start looking after myself, and the time is finally right." The owner then introduced herself as Millie Sheppard. She was a slim, forty-something lady with a nice smile and very good manners. She had short brown hair and a thin, nice-looking face.

After weighing Marie and taking her height, she said, "I think you should start in the morning Pilates class for beginners. Once we see how that goes, we can decide where to go from there."

She then took Marie around the facility, showing her the different machines and pieces of equipment, explaining how each functioned and what was achieved by using it. "The daytime beginners' Pilates class is scheduled for mid-morning. Will that work for you?"

"That will be perfect. Where would you suggest I look for gear? I'm thinking I'll need workout clothing, shoes, and an exercise mat." Millie told her, and she headed out to get it.

It was a lovely June day, not too hot or too cool, with a few fluffy clouds floating across the sky. Arriving home, it dawned on Marie that she had no obligations. Her time was totally hers. Pouring herself a glass of wine, she went out and sat on a lounge chair on the patio in her backyard. *I've never been able to do this,* she thought, and realized that she had been so busy with her family that she just didn't get much time for herself.

Settling in, she started looking around at her surroundings. Everything was green, and the flowers were in full colour. Then her eyes fell on the storage shed that Jorge Gomez had made for her. Taking her glass of wine, she went over and entered the shed.

The wooden shed was unfinished inside and smelled of untreated wood. There was a workbench, windows, and a side double door that allowed the lawn mower or snow blower to be taken out. A gasoline container was sitting on the floor, and cans of engine oil, along with several tools, were sitting on the workbench. Rakes, hoes, shovels, and pitchforks were hanging from strategically placed nails on the wall. Bags of peat moss, black soil, wood chips, and fertilizer were also on the floor. Everything was neat and tidy.

Happy with what she saw, Marie returned to her chair and started thinking about getting back to painting in her studio. *It sure is nice to have control of my own time again,* she thought, *and be able to do what I want to do.* As she was getting ready to go back into the house, she noticed a car sitting on the other side of the street, just down from her house. She thought she had seen it before but went back into the house without giving it any more thought.

The day was getting on when Julie called, telling her, "Gerardo Morelli has a good reputation, and from what I hear, he could be ideal for you. Get a pen, and I'll give you his number." They settled on a date when they would get together for their concert and dinner. Marie then called the number Julie had given her and booked an appointment for an initial meeting with Mr. Morelli.

The following morning, after breakfast and coffee, Marie headed downtown, arriving at the women's fitness centre just before ten. She was introduced to a group of ladies who were there and joined them for her first class. It was not a particularly strenuous class, she thought, but the next morning, she realized she had used muscles that felt like they had never been used before. She was quite stiff and sore. The following day, she went to "the club," as she had learned the fitness centre was known to its members. On Millie's recommendation, she did stretching exercises before working out on a stationary bicycle. Then she was ready as the class began. After showering and grabbing a bite to eat and realizing that there were no after-effects from the class, she left for Markham and her appointment with the prospective lawyer.

$ $ $

AFTER THE FUNERAL, Marie and Ana had asked Michael and Rose to join them at their father's interment in Toronto, but they had begged off. Rose said she was feeling a little off and wondered if it may have been something she ate. She was also thinking about financial matters and hoped that the estate settled quickly so they could get their share of the money and the cottage. She asked her husband, "Do you think we should call Pasquali Bertollini and see if he got the letter?"

"No," Michael replied sharply. "We'll hear in due course, and we don't want him to think we are desperate. I'm sure we'll hear shortly."

"I've been thinking that when things are settled, we could sell the cottage and get a nice home with some land," she told him. "I would love to have a couple of horses." She had always loved horses and, as a child, had hoped that someday she could have her very own Black Beauty.

"Yeah, sounds good to me," he replied.

Michael was spending his days on his computer. The odd time he was in town, he would drop into the real estate office and see how things were going, but as a rule, he was just putting in his time, hoping that the estate would settle quickly.

They never heard back from Bertollini about the money they had asked him to loan them, and so they continued to just get by. Michael thought that once they got the money, they could settle into a nice house. Then his wife could get her horses, and he would get a new car. *We could do some travelling and maybe take a nice cruise somewhere,* he thought. The Mediterranean really interested him, and he was thinking that they could tie that into a visit to Italy again and see his relatives. Of course, his uncle had returned to Italy when he had inherited a family home. Mike would be thrilled to hook up with him again.

CHAPTER **THIRTY-FIVE**

ARRIVING AT GERARDO Morelli's office just after 1:30, Marie was shown directly into his office. As she entered, a fellow in his late thirties or early forties, she guessed, stood and greeted her. He was of average height and on the slender side, dressed nicely in a suit, white shirt, and a very nice red patterned tie. He had black hair, and his smile was nice as he welcomed her.

"Hello, I'm Gerardo, but I have anglicized to Gerard. Most of the time, I'm Gerry. Come and sit and tell me how I can be of service."

Marie introduced herself, and they chatted about their Italian heritage and shared the circumstances under which their families had come to Canada. Gerry's family had come from Bari, the capital of the Puglia region.

He then asked again, "How may I be of service?"

"My father just passed away, and my sister and I are joint executors of his will," she told him. "We have a younger brother, and unbeknownst to us, he had our father write a new will, which gives him the family cottage. Here, I brought you this copy," she said, handing it to him. "Our father had Alzheimer's when he died, and it may or may not be a factor, but my sister and I want to challenge it. Everything else is to be divided three ways, and there is no reason that the cottage should be excluded."

Gerry read the will and asked, "What are you thinking the value of the cottage would be? I've never been to Sauble Beach and have no idea what the property values would be."

"Our father was in the construction business, and being a professional carpenter, he did quite a bit of upgrading and renovating," she replied. "I'm thinking it will be in the 250 to $300,000 range, but it could be more."

"I can certainly see why you and your sister are unhappy. However, your father was completely within his rights to leave what he wanted to whomever he wished," Gerry told her and then added, "There are limited grounds on which a will can be successfully challenged. The first thing you and your sister would do is resign as executors before any challenge is entered. The court would then appoint a new executor. And," he added, "you both would be forfeiting your executor's fees. Based on the value of the estate, they would amount to roughly $50,000 for each $1 million in assets."

"Our brother and his wife moved in with our father when our mother passed, and I'm sure they asked Dad to leave the cottage to them. The fees are really not all that important to us," she replied.

He nodded and continued. "It will take more than a hunch to have a judge look at the case. The grounds for successfully challenging a will are very specific. They are: First, undue influence or duress on the person making the will. Second, the person being without mental capacity to understand what he or she is doing. And finally, fraud and/or forgery."

Reaching into her briefcase, Marie produced a document, which she laid in front of the lawyer. He saw that it was the last will and testament for Yolanda and Clemente, dated about ten years prior, when Yolanda was first diagnosed with breast cancer.

Marie then told him, "I held on to this for our father after Mother passed away, as it was still valid. As you can see, it clearly leaves all holdings equally between the three children."

Gerry pondered for a moment, reading and rereading the will. "This changes things. I think we may have a case," were the next words out of his mouth. He then went on to say, "Here's how it will play out. The lawyer who prepared the new will will present it to the judge and declare that he prepared it and believes it to be the last and current will. We will attend, and then the judge will ask if the named executors are prepared to act in that capacity. I will inform the judge that I am acting for the named executors and that you are not prepared to act, as you are going to challenge the will, and so new impartial executors should be appointed."

Gerry paused and took a drink of water before continuing. "The judge will then approve or probate the will. Under this process, he would declare it to be the legal last will and testament of Clemente Gallorini. He will then direct the clerk to arrange for a qualified, uninterested third party who is willing and able to assume the executor's duties and to have that person appear before him so they can be officially appointed as the executor. Once that happens, we, as the parties challenging the will, would appear and file our challenge. Finally," he added, "all parties who have an interest in the will would have to be notified accordingly.

"Before anything can happen, you and your sister will have to formally engage me. I'll have my secretary prepare a formal engagement contract for you to sign. We can email it to your sister and then schedule a video meeting so she can sign it with you and me looking on. She can email the signed copy back to us, and then we will put the wheels in motion."

"Great. The only thing left to discuss is your fees," Marie said.

Smiling, Gerry replied, "Let's talk."

$ $ $

MICHAEL AND ROSE were going about their daily routine when there was a knock on the door. Upon answering it, Michael found it was a post office courier with a registered letter addressed to him, which required his signature. After signing it, he opened the envelope and found that it was from the County of Simcoe Superior Court of Justice, notifying him that the executors appointed in his late father's will had refused to act, and therefore a new executor was to be appointed by the court. The court was proposing to name Joseph Wittrup, a chartered accountant from Stayner, as the new executor. There was another separate letter enclosed from the same court, advising him that his father's will had been challenged and a hearing date would be set. He would be notified about when to appear. Rose appeared, and he handed the letters to her without saying anything.

She read them, looked at him, and said, "Now what?"

Looking at her, he shrugged and said, "I guess we should get in and see Ken Scholtz to see what is going on and what we need to do." Rose nodded her agreement, so he made the call.

$ $ $

UPON ARRIVING AT Ken Scholtz's law office, Michael and Rose were shown into a small meeting room. Shortly thereafter, Ken arrived. He informed them that he had also received the correspondence and was being directed to appear before the court to certify that this was the last will and testament that he had prepared for Clemente. "I'll attend and swear that it was, to my knowledge, your father's last will."

"I guess you can't represent us," Michael said.

"No, it would not be appropriate," Ken stated. "As I prepared the will in question, it would not be appropriate for me to act on behalf of one of the named beneficiaries."

"Can you recommend someone we could get?" Rose asked.

"I don't think that you will get anyone from town, since several of them have already been involved. You'll probably have to engage someone from out of town, but I can't be involved in that in any way," he told them.

As they were leaving the office, Ken's secretary gave them a card, saying, "I don't know him personally, but I know he practises family law, and you could contact him and see if he would be able to work on your behalf."

Thanking her, they left. When they got into their car, they looked and saw the name on the card was James Grasser, Barrister and Solicitor. His address was in Creemore. They went home, called, and booked an appointment for the next day.

Arriving in Creemore the next afternoon after the twenty-minute drive from Collingwood, they proceeded to James Grasser's office, where they were welcomed by a receptionist who directed them to take a seat. "Mr. Grasser will come and get you shortly," she added. A few minutes later, a small stout man wearing half-lens reading glasses around his neck and a tweed sports coat came out, saying, "Hi, there. I'm Jimmy Grasser. Come and join me in my office."

He seemed to be in his mid-fifties and had a slight, barely noticeable, raspy voice when he spoke. He was short and had a head of grey hair that looked like the ash of a cigar, the way it was piled on his head. His nose was hawklike. After greeting them, he said, "Tell me how I can be of service."

Entering the office and sitting in the two available chairs, Michael and Rose couldn't help but notice that the office seemed to be totally disorganized. There were files piled everywhere, and his desktop could not be seen for all the paperwork and folders. There were more files and boxes on the floor all around the desk. Michael and Rose proceeded to give him an overview of what had happened and gave him their copy of the correspondence they had received from the court as well as their copy of the will.

Looking over everything, he said, "Okay, good. I've done a fair bit of this type of work before involving family disputes over a will, and we should be able to look after you quite nicely. I usually receive a small retainer up front and then will bill you once the matter is concluded."

"How much is the retainer?" Rose inquired.

"A thousand dollars," was the answer.

"Okay, that will work for us," Rose replied.

The lawyer then proceeded to inquire about Michael's sisters and who they were and what they did. They talked about themselves, advising the lawyer that Michael was a retired real estate broker. When all was done, they shook hands, and Grasser told them, "Don't worry. I'll contact the court and advise them that I'm representing you. I'll take it from there."

After giving him a cheque and shaking his hand, they were leaving the office when they heard the secretary say, "That was your last client for the day, Jimmy."

Looking at his watch, he saw it was just after three. Jimmy answered, "Great, now let's see what we are looking at."

# CHAPTER THIRTY-SIX

G ERRY CALLED MARIE, advising her that the date for the initial hearing had been set.

"Should Ana attend?" Marie asked.

"Yes, it will be good for the judge to see you together at the start of the process. It will give your sister a chance to get a feel for what is going to happen. Then, I expect, she won't have to attend again until things are resolved." He saw no point in telling her that he had received a call from James Grasser, who was her brother's lawyer, or that he had checked him out after their brief conversation.

Calling Ana, Marie brought her up to date and told her what Gerry had advised about her attending. She replied that she and David would be there. When they hung up, Marie once again went over everything in her mind and came to the same conclusion. *I can't see Michael asking Dad to leave the cottage to him. He doesn't think that way, and I am pretty sure he would have been happy to have everything divided equally between the three of us.*

She had a hunch that, while they were living with Clemente, Rose had probably taken her father-in-law aside and told him how much it would mean to Michael to have a cottage left to him. She knew that she could never prove it and that they would vehemently deny it if they were ever challenged. But in her mind, there was no other explanation, and Rose was well aware that their father was so proud of his only son that he would do anything for him.

$ $ $

ANA AND DAVID arrived the day before the court case was scheduled to start, on a late flight from Calgary. They were staying at a hotel near the airport, and they drove up to Marie's the next morning in a rental car. They left the rental and drove with her sister's car to the courthouse, arriving fifteen minutes before their case was scheduled to commence.

Gerry Morelli was waiting for them and introduced himself to Marie's sister and brother-in-law. Gerry explained how the proceedings would unfold and assured them that, as this was a preliminary hearing, the judge would be looking to meet everyone involved and determine what their interest was in the matter before him. "Michael's lawyer and I will address the court, informing the judge we are ready to proceed. I will then introduce you ladies to the judge as my clients, and he will then instruct the clerk to schedule a time for the proceedings and notify all parties accordingly. It may seem like a waste of time and effort, but better that the judge finds everything in order now than gets a surprise once the trial commences."

Entering the courtroom, they saw that only the clerk and a court reporter were present. Shortly thereafter, Michael and Rose entered, along with a fellow they guessed was their lawyer, James Grasser. They took their place in the front seats to the left. Ken Scholtz followed and took a seat in the second row, behind Gerard and the sisters. Dave sat in the third row by himself, as he was not involved in the proceedings. Another gentleman, who turned out to be Joseph Wittrup, came and sat beside Ken Scholtz.

Once everyone was in place, the clerk stood and said, "All rise for His Honour, Mr. Justice Alexander Grossmith." The judge arrived and took his place, and then the clerk said, "Please be seated."

The judge then proceeded to read the matters with which the court was dealing. Judge Grossmith then took over and commenced dealing with the matters at hand. He then asked the lawyers to identify themselves and their clients.

Once he established who the parties involved were, he seemed satisfied that everything was in order. He then said, "I have reviewed the submissions by each of the lawyers, and I am scheduling a discovery hearing for six weeks' time." As he rose to leave, the clerk announced, "The court is adjourned."

As they were leaving the courthouse, Gerry asked Ana and David, "How long are you planning to stay?"

"I'll be here for a week, but David has to return in a few days," Ana replied, adding, "It is not my intention to attend any of the hearings unless it is absolutely necessary."

Nodding, their lawyer said, "I completely understand. Give me a minute." He then made a call, and consulting with his secretary, he suggested, "Let's all meet in my office tomorrow afternoon at three."

Everyone agreed.

$ $ $

ARRIVING BACK AT Clemente's house, Michael and Rose decided to have a drink and review what had unfolded so far. After making his wife a gin and tonic, Michael poured himself a glass of Laphroaig and added a splash of water. Jimmy had explained that, during the next step, both lawyers would speak to their clients' positions to the court. After giving things due consideration, the judge would decide if a formal hearing should be held. Jimmy had then assured them, "We are exactly where we want to be, and unless anything unexpected crops up, we shouldn't need to get together before the hearing."

Sitting with their drinks, Michael said, "It looks like everything may work out for us. I've been checking properties in Sauble Beach and think the cottage could bring about 750 to $800,000."

Breaking out in a great smile, his wife replied, "That sounds great. That'll give us lots of flexibility so we can decide about keeping it or selling and wintering in Florida. Maybe, I've been thinking, we could sell it and get a condo somewhere in the Collingwood area."

Taking another sip of his single malt, he added, "We'll have lots of options."

Ten days later, two registered letters arrived simultaneously. The first was from the court advising that the discovery hearing had been scheduled for thirty-three days from the date the letter was written.

The second letter was more troubling. It was from the executor of the will, advising that he was going to start liquidating the estate and consolidating the proceeds in a new estate account. As a result, they were being instructed to vacate Clemente's house as soon as possible and no later than thirty days, as the house was going to be listed and sold. The letter then went on to explain: "Because the will is being contested, the cottage will not be included in these actions until the court has resolved the matter before it."

Mike read the letters and then called Rose and gave them to her to read. "I guess we'd better start thinking about what we should do," he added when she handed it back. "I've wondered if this was coming, and with winter coming, it probably wouldn't be smart to go to the cottage. I'm thinking we should probably return to Fergus and rent there again. It's only an hour and a half from here, and with any luck, I might be able to do some work for Jim. It won't bring in a lot of money," he added, "but with rent to pay every month, a little extra income would prove useful."

"Yeah, that's for sure," she replied.

"Okay, I'll call my old office and see what they can find for rent. I'll tell them we'll be there in two days," he said.

# CHAPTER THIRTY-SEVEN

W HEN ANA LEFT, Marie returned to her routine of going to "the club." She was feeling quite good about her progress, as she was now working out on various machines after the class. Occasionally, as she was finishing, she became aware of a slight pain in her chest but assumed it was a bit of indigestion from her breakfast. Once she returned home, she spent the rest of the day in her studio.

Time passed quickly, and before she knew it, they were returning to court on August 21. Arriving at the appointed time, she found her lawyer waiting for her. They entered together and took their seats. Michael and Rose were already there with their lawyer. Marie acknowledged him with a nod. Shortly, the clerk called on everyone to rise, and Mr. Justice Grossmith entered and took his elevated seat at the front of the courtroom.

The clerk then read out, "The matter before the court is a challenge to the last will and testament of one Clemente Gallorini."

Rising, the judge addressed the parties. "Family disputes are not uncommon, and I am not in favour of this court being used to resolve an internal family matter. No one involved will be happy if I have to make a ruling. I am therefore instructing Mr. Morelli and Mr. Grasser to work with your clients and each other to find a satisfactory solution. Court is adjourned." The clerk then called on everyone to rise, and Mr. Justice Grossmith left the court.

Outside, Gerry said, "I'll get a hold of Grasser and see how they want to proceed."

Marie went home and called Ana, telling her what had transpired. "Gerry had suggested this might happen, as judges, on the whole, are reluctant to deal with this type of no-win issue," she added.

$ \ \ $ \ \ $

IT WAS A warm, sunny fall day, and the trees were starting to turn as Rose and Michael arrived in Fergus. While they had originally planned to go to their cottage and enjoy some time there before they closed it up for the winter, their plans changed when they received the executor's letter.

Waiting for them at the office was their old friend Jim Dielle. He had aged. He greeted them warmly, telling them, "I'm now retired and have turned the company over to my son Angus. When he told me you were coming back and were looking for a rental house, I told him I would look after you. After all, we have history." He laughed and then continued, "The house you rented before is gone, but we've got two other houses in the same part of town for you to check out."

"That's great, and we really appreciate it," Michael said. He then went on to explain, "My father passed away, and until the estate is settled, we decided to come here rather than go to our cottage at Sauble Beach. This is closer, and if things are not sorted by winter, it will be better to drive to Barrie from here rather than from Sauble. They can get some pretty crazy winter weather coming across the lake up there."

"Let's have a coffee and catch up. Then you can go and look at the properties," Jim said, and as they agreed, he poured their coffee, and they caught up.

After finishing their coffees, Jim gave them the keys and directions to the houses. When Rose and Michael checked them out, they found both were in pretty rough condition, but they decided on the one they deemed to be a little more comfortable.

Arriving back at the office, Angus, Jim's son, had a rental agreement ready for them. As they filled in the details, he told them, "The landlord was looking for a $1,000 damage deposit, but because of your history with the firm, he agreed to waive it."

As they were leaving, Rose said to her husband, "I called Dr. Hickling, and he is waiting for me. Why don't you drop me off, and I'll call you when we are done."

"No problem," he responded. "I'll drive around and see how the town has changed. Give me a shout when you are ready, and I'll come right over. We can grab a quick bite of lunch to take out and eat on the way back."

About forty-five minutes after he dropped her off, Rose called, telling him she was ready. He swung around and picked her up, asking, "How'd it go?"

"It was great to see him again. He is such a nice man, and he wanted to know how you were doing and if you were still drinking Laphroaig," she said, laughing. "I assured him you were. He offered me two days a week to start and thought they could increase it fairly quickly once I've settled back in."

They picked up lunch at a local drive-through before heading back to Collingwood to organize their move.

$ $ $

GERARD MORELLI AND James Grasser had been given their marching orders by the judge, and now they had to get busy and explore how this could be resolved. Lawyers generally approached their tasks in different ways, and these two were no exception.

Gerry started to review the facts on which they were basing their case. He thought, *First, the father's previous will, which had been drawn up before his wife's passing, had left everything equally to his three children. Next, upon his wife's passing, the son and his wife moved into the father's house. Next, during the time they lived with the father, he had rewritten his will, leaving a major asset solely to the son. Finally, the father had developed Alzheimer's, but it was not diagnosed until he moved in with his oldest daughter, Marie. Then,* he reasoned, *my first task is to determine if there is any way of determining and proving that the onset of Alzheimer's could have played a part in the writing of the new will and its contents. Next,* he thought, *I need to research past cases that are similar and determine what was decided and why the decisions were reached.*

Jimmy Grasser took an entirely different approach. He reasoned, *The facts are pretty straightforward in that the father has left the family cottage to his son and his wife, and that makes it pretty clean-cut. The will is very clear on his wishes.* He decided that he could wait and see what the other side was presenting before he really had any work to do.

And so it was.

Typically, both lawyers had other cases they were working on and juggled their time to make things work. After about a month, Gerry wrote to Jimmy requesting a meeting so the family members could get together and see if there was any common ground. This took place in early October, and it was clear that nothing was close to being resolved.

Jimmy stated, "It is not illegal or improper for Mr. Gallorini to give his son preference in his will. And further, there is no evidence that Mr. Gallorini has been unduly influenced or under duress when he decided to make a new will."

To this, Gerry responded, "We feel that there is a case to be made because of the change that was made from the previous will. There was also the fact that Michael and his spouse had moved in with Mr. Gallorini and were living in his house when the new will was written."

As both sides were firm in their views, the meeting ended. Gerry had decided not to bring up the Alzheimer's until it was necessary. He had found an expert witness he could call to speak to the fact that the onset of the disease could have played a key role in the rewriting of the will and its contents.

$ $ $

OVER THE NEXT three months, both lawyers worked to solidify their cases, and while they were reluctant to do it, it seemed that the only way out was to go back to the judge and advise him that common ground could not be reached. They called the judge's office and requested a meeting with him. One was scheduled to take place in three months. They were told that because of the court's caseload, the judge would not be available any sooner.

# CHAPTER THIRTY-EIGHT

MICHAEL AND ROSE settled into life in Fergus, with Rose working at the vet's office and Michael helping out in the real estate office. It was a cold winter, but the weather in Fergus was remarkably different from Collingwood or even Sauble Beach, for that matter. Fergus had some snow and cold temperatures, while Collingwood, situated on the shore of southern Georgian Bay, received snow squalls and colder temperatures as a result of the wind blowing off the water. Michael and Rose were in regular contact with their lawyer, who assured them that he had everything under control, and when they appeared before the judge again, he was confident that things would be resolved their way.

Rose, however, was not totally at ease with things, knowing Marie was very strong-willed. If there was a way to have the court decide in their favour, Marie would come up with it.

The full moon was approaching, and as was usually the case each month at that time, Rose couldn't sleep. She lay in bed, thinking and worrying. What would Marie do? How could they stop her? Was she planning to bring a surprise witness to the court? Was it Bertollini? They had never heard back from him when they wrote to him about lending them money. Did she have someone else? Did she contact Uncle Spiffy, and was she bringing him back to testify? How could they stop Marie?

Marie had continued her routine of going to "the club" each morning over the winter. She had noticed that the discomfort in her chest was gradually getting worse, so she cut back on the number of machines she was using after the Pilates class. Finally, about a month before the case was to be taken back to the judge, she decided to take her sister's advice and see her doctor for a thorough physical examination.

Arriving at her doctor's office, she told her doctor, "I've joined a fitness club and have a Pilates class in the morning, and following that, I work out on various machines for about half an hour. I noticed a slight pain in my chest, and it seems to be getting worse."

The doctor took her blood pressure and listened to her lungs and heart with her stethoscope. Then she said, "There is a definite murmur in your heart that we will have checked out. We'll notify the hospital and send them the requisitions for a series of tests, including stress tests. I've requested that they do them today."

At the hospital, Marie spent several hours going through a battery of tests, scans, and lab work. The following Monday, she returned to her doctor and was told, "You have endocarditis, which is an infection of the inner lining of the heart, and it has started to damage your heart valves. Probably the stress of your father's passing and your fitness classes have caused the condition to worsen. I'll refer you to a specialist in Toronto. I'm hoping that surgery to repair the damage is an option, but the cardiologist will explain everything to you once they get a good look at your heart."

Returning home, Marie called Ana and told her. Ana offered to fly over immediately. Marie assured her that that was unnecessary and that she would let Ana know if she needed her. Then, to Marie's surprise, her sister went on to tell her, "I was about to call you. Pasquali Bertollini called yesterday and asked how things were going. I guess he called me because I used to babysit his grandkids. Anyway, he told me he was aware of the court case and if we thought it would help, he would be happy to come and testify. He said he would tell the court that Dad had always thought the cottage should be left to all the children and especially me, since we have children."

"That's great. I always knew Pasquali and Dad were close, and his testimony could be amazing," Marie replied.

Ana then said, "I'm going to let Michael know because he is still our brother, and we should try to put an end to this nonsense, which is a waste of everyone's time and money."

The following day, Marie received a call from her sister-in-law. "Hi, Marie. It's Rose. Ana called us yesterday, and we are sorry to hear about your heart issues. I know we haven't always seen eye to eye, but if there is anything we can do or anything you need, don't hesitate to ask. We are here for you. I'll be off work for the next two days and will drop in to see you."

When Ana had called and informed Michael about Marie's heart murmur, she had told him, "It is quite serious, and she is scheduled to see a cardiologist in Toronto next week."

"Wow, that sounds serious and could be nasty. I appreciate the call, and we are available to do whatever we can to help," her brother had responded. He then relayed the news to Rose.

"Boy, that sucks!" was her response. "I'm going to give her a call and see if she needs anything."

Now, when she finished the phone call to Marie, she thought she would like to see Marie tomorrow by herself so they could have a good heart-to-heart chat. When she told Michael this, he said, "That's cool. Give me a call when you are heading back, and I'll order in supper and have it ready for you." He actually felt happy that his wife was taking steps to get closer to his older sister, as they had never really developed any kind of relationship.

When Rose arrived at Marie's early the following afternoon, they hugged, and Rose said, "God, I am so sorry. That really sucks. Here." Stepping back, she handed Marie a small gift-wrapped box. "I hope this will give you a lift."

Marie smiled, saying, "Oh, that's nice. Will you come in for a cup of tea?"

"Of course, but I won't stay long since it's a good drive back, and I don't want to drive back when it is dark this time of year. You never know what the roads will be like, and your brother is planning to have dinner ready for me," Rose answered, coming in and taking off her coat and boots. They sat and chatted.

As Rose got up to leave, she said, "I'm sorry we are into this court case. I'll talk to Michael to see how they can stop it." Then, after another hug, she left.

Now, Marie didn't have a lot of vices, but her love for chocolates, especially dark ones, had never waned.

She still remembered when her uncle gave her a small box of dark chocolates for her tenth birthday. She had been overwhelmed by how good they were and proceeded to eat the whole box over the next two days, completely by herself. The whole family knew of her love for dark chocolate, and over the years, she had received it for special days like First Communion, graduation, and birthdays.

Her habit was to eat the centre or middle chocolate first and then work progressively to the outside ring. So, when she opened that box and saw six dark chocolate truffles, she couldn't believe her eyes. Sitting down, she poured herself another cup of tea and took the first truffle from the middle. Taking the first bite, she exclaimed to herself, "I think I've died and gone to heaven."

After supper, she settled in to watch a movie and nibbled on her truffles.

# CHAPTER THIRTY-NINE

T WO DAYS LATER, on March 23, the telephone rang at 6:45 a.m. in Penticton. David grabbed it first and answered. The voice on the other end said, "This is Corporal Fisker of the Collingwood Ontario Provincial Police. Can I speak to Ana Kornichuk?" David passed the phone to Ana, saying, "It's for you."

Ana said, "Hello?" and her face turned stark white as she listened but failed to grasp what she was being told.

The voice on the other end said, "Mrs. Ana Kornichuk?"

Ana replied, "Yes."

"This is Corporal Fisker of the Collingwood Ontario Provincial Police, and I'm afraid that I have bad news. Your sister was found dead in her house this morning." As the officer started to tell her more, Ana tuned her out. David could see she was distraught as she handed the phone to him. She couldn't concentrate on anything as she tried to process what she had been told.

Taking the phone, Dave said, "Hello. This is David Kornichuk, Ana's husband. She is in shock and unable to speak to you."

"I'm terribly sorry. I know it is a great shock," the voice on the other end replied. "We received a call from a friend who told us she hadn't seen your sister-in-law, and when she tried, she couldn't get hold of her. We sent a car over to check it out, and they found her body in her house. We don't have any other details at this time, but we found your wife's name on her speed dial."

David replied, "I am retired from the RCMP, so I am aware of the procedure. Give me your number, and I will call you back once we have digested things. We'll probably fly over immediately." After getting the telephone number and being told once more how sorry they were, David hung up. Taking his wife in his arms, he comforted her. They were both devastated and gradually came to grips with what they had been told. They both had questions. Many questions.

Finally, Ana said, "It must have been her heart!" David nodded in agreement. Then she added, "We should get there as soon as we can." Again, he nodded.

"I'll get a flight sorted out if you want to call the kids," he told her.

"Okay. I don't feel like it, but we'd better eat something. It could be a long day," Ana added.

The first flight was leaving in four hours from Vancouver, and David booked it business class to give them a little privacy. They took their coffee and toast with them back to the bedroom, where they each packed their luggage. David knew that the police would have Marie's house cordoned off while they conducted their investigation, so he booked a hotel room in Collingwood and a rental car at the Toronto airport. After calling their kids, they asked their next-door neighbour to keep an eye on things. They loaded their suitcases in the car and headed to the airport.

Arriving in Collingwood in the late afternoon, they called Corporal Fisker and then went to meet her. It was nearing the end of March, and they were glad that they had brought some heavier jackets. The day was cloudy and grey, and the wind off the water was cold. They went straight to the Ontario Provincial Police office, where they were greeted by a thin, very fit uniformed policewoman with short blond hair and a very serious disposition. Introducing herself as Corporal Fisker, she took Ana's hand, saying, "I am so sorry for your loss," and led them to an adjacent interview room.

As they settled in, the corporal informed them, "Your sister's body wasn't found for two days. We received a call from the manager of her fitness centre, who had become worried when she did not turn up for her class and hadn't called to say she wasn't coming. The manager had tried to call her, but getting no answer, she became concerned, and not knowing who else to call, called us. We found her body, and after the coroner examined it, it was taken directly to the morgue at the hospital. We called in a forensic team, and they are at the house now."

"Have you notified our brother in Fergus?" Ana inquired.

"Yes, we called him right after we spoke with you. He told us they would come up tomorrow. There is one thing you should know, however. It appears that foul play could have been involved. I'll let you know when we finish our examination, but for now, it is being treated as a murder investigation."

Ana and David were caught completely off guard. They didn't know what to say. Finally, David asked, "Where is the body now?"

"It is at the hospital, and we are expecting to hear from the pathologist tomorrow. As soon as we hear, I will let you know."

Ana was on the verge of telling her that her sister had a heart murmur and was scheduled to see the cardiologist in Toronto because she had been diagnosed with endocarditis but decided it wasn't relevant, and as they got up to leave, she said, "We are staying at the Blue Water Inn for now, and we'll start making the funeral arrangements."

"That will be fine," the corporal responded, adding, "We should be done sometime tomorrow. I'll let you know. And, again, I am so sorry for your loss."

Thanking her, Ana and David left and headed to the motel.

$ $ $

"ROSE, YOU WON'T believe it. The police called and said they found Marie in her house—dead," Michael said as he hung up the telephone.

Thinking for a minute, Rose replied, "Her heart must have given out. That's terrible. She was probably under a lot of stress with the court case."

"Yeah, for sure. It was all on her shoulders," he added. "I told the police we would go up to Collingwood tomorrow. I guess Ana and Dave are flying in this afternoon."

They had been focusing their attention and thoughts on the upcoming court case that was rapidly approaching, as they had just received a call from their lawyer. He had advised them that he had just received a call from Gerard Morelli, and there was a new development. He had then continued, "Gerard advised me that he had been contacted by a Pasquali Bertollini. It seems he was aware of the court case and the new will. He went on to tell Gerard that, as an old family friend and business partner, he was prepared to come to court to testify because he knew that Clemente would never agree to have any of his children treated differently than the others. Apparently, he also told their lawyer that he and Clemente had talked about their families many times over the years, and he knew Clemente and Yolanda were of one mind that their children were equal. And finally, Mr. Bertollini told him that he and Clemente had talked just before Yolanda's passing. Your father had said that as he had disposed of most of his holdings, he was drawing up a new will to ensure everything that was left would go equally to each child.

"This throws a whole new light on things. We had better get together and review our options."

But now, as they had planned to go to Creemore the following day, they immediately called Jimmy's office and advised his secretary that they would have to postpone their meeting for a couple of days due to a death in the family.

$   $   $

THREE DAYS LATER, Michael and Rose met with their lawyer in Creemore, and Jimmy repeated what Gerald Morelli had told him. He said, "This is not looking good for our case. With Mr. Bertollini's testimony, Morelli will argue that it is apparent that after Mr. Gallorini's wife passed, he was at a total loss without her. He will further state that you moving in with him presented the opportunity for one or both of you to influence him to write the new will that favoured you."

"Can he do that?" Rose asked.

"It would be up to the judge, but if Mr. Bertollini does testify, I think there is a very good chance that the judge will take his word and will rule against you and throw the new will out. In light of this new development, my advice is to settle. In a lengthy trial, the legal costs could be extensive, and if you lose, there would be a very good chance that you will have to pay all the trial costs."

Michael was speechless. He didn't know what to do. He knew they were banking on winning the court case. Rose had not yet told him about her conversation with Marie. As they sat there looking at each other, Jimmy went on to inform them, "I have done a lot of research on similar cases, and from what I can see, your chances of winning have just gone from good to very bad. I suggest that we meet with Ana and her lawyer and agree to have the estate divided equally."

"With Marie's passing, will things be divided between Ana and Michael?" Rose inquired.

"No," was his reply. "Marie's estate will receive her share, which will then be disbursed as per the instructions in her will."

"Are you aware of the provisions in her will?" Michael inquired.

"I have no knowledge of that," Jimmy replied.

When Michael, Rose, and Ana met two days later with their lawyers, it was agreed that Clemente's estate would be divided equally between his three children. It was further agreed that the cottage would be sold and the proceeds from the sale would be included in the disbursement. It was further noted that Marie's share would be paid to her estate and would then be disbursed as per the direction of her last will and testament. The appropriate legal documents were then signed, and Gerard said he and Jimmy would file them with the court immediately.

As they were about to leave, Rose inquired, "Can you tell me two things? First, when will the estate be able to disburse the money to the beneficiaries? And second, what does Marie's will say?"

Looking her in the eye, Gerard replied, "The estate could take up to a year to be finalized, depending on what progress the executor has made and when he receives the tax clearance certificate. On your other question, I am not in a position to discuss the provisions of Marie's will."

CHAPTER **FORTY**

L
ATER THE NEXT day, Ana received a call from Corporal Fisker advising that the forensic team had finished with the house, and she and David could come over anytime to pick up the keys at the front desk. Little did she know that within a short period of time, the house would become her property.

When they went to collect the keys, the corporal was waiting for them and told them her inspector would like a word with them. She took them upstairs and into a boardroom with a large table. They sat and were left for a few minutes. Then, a young, smart-looking fellow in an officer's uniform entered and introduced himself as Inspector Berube. He was just over six feet tall with a slim build, short rust-brown hair, and a thin moustache.

"I'm terribly sorry for your loss," he said directly to Ana. "It is a real tragedy. We just received the report from the hospital, and we are now treating it as a murder investigation. The cause of death has been confirmed as an injury to the head. Corporal Fisker will no longer be directly involved, and the investigation will be headed up by Detective Sergeant Bill Teche. He is waiting for you in his office. I'll take you down if you don't have any questions."

Entering the office back on the first floor, the inspector introduced them to a short, husky fellow with a round face and a brush cut. He thanked the inspector, who turned and left, and invited them to take a seat.

"I can't believe this happened, and I am so sorry for your loss," he said to Ana. Turning to Dave, he continued, "Welcome to our detachment, sir." Seeing the surprised look on Dave's face, he added, "When you told Corporal Fisker on the phone that you had been with the RCMP, we ran you through our system. Your background came up immediately. I haven't shared this with anyone and didn't know if you wanted me to keep it to myself or let the inspector know."

"Well," David answered slowly, thinking as he spoke, "I don't see how it can hurt, but this is your investigation, and obviously, I will do anything I can to assist, but I certainly have no intention of getting directly involved unless I am invited."

Smiling with relief, Bill became much more relaxed. Dave then went on, "My wife and I are going to move into the house this afternoon, and the funeral is tomorrow. I'm not sure how you want to proceed, but I would appreciate getting updates, and if there is anything you need to know or want us to do, don't hesitate to ask, but again, to be clear, this is your investigation."

They stood and shook hands, and Bill said, "That is good to know. Thank you." He ushered them down the hall to the main reception. "I'll be in touch as soon as we know anything," he added.

Ana and Dave moved into the house that afternoon and quickly settled in. The following day, they drove to Toronto for Marie's funeral. Her body had been cremated, as she had told her sister many years earlier that was what she wanted. Ana was completely devastated by her sister's passing. Dave knew how close they were and how much Marie meant to Ana. She broke down at the ceremony, and he took her in his arms and held her, telling her that Marie had been an amazing sister and he understood her loss.

They returned to the house and called their children, bringing them up to date with what was happening. Over the next few weeks, they occupied themselves with sorting through Marie's things. When they went into her studio, they saw the painting that they had purchased in the north and given to her as a housewarming gift. The artist was a former priest who had left the priesthood and married a local girl. They had settled in a small northern community called Coville Lake, where he built a log Catholic church and a fishing lodge. Over the years, he had developed into a talented and respected artist. His name was Bern Will Brown, and the painting was of an Inuit dog team headed over the ice and into the setting sun. It was done in oil and was very impressive.

As soon as Marie's will was probated, they set about transferring her property, car, and belongings into Ana's name. She also took over Marie's membership at the women's fitness centre, while Dave joined the local YMCA to take advantage of their gymnasium and pool.

As they went through Marie's things, they decided to take her clothing to a local women's shelter. They went slowly and methodically through her files and papers. They took the same approach with her jewellery. As she was looking, Ana said, "I don't see some of the nicer pieces, including the beautiful sapphire and diamond necklace that Favio's wife had given her before they left." She could see the blank look on her husband's face, so she added, "Apparently, it had been Uncle Spiffy's mother's, and since they had no children to leave it to, she gave it to Yolanda as the oldest daughter of her husband's nephew. It was considered a family heirloom."

CHAPTER **FORTY-ONE**

I T WAS COMING on two months since the murder was discovered, and the weather was slowly turning nice. Early in May, Ana and Dave had a knock on the door from a fellow who identified himself as Carlos, Marie's gardener. He was tall and very skinny and had a head of hair that Dave thought looked like a blob of licorice cotton candy. Carlos told them he did all of Marie's yardwork and asked if they wanted him to continue looking after the property. They looked at each other for a moment, and Ana said, "Yes." She did not know how much time or effort they would be able to put into the yard with all the things that were lurking on the horizon. Carlos informed them of his compensation, and they agreed. He also mentioned that he was subcontracting for a landscape company owned by Jorge Gomez, who had done the original layout and landscaping of the yard.

Dave had left it with Bill to call him when he thought a briefing was appropriate. When he did go in for his first update many weeks later, he was surprised to be called "sir" by everyone. There wasn't a great deal of new information about the case, so Dave thought he would have coffee with Inspector Berube and share his thoughts with him. He told Bill, who called and made sure the inspector was available and then directed Dave upstairs. The inspector's secretary asked what he took in this coffee before taking him into the inspector's office.

"Great to see you, Dave. How are things going?" Inspector Berube asked once he had settled into a chair at the work table adjacent to his desk. "Oh, by the way, I'm Charles, but everyone calls me Sandy." And so they chatted, and Sandy was quite intrigued by Dave's northern experience.

Finally, Dave said, "I told Bill that I wouldn't involve myself in his investigation, but he seems to have reached a point where things are slowing down. I'm at a point with the estate where I've got time available, and I wondered what you would think if I offered to join his team as an unpaid consultant. I would work for him under his direction and report to him. I do have my private investigator's licence in BC, but I thought this other route would be more advantageous, as I don't want to be seen as horning in or trying to take over."

Thinking for a moment, the inspector replied, "I like it, but let me check with HQ in Orillia first. I don't want to step on anyone's toes. I'll get back to you in a couple of days."

"That's good," Dave replied.

True to his word, Sandy's secretary called a few days later and asked if Dave was available to come over to the detachment. Dave went directly over and was again ushered to the inspector's office. Sandy was waiting, and once they settled in, he said, "Your offer caught them off guard, but once they got their heads around it, they agreed, with one stipulation. You cannot, under any circumstances, let it be known, especially to the press, that you are working for us. They said if it comes up, it should be said, very clearly, that you are working 'in conjunction' with us."

"No problem there," Dave replied. "I realize the press could blow things out of proportion if they got wind of it, so I'll just keep my head down and do things out of the limelight."

Sandy then continued, "I've told Bill, and he is waiting for you in his office. He is thrilled, by the way."

Entering Bill's office, Dave was greeted with an enthusiastic handshake, followed by, "Welcome to the team. Glad to have you." Sitting down, Bill went over what direction they had taken with their investigation. "Not much has come to light, and we still have to talk to the family members. Rose is definitely a person of interest, as she was the last person to have contact with the victim."

"Okay," Dave replied. "Why don't you let me do that? I know Mike and his wife and can probably get things out of them in pretty short order. Do you want me to brief you daily or weekly? I will be doing some travelling to the city, so weekly may be a bit more practical, but if I get anything, I'll let you know right away."

"Sounds good. Thank you for doing this. We really appreciate it," was the reply.

Dave went home and told Ana what was happening and that he would need her help. "Things like this missing jewellery, for instance, may be very important, and your knowledge of these family things could be crucial to us getting to the bottom of what went on."

The following morning, they sat down to collect their thoughts and decide how to approach things. Dave told his wife that, in his experience, there were certain truisms when working a case. "First," he explained, "a crime that involves a family is usually committed by someone close to the victim. Second, follow the money. When money is involved, who stands to gain the most is important. So, my first thought is to your brother and his wife. But before we go off chasing shadows, we should put together a list of people we want to interview because they may have information or knowledge that will be valuable to us."

Ana paused for a moment before saying, "This should be quite an undertaking. I am looking forward to seeing my amazing husband at work."

Just then, the telephone rang. Ana answered it, saying, "Yes. Hi there. Okay, thanks. We'll watch for it." Turning to David, she told him, "That was Gerry Morelli. He's mailed a registered envelope to me containing a letter and Marie's will."

"Now, let's see who we should be talking to," David said.

"Well," she responded, "I've always wondered about that guy she worked with at the accounting firm where they snubbed her because she was an Italian female. I think his name is Bill Brown, and I guess he wasn't very happy when she broke it off with him."

"That's great. That's what we need," he replied.

Ana felt good as they continued brainstorming about other people they should talk to. Then David said, "I know the OPP folks should have talked to the neighbours, but I think we should make a point of talking to them, just to make sure no one was missed."

And so they developed their initial list, which included the owner of the woman's fitness centre, Danilo, and the staff at Marie's accounting practice, Bill Brown, and Marie's friend at the accounting firm. As they were mulling over who else they may want to talk to, Dave said, "And of course, we should start with your brother and Rose. It will be interesting to hear what they have to say."

At that point, they stopped and had lunch. In the afternoon, they called Danilo and arranged to meet him and his senior staff the next morning in their office in the city.

As they were getting ready to leave, the mail arrived. Ana signed for the registered envelope and, opening it, read it to herself. Then, without saying a word, she passed it to her husband. He read it, and the first words out of his mouth were, "Sweet Jesus." He had just read that his wife's sister had left everything to her . . . her house, her car, her share of their father's estate, her savings—everything. "There's well over a million here," he commented.

Getting in the car, Dave said, "Let's plan to have dinner in the city tonight, in memory of and to thank your sister. You have some thinking to do."

"Yeah, good idea," Ana responded. "A very good idea. I really miss her." Holding back her tears, she continued, "She was such a huge part of my life, and I learned a lot from her. She always looked out for me."

$ $ $

IT WAS A lovely sunny day with a breeze that kept the temperature very comfortable. It was a great day for a trip, and they proceeded to Marie's old accounting office, where they met with Danilo and the senior staff. After hearing of their shock at Marie's untimely and unfortunate passing and accepting their condolences, Ana and Dave asked if there was anyone—a former employee or client—who may have had a problem with or held a grudge against Marie. There was none. "Everyone liked her and respected her," Danilo told them, and the others nodded in agreement. Thanking them, Dave asked them to call if anything came to mind. Then they left.

They decided to go to the Italian restaurant in Vaughan where they had stopped for dinner after their father's funeral. Ana remembered it was called Ristorante Positano, and it was owned by Santino Scaini. Santino recognized them when they arrived and was sorry to learn of Marie's untimely passing. He then served them a wonderful meal in her honour.

As they ate, Ana told her husband, "Yes, I did some calculating, and you were right. We are looking at more than a million dollars from Marie's estate."

"Yes, I thought so. But I would much prefer her still being with us," Dave replied. "She was a pretty amazing lady, and I always respected and admired her."

When they left, Santino saw them out. They insisted on paying for their meal, despite his objections.

"We'll certainly be back again," she told him in Italian. "Again, it was an amazing meal. *Grazie.*"

The following morning, it was raining. Dave was going to brief Bill Teche on their visit to Marie's former business. Ana was heading to the club for a workout on the equipment. As they were leaving, Dave suggested, "Have a sniff around and see if anyone ever saw or heard Marie say anything that may be of interest."

"No problem," she replied as they left the house. After she dropped her husband at the detachment, she headed to the club. When she arrived, everyone gathered around to tell her how terrible Marie's passing was and how sorry they were. Ana thanked each person individually and used the opportunity to ask if they had heard or noticed anything. The only thing that came up was from Millie, who told her, "One day, not that long ago, Marie mentioned she had the feeling that someone was following her. She said everywhere she went that morning she noticed the same vehicle just sitting there."

"Did she give you any details or say anything about the vehicle?" Ana asked.

"Not really. She said it stayed pretty well back and was certainly a dark-coloured car, as I recall."

"Did she say how often she thought it happened?"

"No, just that it had happened a few times before. Oh, I remember, it was the day she came back after seeing her doctor."

"That's great, thanks, Millie. If you think of anything else or if any of the other girls do, let me know, would you? I'd better get to work on the machines." And with that, Ana headed over to the treadmill to start her workout.

When Ana picked David up at the detachment, it was still raining. As they drove, she relayed the conversation to him.

"Great," her husband replied. "That is what it takes—finding out the little things, one at a time. How about we head to the city tomorrow and visit the firm? What was her friend's name?"

"Julie something. I don't think I ever heard it. Let me call down and find out who she is, and then I'll speak with her and see if she is free for lunch."

Arriving back at the house, they saw the neighbour across the street wave hello to them. While Ana went in to make the phone call, Dave walked over and introduced himself to the neighbour, who was waiting under an umbrella. Returning to the house as Ana was hanging up, he said, "Her name is Schmit, and she would love to have coffee with us when we get back."

"Okay. Julie is good for lunch tomorrow and will be expecting us around twelve-thirty. Her family name is Henderson."

"Great. Let's plan an early breakfast so we can leave in good time. That's quite a talkative neighbour, by the way," he added. "She's been down east looking after a sickly aunt and just got back. She told me that she 'keeps an eye on things.' I asked her if the OPP had talked to her, and she said that she was away when they found Marie's body and she hadn't talked to anyone about it. So, I told her we were away tomorrow but that on Friday we could have coffee. Oh," he added, "her name is Laura Schmit."

The following morning was still rainy as they left. They arrived at the accounting offices shortly after noon. It had rained off and on during their drive. They saw the firm was called Ferguson and Associates Chartered Accountants. As they entered the foyer, a woman in her early sixties with medium grey-brown hair and a round face was waiting for them. Shaking Ana's hand, she said, "Hi, I'm Julie. You must be Ana. I've heard a great deal about you. And this is your husband?"

"Yes, this is David, and I am Ana. Nice to meet you. I remember my sister talking about you when she worked here. Where would you like to go for lunch?" And with that, they left, chatting about Marie and how badly everyone who remembered her was feeling.

"I have worked at Ferguson's since college and am planning to retire in three years," she told them. Then, during lunch, Julie filled them in on

Bill Brown and the issue with selecting a new partner, which resulted in Marie's sudden departure.

"Did she ever have any further contact with Bill Brown?" David asked.

"No, I understand he tried, but she had lost total respect for him and wanted nothing more to do with him. He didn't take it very well and tried to reach out to her several times. When that didn't work, apparently he resorted to sending her birthday and Christmas cards every year. She told me she threw them out without opening them."

"Where is Bill Brown now?" David asked.

"Oh, he retired to Huntsville. He had a family home there, and as far as I know, he is still there. He never married and retired about three years ago. Talk around the office was that he never got over Marie or what happened when she was passed over for the senior partner's kid."

"Offhand, would you have any idea what type of vehicle he drives?" David inquired.

"Not offhand, but give me a minute and I'll find out." With that, she took out a cellphone, made a quick call, and then said, "It's a dark-coloured Ford or Mercury sedan. They think it may be a Crown Victoria. He liked a bigger car but not too flashy. Apparently, he'd never get anything like a Lincoln."

"Thanks, that's quite helpful," David added as he signalled to their server to bring him the bill.

After saying their goodbyes and thanking Julie again, they headed back to Collingwood just in time to avoid the afternoon traffic heading north. The rain had stopped, and the sun was just trying to break through the dark clouds.

The following morning after breakfast, Dave suggested that he would go and see if their neighbour would like to come and have a visit over coffee. Ana agreed, saying, "Okay, once I get the breakfast things put away and the kitchen tidied." Dave pitched in by packing the dirty dishes in the dishwasher and then headed across the road to Laura Schmit's house.

Shortly after, Dave and Laura arrived back, and it being a lovely day, they decided to sit out on the patio. Laura said she heard about Marie as soon as she returned from PEI and how sorry she was.

They chatted about the neighbourhood, and during the conversation, Laura told them how surprised she was with the number of people who came to see Carlos, the gardener, while he was working on Marie's property. "They drive up and stop. He will go over to see them. They have a short visit with him, and then they leave. Quite often, five or six cars come by."

"No one ever gets out?" Dave inquired.

"No, not that I saw. But about once a week, the other fellow, Carlos's boss I think, comes by and talks to him, and then they carry things into the storage shed," she continued. "His name was Mandez or something like that."

"Gomez, Jorge Gomez?" Marie asked, remembering what Carlos had told her when they first met.

"Yes, that's the name. And the only other thing I saw was that every once in a while, a dark-coloured car came and parked down the street a bit and sat there for an hour or so. Then it would just leave."

"Did you ever get a look at the driver?" Ana asked.

"No," Julie answered. "It was too far away."

"Was Marie at home when the car was there, do you know?" was Ana's next question.

"Oh yes, always. I like to keep an eye on the happenings around the neighbourhood, and I thought that was odd."

"Well, that is great, and we are happy to know that you are keeping an eye on things," Dave said, standing to show her out.

"If I see it again, I'll give you a call. Thank you for the coffee, and it was nice to meet you both. Are you planning on staying long?"

"We have some things to wrap up here, so we'll see. Thanks for coming and for the information. Bye."

Once she was gone, Dave turned to Ana. "That's what I call a nosy neighbour. Some interesting things, though, and I have a hunch that the lurking car may have been Bill Brown."

They looked and found that his telephone number was unlisted, so they called Julie, and she gave them his phone number and address in Huntsville. They then decided to drive and see him, so after the weekend and when Dave had touched base with Bill Teche, they headed up to Huntsville.

"Should we have called him?" Ana asked as they drove.

"I don't think so," Dave answered. "We don't know anything about him or what he's been up to, so I think we want to arrive unannounced so we get a feel for him and what he's doing."

"That makes sense. Do you think he is some kind of weirdo who was obsessed with her? I remember Marie saying—and didn't Julie mention it too?—that he kept sending her Christmas and birthday cards."

"Yes. The more we hear, the more I'm thinking that he is the mystery stalker in the dark sedan."

As they drove north, not too far from Orillia, they crossed a bridge, and a sign identified the river as the Severn. They were both surprised by how the landscape changed immediately on the north side of the river. The outcropping of rock became very evident, and the trees were more pine and spruce instead of maple.

They had entered northern Ontario.

## CHAPTER FORTY-TWO

ANA AND DAVE pulled up to the house at the address that Julie had given them just after eleven. It was a very plain-looking two-storey brick house with minimal landscaping. The garage door was open, and a black Ford Crown Victoria was parked inside. They decided that Ana should stay in the car and Dave would go to the door and use her presence in the car as bait to get them invited in. *But,* he thought to himself, *I have to read this guy and see where his head's at.* So he went to the door and knocked.

The door opened a crack, and a voice said, "Yes?"

"Oh, hi. Are you Bill Brown? My name is Dave Kornichuk."

The door opened wider, and an older fellow with heavily rimmed glasses, a large nose, brown-grey hair, and a thin face replied, "Yes, I'm Bill."

As Dave got a better look, he could see that Bill was slightly built and about five feet nine. "I'm Marie Gallorini's brother-in-law, and her sister Ana is waiting in the car." He motioned with his head as he continued, "We didn't want to barge in, but Ana would love to meet you. We are hoping you might be able to help us. Can we come in for a chat?"

Thinking for a moment, Bill replied, "Yes, I guess so. I don't know how much help I can be."

Dave turned and signalled to his wife to join them. As Ana came up to the door, Bill stepped back and said to her, "Do come in," and showed her into the living room, which was small but tastefully furnished. Dave followed. "Have a seat. Can I get you anything to drink?"

"No, thank you," Ana replied. "My sister had told me about you when you were working together, and I wanted to meet you. We are devastated by her loss and wondered if you had any thoughts on what could have possibly happened. David has offered to help the police with their investigation, and we thought we would pick your brain to see if there is anything you think we should know."

Bill, looking down at his feet, answered, "I feel sick about what happened. Do the police have any leads yet?"

*I wonder how he knows,* Dave thought to himself, and then said, choosing his words carefully, "Nothing to speak of. We are fully aware you weren't close anymore, and we are wondering if there is anything from her past that you think we should be looking at."

Glancing at Ana again, Bill said, "I am completely to blame for our falling-out. I really loved your sister, but when she was passed over as a partner, I didn't want to jeopardize my position as a junior partner by challenging the big guy. In retrospect, I should have, but I didn't. Your sister couldn't accept that. We were good together, and I was going to ask her to marry me. It's my fault. I've been watching out for her ever since, making sure that she was never threatened. I watched her house, but her neighbour, who I've dubbed 'Nosy Parker,' became aware of my presence, and I didn't want her to tell your sister, so I cut back my surveillance. And when I did go, I parked further back. On the night it happened, her sister-in-law visited, but then she left, and so did I." He looked away and wiped a tear from his eye. "I really loved her, you know."

Ana came over, sat beside him, and put her arm around him. "I think you would have been good with her. We're sorry it didn't work out. Did you see anything else that caught your eye while you were watching?" she asked, glancing over at her husband.

"The only person that was around much was her gardener. His boss dropped in from time to time. Come upstairs, I want to show you something," he said to Ana.

"Can David come?" Ana said, taken aback and unsure what was going to happen.

"Sure, if he would like. It'll just take a minute."

Following him up the narrow staircase, they came to a small room on the next floor. Bill opened the door, turned on the lights, and without saying a word, motioned them inside. They couldn't believe their eyes. The room was a shrine to her sister—photographs everywhere, candles, and a scrapbook filled with his memorabilia of her. They were speechless.

Bill left them to peruse the contents of the room and returned downstairs. When they came down, he told them, "She was a wonderful person, and I am so sorry that she is gone. Is there anything else I can tell you?"

They said no, and, thanking him for his openness, they left.

## CHAPTER FORTY-THREE

O N THE WAY back from Bill Brown's, Dave said, "Let's stop in Barrie. We can grab a bite of lunch and see if there are any pawn shops we can check out. I've been thinking about the missing jewellery, and I'm wondering if it could have ended up in a pawn shop. If it was stolen for the money—and it probably was—they certainly wouldn't try to get rid of it in Collingwood. I don't know if there are any pawn shops of any size in the area. I think Toronto would be the closest, so let's check around and see."

After lunch, they walked around, looking for pawn shops. They saw one and went in and had a quick look around. There was nothing of interest. The owner asked if he could help them find anything, and Dave asked about other pawn shops. The fellow told them there was one other two blocks away and gave them directions. Thanking him, Ana and Dave left, got their car, and drove over to the other shop.

This establishment looked a little more rundown than the first one. Dave and Ana entered, and there was a man behind the counter who glanced up from the computer screen he was focused on, took a quick look, and then returned his attention to the screen. They were walking around, examining the contents of the cabinets, when Ana spotted it. She didn't say anything but nudged her husband and pointed at it. There it was: the beautiful sapphire and diamond necklace. Nodding, they left the shop and returned to their car.

Dave called Bill Teche, telling him, "We are in Barrie and were checking out local pawn shops when Ana saw a family heirloom that belonged to her sister. Can you arrange for a search warrant and any other paperwork we need to go back and secure it and anything else we find?"

They waited in their car, and within the hour, an OPP cruiser pulled up. Two members got out. Dave and Ana introduced themselves, and one of the officers advised them that the Collingwood detachment had called and requested their assistance. Dave briefed them, and then they all proceeded into the shop. Approaching the fellow behind the counter, who was now fully focused on the group that had entered his store, Dave stated, "I'm Dave Kornichuk, and I'm working with the OPP. We have a warrant to search your premises." One of the constables produced the search warrant and gave it to him.

Ana then led them to the display case, where the constables instructed the sales clerk to put on a pair of jeweller's gloves and carefully place the necklace in the evidence bag one of the constables was holding open. "We want to see your records of who brought in that necklace," the constables told him. The sales clerk showed them, and one of the constables took a photo of the page showing the details.

Dave then asked, "Do you remember who brought it in?"

The answer was, "Yes."

"Can you describe him?"

Again, the answer was, "Yes." The sales clerk was small with an oblong face and a goatee. As he started to speak, his accent became apparent. Dave thought it could be Serbian or another eastern European dialect. He went on to tell them, "He was a young, tall, thin fellow with a pile of black hair on top of his head. He was wearing jeans, a plain shirt, and a baseball cap."

"What else did he hawk?"

Remaining very calm, the shop clerk started to read from his book, and Dave interrupted him, saying, "Show us."

He then proceeded to point out five other items in the cabinets. "Is that everything?" he was asked.

"That's all. Honest to Christ," was the answer.

Ana confirmed that she was pretty certain they were her sister's, and again, the fellow put on the jeweller's gloves and placed them individually in other evidence bags.

Dave then asked the officers to give the fellow, who turned out to be the shop owner, a receipt before they left. He then thanked them for their assistance, and he and Ana got in their car and drove back to Collingwood.

Arriving in Bill's office, Dave gave him the bags and the paperwork, explaining how things had unfolded. Bill said that each piece would be checked for fingerprints. Dave went on to tell him, "The owner gave us a description, and it sounds like Carlos, the gardener, hawked them. You can check and see if Carlos's prints were on file. His last name is Menendez. My wife was going through her sister's cancelled cheques and saw one made out to him. We are thinking that we'll go to Fergus and chat with my brother and sister-in-law. Bill Brown, by the way, referred to our neighbour as 'Nosy Parker,' and she certainly keeps an eye on the comings and goings in the neighbourhood. She told me that our sister-in-law visited Marie on the night she was murdered. We'll check the details with Rose and see if anything seemed not right to her. Anything else you can think of?"

"Sounds like you've got all the bases covered," Bill replied. "Is this Bill Brown guy a weirdo? Should we be keeping an eye on him?"

"No," Dave replied. "I think he is a little man who let things get the better of him, and he regrets that he didn't deal with them head-on. As a result of his inaction, he lost the love of his life. Too bad—he doesn't seem like a bad person, and he could have been a part of the family if he had stood up for his girlfriend."

"We really appreciate your assistance," Bill told him. "Your past experience and having the inside family knowledge are making a huge difference."

"No problem. All in a day's work," was the answer. "Let me know when you get word on the prints. Cheers."

When they returned to the house, Dave called Mike, saying, "We thought we would come down and take you out to dinner tomorrow, if you are free."

"I'll check with Rose when she finishes work, but I think tomorrow would be fine," he responded.

It was an overcast, grey day as they headed out. Neither of them had been to Fergus, so they thought they would go early and have a look around before meeting up with Rose and Mike. "I would really love to know if she talked your father into doing that dumb will," Dave commented as they were driving along.

"I have a feeling that she did, and with the Alzheimer's taking hold of his mind, he agreed to please her. But I know she'll never admit it. I think she had high hopes for her life with my brother, but I've watched them fade away over the years. This was probably a last attempt at getting the lifestyle she strived for. I think Michael was behind her, cheering her on, so to speak."

"Hmm." He thought for a minute and then said, "You are probably right. How did he end up so rudderless while you and your sister were so focused?"

"I hate to say it, but Dad spoiled him. He never held Michael accountable. Mom was always teaching and steering Marie and me."

Arriving, they had a good look around Fergus, and its Scottish heritage was very evident. Then they found Mike and Rose waiting for them in the restaurant they had suggested. After the hellos, they settled in.

Dave got right to the point, and in answer to his question, Rose replied, "Yes, I visited Marie and took her a box of dark chocolate truffles. I looked at it as a peace offering after the will and all the court stuff. I was worried about her health and wanted her to know that I—I mean, we—didn't hold any grudges and that we were there if she needed us. And yes, she was pretty uptight with everything that was going on," Rose added.

Then, to their surprise, Michael spoke up and said, "I mentioned to Dad that we would love to get the cottage but never thought for a minute that it would turn out to be such a bone of contention."

Ana was on the verge of saying something condescending, but sensing it, Dave jumped in and said, "Well, thank goodness it's over and we can get on with things."

Getting the subtle message, Ana asked, "How's your job going, Rose? I'll bet the vet is glad to have you back. From what we hear, you are a natural with the animals."

It turned out to be a lovely dinner, and as they drove home later, Ana said, "Thanks for getting into that conversation before I said something that I would have regretted."

"No problem," he answered. "I thought we should try to keep things civil."

CHAPTER **FORTY-FOUR**

H AVING RULED OUT Rose and Michael, Dave and Ana—who was thoroughly enjoying working with and helping her husband— felt they had narrowed things down to the property care team. They knew, however, that they still had to find the motive or trigger for the death and then prove who did it.

There were many fingerprints on the necklace, and unfortunately, Carlos's weren't in the system. So, David came up with a plan.

Carlos was working at the house about three times a week for two to five hours at a time. The next day he worked was hot and sticky. Ana invited him to have a glass of lemonade as he was finishing. He joined them on the patio and proceeded to guzzle the glass of lemonade in short order. Ana refilled it and asked, "How long have you been in Canada?"

"Six years," Carlos responded.

"Did you come from Mexico?"

"Yes, just outside Guadalajara."

"How do you like it here?"

"It's wonderful," Carlos said, adding, "It's very different from home, but I love the four seasons, and I'm planning to learn how to ski this winter."

And so the small talk went on, with Dave telling Carlos about their time in the Canadian north. After about half an hour, Carlos thanked them. Ana gave him his cheque for the week's work, and he left. Dave immediately and carefully placed Carlos's glass in an evidence bag, saying to his wife, "I'll just run this over so they can get his prints."

Back home, as they sat out on their back patio waiting, Dave was thinking, and then he said, "The neighbour Nosy Parker had told us that

Carlos was visited several times while he was working. He must be dealing, but where would he keep his supply?" As he turned it over in his mind, he assumed that it had to be somewhere in the garden shed.

"Did Marie tell you that Gomez built the shed for her when he was doing the landscaping?" he asked Ana.

"Yes. I was with Dad when she told us."

Dave then headed over to the shed to have a look around. It was well-constructed with unfinished cedar. It held all the yard and garden maintenance tools, including a gas-powered lawn mower, a snow blower, and several smaller tools. There were cans of gasoline and oil on the floor. There was a workbench under the south-facing window and a large deep drawer built in underneath the bench top. Dave opened the drawer and found nails, screws, string, and cords. Examining it more closely, his trained eye saw that the drawer had a false bottom. It was deeper than it appeared. Removing the drawer and examining it carefully, he saw the last quarter of the false bottom could be lifted off, exposing a hidden storage compartment. In it, he found a large plastic box containing a number of pills, which he assumed were fentanyl, and small packages of a white powdery substance that Dave thought was heroin or cocaine. *No wonder Carlos has so many visitors,* he thought. *He's got quite a stash here.*

He put everything back exactly as he found it and left the shed. "You won't believe what I found in the shed," he said, and he went on to tell his wife of his discovery.

"Can you arrest him?" she asked.

"Not yet," Dave replied. "We still have to catch him in the act of selling, but before that, we have to get his fingerprints identified so we can prove that he took your sister's jewellery to the pawn shop. I think there may be more to this than meets the eye, so we'll have to dig a little deeper. We need to determine why your sister died. What happened to cost her her life?"

He decided to share his findings and thoughts with Bill and see if he had the results of the gardener's fingerprints yet. Learning that they weren't in the system, he briefed Bill and outlined his thinking to him. As he headed home, he walked across to Laura Schmit's and rang her doorbell.

"Can we chat?" Dave asked when she answered the door.

"Of course," was the immediate response, and he was shown in.

Half an hour later, he left and walked over to their house, where Ana was waiting. "You won't believe how excited Nosy Parker is." He then went on to tell her what he had done.

$ $ $

OVER THE NEXT week, Dave and Ana went about their normal routine. Carlos came and went about his yardwork. Nothing appeared to have changed, and that's what they wanted. The weather was now hot and a touch humid . . . a perfect summer.

The following week on the Friday, two casually dressed men arrived at their kitchen very early in the morning. Ana made them coffee, and they waited.

When Dave visited Laura two weeks before, he had asked her to keep a detailed account of who visited Carlos that week. Then he had asked her to come over with the notes he had asked her to make. He had sworn her to secrecy. After he complimented her on a job well done, she left. Dave showed Ana the carefully compiled notes on the visitors Carlos had seen the previous week. Laura had recorded the day, the time of day, the make, model, and colour of the vehicle, and the number of passengers inside. When possible, she recorded the licence plate number. Ana was impressed.

Based on this, it appeared that Friday was the most active day. So, on the following Friday, which just happened to be just before the Labour Day weekend, two plainclothes OPP detectives, who were now waiting in Dave and Ana's kitchen, had arrived. They were waiting, and when the time was right, they would quickly descend and apprehend the first car to arrive as well as Carlos.

At 10:43 a.m., a vehicle arrived, and as Carlos was standing and chatting with the occupants, the detectives moved in and arrested them. They were quickly handcuffed, placed in two cruisers that were standing by, and taken to the OPP station. The vehicle was also towed away immediately.

As suspected, Carlos was selling drugs to his visitors. Apparently, they would call him and place their order. He would get the drugs they wanted from his supply in the garden shed, and when they arrived, the transaction was completed.

The results of his fingerprints taken from the lemonade glass had come back, and they were a match to fingerprints found on Marie's jewellery.

The drug buyers were charged and released after a brief court appearance. Carlos was held in a cell, awaiting further questioning.

CHAPTER FORTY-FIVE

THE INTERROGATION WAS conducted by a heavy-set OPP detective inspector, Pierre Larocque. He was just over six feet tall and had sandy red hair, which was parted in the centre and combed to each side of his head. He had a matching waxed moustache and a very serious face. Joining him was Bill Teche. David attended as an observer.

After the formalities, Carlos informed them he did not require a lawyer. The inspector then got down to business by questioning him about the drugs he was selling and where he obtained them. Carlos was very evasive with his answers and revealed nothing.

DI Larocque asked, "How long have you been selling drugs?"

"About two and a half years," was the reply.

"Where do you get them?"

"I purchased them from a fellow named Smoky. I don't know Smoky's name or anything about him. We never talked when we met. When I needed more product, I sent a text to an unknown mailbox. I received a message back telling me when and where to pick them up," Carlos told him.

"Can you describe this fellow, Smoky?"

"He was a white guy, about twenty-five, with long black hair tied into a ponytail. He's about five feet eight or so and wears a Blue Jays hat, a brown jacket, and blue jeans."

*Wow. That could be anyone,* Dave thought. *He's obviously being well briefed on what to say.*

Things took a turn when the inspector produced Marie's jewellery and, showing it to Carlos, asked him, "Have you seen these items before?"

Carlos hesitated, not expecting this, and then answered, "Yes."

"Tell me how they came to be in your possession," the DI asked.

"I found them in a bag on the side of the road when I was walking to the convenience store," was the answer.

"Did you know where they came from or who they belonged to?" the DI asked.

"No," Carlos replied.

"What did you do with them?"

"I took them to a pawn shop and sold them," Carlos told him.

"Where was the pawn shop?"

"In Barrie," was his answer.

"Why Barrie? Why not Collingwood?"

"I thought I could get more for them in Barrie because there is more than one pawn shop, and so there was a bit of competition," Carlos said.

"And you have no idea who they belonged to or where they came from?"

"That's correct."

"You worked for Marie Gallorini. Is that correct?"

"Yes," he replied, nodding.

"She was found dead in her home, and your fingerprints are on this jewellery, which belonged to her and which you sold at a pawn shop." He paused, taking a drink of water, and then continued. "Carlos Menendez, I am charging you with the murder of Marie Gallorini." And with that, the inspector proceeded to read him his rights. "Do you wish to arrange for a lawyer before we proceed?" was the next question.

"Yes," was Carlos's reply. He was visibly shaken.

"Very wise decision," the inspector said. He opened the interview room door and said to the guard who was stationed there, "Take him back to his cell."

When they were alone, Dave advised them, "I don't think we have our man. You saw the look on his face. That was a look of complete surprise and fear." The others nodded in agreement.

"I didn't buy that cock-and-bull story about him buying the drugs from some unknown middleman," Inspector Larocque added. "Once he gets a lawyer, we'll have him back here and turn up the heat."

## CHAPTER FORTY-SIX

THE FOLLOWING DAY, Dave had Bill Teche and the inspector come to his house, where he showed them the hidden drawer in the garden shed. "We don't know when it is being replenished. I've told you about our neighbour who keeps an eye on the comings and goings, and she tells me that she has never seen anyone come to the house at night. Of course, that doesn't mean that things couldn't occur late at night when everyone is asleep. Let's go over so you can meet her and see what you think."

Arriving at Laura Schmit's door, which opened before they knocked, the inspector introduced himself, telling her, "I wanted to thank you for helping us with the drug bust. I am wondering if you ever see anyone else, besides the gardener, arrive and go into the garden shed?"

"Well, that landscape fellow comes by periodically and drops things in the shed. I didn't get a good look, but he seemed to be dropping off gasoline and oil," was her response. "Can I interest you in a cup of tea and a scone?"

"That sounds wonderful," Bill answered, "but we have a few things that need attending to, so we'll have to take a rain check. Thank you for your information. It is quite helpful." They left.

As they were getting into their car, Dave asked, "Can we get a forensic team over and see if they can lift any fingerprints off the gas or oil cans?" And then Dave said to Bill, "Can you check and see if you have anything on Jorge Gomez on file?"

"No problem." Then the inspector added, "Okay, let's go and see if we can get anything else out of Menendez."

Arriving back at the station, they were informed that Carlos had appeared before a Justice of the Peace and had a court-appointed lawyer assigned. Subsequently, he had pled not guilty to the second-degree murder charge. Bill had already called the office, advising them of their intent to question Carlos again.

The lawyer, Zolton Gyarmathy, was waiting when they arrived. He was a small man, about forty, Dave guessed. He had neatly combed black hair, a very serious manner, and a hint of an accent. After introducing himself, he joined them in the interview room as his client was escorted in by a guard.

Again, Inspector Larocque took the lead, and addressing Carlos, said, "You have pled not guilty, so let's start by looking at what we have. First, you worked for Marie Gallorini as her gardener. Second, you were in possession of jewellery that was stolen from her house. Third, you pawned the said jewellery at a pawn shop in Barrie. And finally, Marie was found dead from trauma to her head." He paused to let things sink in before proceeding. "So, here's the deal. If you are not honest and upfront with us and tell us why you had the jewellery and where you got it, we will proceed with the murder charge against you. Also, we will recommend to the Crown that you be deported and serve your time in Mexico. We are sure we can arrange that since you are not a Canadian citizen. Just think of how you will fare in a Mexican penitentiary. Especially if you are associated with or have ties to a cartel, which we think you probably do."

Again, he paused and had another drink of water before continuing. "Now, if you are upfront with us and tell us exactly who gave you the jewellery and what instructions you received, we will ask the Crown to proceed with a drug trafficking charge only. Since this is your first offence, if you cooperate with us, we will ask them to recommend time served and probation." As he paused, Dave tapped him on the shoulder and then whispered in his ear. Continuing, Inspector Larocque said, "We'll also ask to see if you can be assisted in relocating to another part of Canada. What do you say?"

Looking at Carlos, his lawyer then responded, "I would like to confer with my client. Can we have time alone?"

"Of course," the inspector answered, and the three men left the room.

After some time, they were waved back in. Once they took their chairs, Mr. Gyarmathy addressed them, saying, "I have conferred with my client, and he would like to make a statement."

He then nodded to Carlos, who, after clearing his throat, proceeded to tell them, "First, I want it to be clear that I did not murder or rob Marie Gallorini. I worked for her, and I liked her. She treated me with respect."

Then he went on, laying out for them what had transpired.

# CHAPTER FORTY-SEVEN

W HEN THE FORENSICS team finished in the shed, they had two predominant sets of fingerprints. One set belonged to Carlos. The second was unknown, as it was not in their system. Realizing that they would not get Gomez's prints easily, Dave had a thought about how they might get them. "I think that we could ask our neighbour Nosy Parker to arrange a meeting with Jorge Gomez. She can tell him how impressed she was with the work he had done for Marie and ask if he could drop by and give her a rough price to have a pergola installed over her patio. When he arrives, she can show him her patio and have him suggest what it would involve and how much it might cost. At some point, probably when he is finishing, she can offer him a glass of iced tea or an alternative summer beverage. We will impress upon her that he has to take the vessel he is going to drink from and pick it up with his bare hands. What do you think?" he asked.

"Well, it sounds like it could work, but she will have to understand that she is doing this to get us his fingerprints," the inspector replied as Bill nodded in agreement.

Dave then went over to see Laura. She was thrilled to be involved and enthusiastically agreed. "We need a set of his fingerprints, and you should only touch the glass when necessary. Once he is gone, I'll give you a pair of official gloves for you to put on when you touch it." Laura was obviously excited, and Dave suspected that the idea of giving her a pair of "official police" gloves to use made it all the more appealing. He also left her an evidence bag in which to place the glass once she had the prints on it and Jorge had departed.

Later that afternoon, Laura knocked on their door and handed Ana a bag containing an empty prosecco bottle. She then accepted Ana's invitation to join her on their deck, where Dave and Bill were waiting for her.

Arriving and grinning from ear to ear, she said to Dave, "I hope this works for you. He refused my offer for a summer drink, so I took a bottle of prosecco I had on standby and pretended to trip, spilling it and dropping the bottle in his lap. It was pretty messy, and he was pretty upset, but he did pick the bottle up and hand it back to me, so I think we have his prints. Oh, I also had him sit in a chair with arms, so if he didn't touch the bottle, he probably would have left a set of prints on the arm of the chair."

Dave and Bill chuckled. "Wow, that was good thinking," Bill said, taking the bag with the bottle in it from Ana. "Thanks for your help. I'll get this down to the office right away."

"You're welcome to stay and visit," Ana said. "Dave is going to barbecue some of his homemade burgers in a bit, and we would love for you to try one."

"I would be delighted," Laura replied, still grinning.

"Great, how about a glass of unspilled wine?" Dave asked, laughing.

The results came back the following day, confirming that the prints on the bottle were the second set of the most recent prints on Marie's jewellery as well as the oil and gas cans in the shed. Based on that, plus Carlos's statement, the inspector and Bill proceeded to his place of business and arrested Jorge Gomez for drug trafficking and Marie's murder.

He immediately said, "I want to call my lawyer."

"You can call him from the detachment," was the answer.

When the lawyer arrived, he was informed of the charges against his client and shown into the interview room. Jorge was brought from his cell and joined him shortly thereafter. They were left to confer.

After a fairly long interval, Jorge's lawyer finally informed them they were ready to talk. The interview team arrived, and again, Inspector Larocque took the lead, saying, "Well, Jorge, things are not looking very promising. We can sit here and play Whac-A-Mole, trying to get the truth from you, but I prefer to be more direct. So, here is what we have: Your subcontractor, Carlos Menendez, was selling drugs. You provided him with the drugs. On the night Marie Gallorini died, you were at her house and stole her jewellery." He paused and let that sink in before proceeding. "You subsequently gave the jewellery to Carlos Menendez and instructed him to get rid of it in Barrie. You told him that the jewellery was given to you to settle a debt and that you would let him keep half of what he got from a pawn shop. Based on this evidence, we are hereby charging you with the death of Marie Gallorini as well as trafficking in drugs. We have no doubt that you will be found guilty, as Carlos has agreed to testify against you." He paused again to let things settle in, and then he continued. "We can't make any promises, but if you cooperate, we will try to get you a better deal. On the other hand, you could be sent to Mexico to do your time, and as a cartel member, you know how long you will probably last there." He then stopped and folded his arms and waited.

Zolton Gyarmathy then said, "I would like some time with my client."

"Take all the time you need," Bill said as the interrogation team left the room.

It was late in the day when they were summoned back to the room. Sitting down, Jorge's lawyer asked, "What exactly are you offering for my client's co-operation?"

"We are not in a position to offer anything, but we will certainly inform the Crown attorney that he co-operated and we recommend consideration," the inspector responded.

The lawyer huddled with his client for a minute, and then Jorge spoke for the first time. "Okay, here's what happened. Carlos was running low on product, so I came over around eleven at night to leave what he needed in the garden shed. As I was walking up the sidewalk, it was dark, and I tripped over a small garbage can that had been left on the sidewalk. I stumbled and was picking up what I dropped when the door beside me opened, and Marie asked me in a very loud voice what I was doing. I was caught off guard. I was trying to pick up the product without her seeing it and at the same time get to my feet. As I was rushing, I lost my balance and fell into her. She fell backwards and hit her head on the edge of the table. When I went to help her, I realized that she had stopped breathing. I panicked and thought I should make it look like she was killed during a robbery, so I went up to her bedroom and took the jewellery. I felt bad, as I had no intention of harming her. I thought that she was a nice lady."

The inspector replied, "We'll get you to put that in writing. We'll review it and speak to the Crown and some others and see what we can work out for you. The RCMP will probably want to talk to you."

Dave nodded. While he was sick with the loss of his sister-in-law, there was now a little satisfaction in knowing that it was an accident and she was not murdered intentionally. Now he could share with the family what had happened.

CHAPTER **FORTY-EIGHT**

S EVERAL MONTHS LATER in the summer, Michael received a cheque from the executor for his share of his father's estate. It was for $319,233.00.

He called Jimmy Grasser, saying, "Jimmy, it's Mike Gallorini. I just got my cheque from the executor, and I need you to have a long, hard look at the invoice you sent me. It's pretty steep for zero results."

Michael listened while Jimmy talked and then replied, "Okay, if that's the best you can do. I'll talk it over with the boss, and if she is okay with it, we'll get the cheque to you." He hung up, and turning to his wife, he said, "Grasser dropped the amount to $141,800, and we need to make the cheque payable to his wife. Oh, and we are to destroy the invoice he sent us."

Marie thought for a moment and then nodded her agreement.

The following day, they took a cheque in the amount of $141,800, payable to Jimmy's wife, and delivered it in a plain brown envelope to his office.

This left them with $197,833. They were relieved that things were finally over, and after talking it over, they decided that they would leave Fergus. Mike spent a few weeks scouring real estate ads and finally made a suggestion to his wife. "I don't think that we want to spend everything on a house and am thinking that we could check out a double-wide in a mobile home park that I came across between Shelburne and Mount Forest. It looks like it's a nice-sized park, not too big, and the home would be the perfect fit for us. It's very central, so we won't be stuck out in the boondocks somewhere." Rose reluctantly agreed to look at it, and after finding something that would work for them, they moved.

Once they had settled in and got a feel for the place, they paid a visit to Sauble Beach. After looking around and checking things out, they made an offer on a trailer that was situated in a trailer park. It was a few blocks from the lake, and they were warmly welcomed by their new neighbours.

They were left with just over $75,000. They reasoned that once their old-age security started, they could live comfortably, and as Rose told Ana later, "We loved the beach, and now have the best of both worlds."

It was now early December, and Dave and Ana were getting ready to leave Collingwood and return home. They had sold Marie's house, her car, and quite a bit of her furniture and gardening tools. What they hadn't sold, they donated to local charities that ran homes for battered women. They had been in constant touch with their son and daughter, who were eagerly awaiting their parents' return. Ana had suggested that they gather for a family Christmas, and this was enthusiastically welcomed.

Ana and David also received $319,233 from the executor as their share of Clemente's estate. They also received Marie's share of $319,233 over and above the $739,000 from the sale of her house and car. On top of that, they had received her investments and cash in her bank accounts. They had discussed things thoroughly and had decided to give each of their children $350,000 at Christmas in memory of their aunt. The only other thing that had been talked about was a visit to Italy to meet Ana's relatives, visit with Favio and Ana, and swing through Ukraine to see Dave's homeland. He didn't think he had any relatives that he should visit but said that he would check with his mother and father to make sure.

Dave was considering giving up his private investigator's licence, as he and his wife planned to enjoy their retirement. Working on his sister-in-law's case had taken a lot out of him. As he mulled it over, and on his wife's advice, he had decided to put the decision off until they returned from their trip to Europe.

Arriving home, they were happy to be back in BC and in their own home. The weather was pretty typical for December—rainy with some wet snow. The temperatures were coolish but stayed above freezing. A number of vineyards had been established in the area because of non-frigid winters and good soil, and they were flourishing.

The week before the children were to arrive, Ana called Kathy Alexander one morning to see if they could get together for lunch. Kathy agreed, so Ana told Dave, "Kathy and I are going for lunch. I should be back by four, and I thought we might barbecue some pork chops for supper."

"Great idea," Dave replied. "I'll get them out of the freezer and have them thawed and basted by suppertime. Take your time and give my regards to Kathy and Cal."

She had driven through Penticton and was on her way to Naramata when a vehicle came tearing out of the driveway of one of the vineyards and hit the side of her car. The force of the impact drove her car off the road, and it rolled over several times. She was rushed to the hospital but died on the operating table. The police informed Dave that the driver who hit her was leaving the vineyard under the influence and didn't slow down as he turned onto the main road. He didn't see Ana's car until it was too late.

The children rushed to their father's side as soon as they learned of the accident. The family was devastated and leaned on each other for support. The funeral Mass was held shortly after the accident, and her body was interred in Penticton. The children stayed with their father through Christmas and left just after the new year. They received the cheques from their father on Christmas morning and were surprised but subdued. Their father told them that it was their mother's decision to give them the money, and while they were pleased, there was a definite cloud over the gifts.

Dave shook his head when it struck him that he had ended up with the bulk of the Gallorini family estate! He gave it a great deal of thought and decided to make two significant donations in his wife's name rather than a number of smaller gifts. He donated the bulk of the money to the hospitals Ana had worked for in Vancouver and Yellowknife.

C ARLOS MENENDEZ, WITH Dave's assistance, relocated to a community in the Northwest Territories, where he was employed by a municipality.

Jorge Gomez was turned over to a joint RCMP/FBI task force investigating the Mexican drug cartels. It was reported later that year that the Combined Forces Special Enforcement Unit arrested five individuals in Canada with an international arrest warrant.

Laura Schmit continues to live in the neighbourhood in Collingwood and keeps an eye on the comings and goings.

David retained his private investigator's licence, and with support from Kathy and Cal and his children, he gradually got over his loss, although he never fully recovered from it. A couple of Christmases back, Ana had given him a series of books by Bernard Cornwell, a British author. They were part of the Sharpe series and followed the life of a street urchin, Richard Sharpe, who joined the British army to avoid being arrested. The books followed his career as he participated in the major British campaigns over the years. After things settled, David decided to read the series as a way to remember the thoughtfulness and kindness of his late wife. He also took on some work as a private detective whenever the cases were of interest to him.

Leo was a successful civil engineer working for a consulting firm in Vancouver. He loved to fly and would often rent a small plane to explore different areas of the province in his free time. When he received his gift, he purchased his own Cessna. He then set himself up as a consulting engineer and flew to various smaller communities that could not afford—and had no ongoing need—to hire an engineer to do work for them. He frequently flew his father on fishing trips to out-of-the-way areas of the province. He met and married a young advertising executive named Georgina Moore. They bought a house in Surrey and raised a family of four.

Suzie took her gift and bought a restaurant in Kelowna. She had developed a relationship with her previous manager, and together they established and developed it into one of the finest eating establishments in the Okanagan region. They never married, although they spent their lives together working as a team.

9 781038 340863